100 FATHOMS BELOW

Other Books by Steven L. Kent

The Clone Republic
Rogue Clone
The Clone Alliance
The Clone Elite
The Clone Betrayal
The Clone Empire
The Clone Redemption
The Clone Sedition
The Clone Assassin
The Clone Apocalypse
Star Crusader
Wing Commander III
The Making of Final Fantasy: The Spirits Within
The First Quarter: A 25-Year History of Video Games
The Ultimate History of Video Games
Star Wars: Galactic Battlegrounds
The Making of Doom 3

Other Books by Nicholas Kaufmann

Walk in Shadows: Collected Stories
General Slocum's Gold
Hunt at World's End
Chasing the Dragon
Still Life: Nine Stories
Dying Is My Business
Die and Stay Dead
In the Shadow of the Axe

STEVEN L. KENT and NICHOLAS KAUFMANN

100 FATHOMS BELOW

BLACK
STONE
PUBLISHING

Copyright © 2018 by Steven L. Kent and Nicholas Kaufmann
Published in 2018 by Blackstone Publishing
Cover and book design by Blackstone Publishing

Printed in the United States of America

First edition: 2018
ISBN 978-1-5385-0763-6
Fiction / Horror

1 3 5 7 9 10 8 6 4 2

CIP data for this book is available
from the Library of Congress

Blackstone Publishing
31 Mistletoe Rd.
Ashland, OR 97520

www.BlackstonePublishing.com

This book is dedicated to the memory of
John Piña Craven, a Renaissance man and an
authentic American hero.

—Steven L. Kent

LOS ANGELES–CLASS SUBMARINE (SSN-688)

1. Engine room
2. Reactor compartment
3. Operations compartment
4. Torpedo room
5. Sonar array
6. Main ballast tanks
7. Sonar room
8. Auxiliary machinery
9. Crew's mess

PROLOGUE

Naval Station Pearl Harbor, November 16, 1983

USS *Roanoke*, SSN-709, sat moored to the dock, half submerged in the calm waters of the harbor. In the dim twilight, when colors and details began to fade to the same flat gunmetal gray, the submarine might have looked to an outsider like some gigantic sea creature, lashed to the dock by thick ropes and braided steel cables, its tower standing tall like a dorsal fin. But not to Warren Stubic, petty officer third class. To him, it looked like where he was going to call home for the next three months.

Roanoke was scheduled to launch tomorrow at 1530 hours. After that, he was staring at an underway spent entirely at sea. Three months without the sun. Three months without liquor. Three months of hot-racking— sharing a bed with three other guys in six-hour sleeping shifts because there wasn't enough room on a submarine to give every enlisted man his own rack.

Three months without women. That prospect in particular struck him as intolerable.

He had only one thing in mind for the night before the launch, and that was to have fun. But unlike other sailors, he didn't see the fun in drinking until he puked. For Stubic, fun meant getting his dick wet.

Waikiki, ten miles away, was the closest center of nightlife. By the time he got there, the last purple tinges were fading from the sky as darkness settled in. He was surprised to find the city hopping even on a Tuesday night. Servicemen from Naval Station Pearl Harbor, hard to miss in their flattops and buzz cuts, towered over most of the locals. The strip along the beach had been developed for tourists and people with money to spend, neither of which accurately described Stubic, although tonight he had enough cash with him to afford all the fun he wanted. On sidewalks as crowded as any in Tokyo or Hong Kong, he walked past fancy hotels with liveried doormen, sushi restaurants and fish houses, tacky gift shops, and kiosks selling oysters that supposedly had pearls in them, not that he'd ever been dumb enough to buy one and find out.

There were girls everywhere, and the kind he liked: Polynesian, with long hair and short skirts. But they were local girls, and he had already discovered the hard way that local girls came to Waikiki looking only for local guys. His fellow servicemen had figured this out too, and now mostly had an eye out for tourist girls—of which there were always plenty at Spats, the popular dance club on the first floor of the Hyatt Regency. Gaggles of interchangeable blonds with sunburned faces and peeling skin. None of them interested Stubic the way the local girls did. Luckily, he had discovered a way to satisfy his appetite for local flavor without risking any more rejections from Waikiki girls or having to settle for some drunk American tourist.

He turned off the strip and onto a side street, where the mega hotels gave way to smaller inns and apartment buildings—three- and four-story affairs that looked shabby compared to the beachside properties. He pulled a card out of his pocket and checked the address printed on it. A pretty Filipina—a dark-haired slip of a thing in a bikini top and denim shorts—had given it to him the last time he came to Waikiki. He had tried to pick her up on the strip, but she wasn't interested. Instead, she handed him the card with a twinkle in her dark-brown eyes, telling him this was where he needed to go if he liked local girls.

"Pretty girls for good prices," she had told him in a detached, indifferent voice. Hawking different merchandise, the well-practiced catchphrase wouldn't be out of place on a grocery store circular.

He found the brothel at the far end of a quiet alley, illuminated only by the stars above and an aisle of lit candles along the floor. He looked around nervously to make sure no one was watching. Honolulu had plenty of brothels, especially near the naval station, but that didn't mean it was legal. If anyone caught him, he would spend the night behind bars and face disciplinary action in the morning. But luck was on his side. The street was empty. He hurried into the alley and through the door.

Inside was a large, softly lit waiting room decorated with erotic paintings and sculptures. A wizened old woman sat behind an ornately carved wooden table. She was Filipina too, like the girl who had given him the card. Stubic saw enough of a resemblance in the old woman's face to wonder whether this was a family operation. When he closed the door behind him, she looked up and welcomed him, but that was both the start and the end of any small talk. No point in wasting time—they both knew why he was here.

"What kind of girl are you looking for tonight?" the old woman asked. "She can be whatever you want her to be."

Stubic was surprised by her perfect English, a stark contrast to the terse, clipped pidgin that so many of the Filipino immigrants spoke. He told her what he wanted—petite, long hair, young but not jailbait young—and realized he was describing the girl on the strip who had given him the business card. The old woman's expression remained stoical as she picked up the phone on the table and spoke into it in a language Stubic didn't understand. It didn't sound like Ilocano or Tagalog, the two main Filipino languages spoken in Hawaii. Something about it sent an unexpected chill down his spine.

"It will just be a moment," the old woman said, hanging up. "Please make yourself comfortable."

While he waited, Stubic looked at the art on display around the room. He felt himself particularly drawn to the only figurine that wasn't of a naked woman or a sensually embracing couple. It looked like a mask of some kind, composed of feathers, or maybe they were flames. The features were human but also not, in a way he couldn't quite pinpoint. Its lips were peeled back in a terrible, angry grimace.

As the seconds ticked by, he became uncomfortably aware that he was the only customer in the waiting room. He didn't hear anyone elsewhere in the brothel, either. He'd been in enough of them to know that usually you could hear men's voices talking or, if it was their first time, laughing nervously. This place was dead quiet.

To fill the awkward silence, Stubic pointed to the strange sculpture and asked the old woman, "What is this?"

"*Aswang*," she said.

"*Aswang*," he repeated. "What does it mean?"

But the old woman just smiled at him and pointed to a door in the wall behind her. "She is ready for you now."

He walked past her table to the door, uncomfortably aware of the old woman's eyes following him, watching him closely. Stubic opened the door and stepped through into the next room, which was lit only with the soft, warm glow of candles. And, like a dream, there she was, the girl from the strip. She had traded in her bikini top and shorts for a beautiful silk kimono. Her jade-green eyes sparkled. Stubic paused. He didn't remember her having green eyes before, but when she smiled and took his hand, her skin soft and warm on his, he didn't care anymore what color her eyes were. More titillating art decorated the walls of the room. Off to one side, a hallway, dark as a cave, led deeper into the building. She sat down on a red plush couch against the wall and patted the cushion beside her.

"I can't believe it," he stammered, sitting beside her. "It's … it's *you*."

She looked even more enticing than when he first saw her. He was already imagining doing everything with her that his money could buy.

"You're from the naval station?" she asked.

"I am," he said, sliding closer to her. "I'm sailing out on a submarine tomorrow and thought I'd give myself one last hurrah."

"All those men on the submarine," she said in a wistful tone. "It must get very lonely without any girls."

"You have no idea," he said, putting a hand on her kimono-draped leg. The silk felt smooth and alluring under his hand.

"So much time in the middle of the ocean, deep underwater, surrounded by the dark," she said. Her green eyes flashed. The top of her kimono drifted open just enough to reveal the curve of her breast. "Don't you ever get scared?"

"Of the dark?" he asked.

"Of everything that could go wrong on a submarine," she said. Her hand traced lazy circles across his chest.

"There's ... there's nothing to be scared of," he stammered, growing more aroused at her touch. "We train and we drill. We know what to do if anything goes wrong."

"So, nothing scares you?" she asked.

He could tell from her smile that she was teasing him. "Not a thing," he said.

"Good." She stood up and walked into the adjoining hallway, disappearing into the inky darkness. "Aren't you coming?" she called back to him.

He stood up and went to follow her, but something made him pause at the mouth of the hallway. The darkness that filled it was absolute. Not even a glimmer of ambient candlelight filtered in from the room. It was like staring into a black hole. Then, farther down the hallway, two eyes glowed, like a cat's eyes reflecting the light—except that there was no light to be reflected, only the stygian darkness around them. For a moment, he thought he was dreaming.

"Baby ...?" he called.

The girl didn't answer.

"Baby, is that—is that you?"

He took a step forward into the hallway, then another, and then the darkness swallowed him whole.

CHAPTER ONE

Without a doubt, the most insidious dangers were the ones that hid in plain sight, camouflaging themselves inside the minds of rational men. Petty Officer First Class Tim Spicer of USS *Roanoke* knew this all too well. He had seen men—good men, strong men—who thought they were equipped to handle life on board a submarine discover otherwise after being crammed into a three-hundred-foot tube in the depths of the ocean with over a hundred other men. Most underways lasted three months, some longer, and in that time even the sharpest minds could crack under the pressure.

Case in point, *Roanoke's* previous planesman. Petty Officer Second Class Mitch Robertson had been fresh out of BESS, the Basic Enlisted Submarine School, which had opened just a year before in Groton, Connecticut. He thought he was ready for everything the ocean depths could throw at him, but his first underway had been a long one—nine months escorting a carrier group around the tip of South America and into the Atlantic. Robertson had lasted only the first three months, growing more frantic and disheveled as time passed. In the mess, he kept to himself, eating less and less until he stopped altogether. In the control room, his response to orders became sluggish. Not seeing the sun for months, not breathing fresh air or seeing any new faces had driven him to the edge. But nothing went unnoticed on a submarine. As a matter of course, the officers kept a close eye on the crew, watchful for signs of fatigue. They had to. Everyone's lives depended on their recognizing it in time, and they caught it right away in Robertson. On long underways such as that one, *Roanoke* would visit port every three months to stock up on food, since she could only carry a hundred days' worth at a time, and Captain Weber had decided to swap Robertson out at the next port. When Robertson found out, he went to his locker and got his toilet kit, went into the head, and slit his wrists with his shaving razor in one of the stalls. Maybe he was ashamed that he didn't have what it took, or maybe something deeper and darker inside him drove him to it. Tim never knew. It was he who found Robertson there, slumped over in the stall, blood from his wrists pooling on the floor—more blood than Tim had ever seen, so much that his gorge rose at the sight. He had rushed to get the hospital corpsman, who, fortunately, had been able to patch Robertson up in time. Afterward, Roberston was transferred to one of the carriers, where they had the doctors and medical facilities to look after him, and Tim got a lot of pats on the back from the crew for saving the man's life.

So when Captain Weber summoned him to his stateroom shortly before *Roanoke* was set to pull out of port, Tim thought maybe it had something to do with Robertson. A personal meeting with the captain wasn't something most petty officers ever experienced, especially with Captain Weber, who was notoriously standoffish with his enlisted men. The summons had sounded urgent, and Tim double-timed it, worried that the captain would tell him Robertson had tried to kill himself again—or, worse, had succeeded this time.

Roanoke was a 688, a Los Angeles–class nuclear-powered fast-attack submarine, outfitted with three levels that housed the crew's living spaces, weapons systems, and control centers. Captain Weber's stateroom was on the top level, forward of the control room, in a short corridor known as the captain's egress.

When Tim got there, he found the stateroom hatch open. The space inside was small and cramped even though it belonged to the captain.

There just wasn't enough room on the boat for anything larger. Inside, Senior Chief Farrington, chief of the boat and highest-ranking enlisted man aboard, was deep in conversation with the captain. Farrington was a no-nonsense career sailor, an aging senior chief petty officer with scant hope of making master chief before retiring. Word on the boat put him at fifty, maybe even fifty-five. Old enough to have grandchildren back home, and certainly the oldest man aboard *Roanoke*. As COB, Farrington was the primary liaison between the commissioned officers and enlisted men such as Tim, which meant that he too had to be present for this meeting with the captain.

Captain Weber, a short, roundish man in his forties, sat at the desk that folded down from the wood-paneled wall. A calendar had been pinned up, the days X-ed off up to today—Thursday, November 17, 1983.

"You sent for me, Captain?" Tim said, standing at attention in the doorway. Saluting was never done indoors, not even for the captain.

"Come in, Spicer," Captain Weber said, barely looking up from the papers strewn across his desk.

Not the warm-and-fuzziest commanding officer Tim had ever seen, but not the kind who spent the entire tour yelling at crewmen, either—even though he did have stringently high standards, which he expected his men to meet. He was more the strong-and-silent type, like John Wayne, only in Barney Rubble's body. Tim stepped into the stateroom, then waited to be addressed before speaking. A file folder was open in front of the captain. Tim read the name across the top, upside down: *White, Jerome: Petty Officer Second Class.*

"Have you met your new planesman yet, Spicer?" Captain Weber asked. "PO2 White?"

"I've seen him, sir, but we haven't spoken," Tim replied.

"What have you heard about him?"

"Nothing yet, sir."

Senior Chief Farrington, leaning against the wall with his arms crossed, said, "What if I were to tell you our new planesman suffers from a bad case of CRIS, Spicer?"

CRIS was seaman's jargon: cranial-rectal insertion syndrome.

"Sir?" Tim asked the captain.

Captain Weber sighed and leaned back in his chair. "What Farrington is trying so colorfully to say is that it appears White comes with some baggage. There was an incident on his last boat, USS *Philadelphia.*"

Philadelphia was a Sturgeon-class sub, Tim knew. Sturgeons were real workhorses, but they were old. They were already being phased out in favor of Los Angeles–class subs like *Roanoke.*

"White lodged a formal complaint against his XO, an officer by the name of Frank Leonard," Weber continued. "I don't know the details of the complaint, but it wound up costing Leonard a promotion."

"Permission to speak frankly, sir?" Farrington asked.

The captain nodded. "Of course, COB."

"I know men like White, sir," Farrington said. "They don't respect authority, they're lazy, they don't want to perform their duties or run their drills, and as soon as an officer gets tough on them for it, these mama's boys run off to lodge a complaint." He turned to Tim. "White got what he wanted, and the lieutenant commander was passed over for promotion. Unfortunately, it was the third time he got passed over."

Tim winced. When an officer was passed over for promotion three times, his career with the navy was over. Whatever had happened on *Philadelphia,* it cost the XO everything.

"Except that we don't know for sure that's the kind of man White is," Weber cautioned. "He also happens to be responsible for singlehandedly saving *Philadelphia* from catastrophe. Something went wrong in the auxiliary engine room—some aging piece of equipment failed and a fire broke out. According to the report, White didn't even hesitate. He grabbed a pair of fire extinguishers and charged into the room while everyone else was running away from it. He spent the next month in a hospital being treated for burns.

"Whatever happened between White and his XO, it's clear he showed extraordinary courage, selflessness, and initiative in saving *Philadelphia.* That's ultimately why I accepted his transfer for *Roanoke.* But I share some of the COB's concerns about who PO2 White is when there *isn't* a fire. I need someone to keep an eye on him, and let Farrington or me know if there are any problems. I believe that you, Spicer, are the man for the job."

Tim gulped. "Me, sir?"

Captain Weber arched an eyebrow. "Is that going to be a problem, Spicer?"

"No sir. Sorry, sir," Tim said quickly.

He knew why the captain had chosen him. He had saved one man's life, and only by being in the right place at the right time, but apparently now he was the go-to guy for keeping an eye on potentially difficult sailors. He supposed he should feel flattered, but he couldn't help wondering whether this was a good idea. What did he know about keeping White— or anyone, for that matter—on the right path? He was a sonar tech, not a shrink.

"See to it I didn't make a mistake accepting White's transfer to *Roanoke*," Captain Weber said. "Dismissed."

"Aye-aye, sir," Tim said.

He turned and started out of the stateroom.

"Actually, Spicer, hold on a moment."

Tim turned back to him. "Yes, Captain?"

Captain Weber stood up from the desk. "Meet me on the bridge when we launch this afternoon."

Tim blinked, unsure he had heard properly. The captain usually had officers and essential personnel with him on the bridge when *Roanoke* pulled out of port, but a petty officer? That would be a first.

"Aye-aye, sir," Tim said, barely able to contain his smile.

The captain nodded. "Be there at fifteen hundred hours sharp, or you'll miss your last chance to say goodbye to the sun."

***

When Tim was in high school, he had a summer job in a produce warehouse, lugging crates of fruit and 50-pound bags of potatoes from the storage aisles to the loading dock, eight hours a day. It had been hard work—thirsty work, his grandfather had called it—but it had also been gratifying work. Not just for the paycheck, although as a teenager it had been nice to have some spending money, and not just because the manual labor had honed his muscles and built up his strength, but also because it had taught him how to move quickly and easily through cramped spaces. The warehouse had been as big as a football field, but around harvest time they would ship out so many pallets of potatoes, he could barely fit between them. That was how it felt inside a Los Angeles–class sub every minute of every waking hour. *Roanoke* was barely longer than a football field and only 33 feet across at her widest, on the middle level. The top and bottom levels were even narrower. It wasn't a lot of space to begin with, and most of it was crammed tight with workstations and equipment.

The middle level of the submarine was devoted to the crew's living spaces. At the forward end sat the officers' staterooms, in an area the enlisted men referred to as "Officer Country." It was where the officers slept in their dorm-like rooms, much to the envy of the enlisted sailors, who were forced to hot-rack for the duration of the underway. The middle level also held the head, the berthing areas where the enlisted men slept, the wardroom where the officers took their meals, the galley, and the mess where the enlisted men ate, which was at the aft end of the corridor, up against the bulkhead that separated the forward compartment from the nuclear reactor and engine room aft. Tim walked briskly through the middle-level corridor while enlisted men hurried back and forth on either side of him in their poopie suits—the unfortunate nickname given to their submarine uniforms: blue coveralls designed to contain body heat in the event of a flood. No one knew where the nickname came from, but they were pretty sure it wasn't anything good.

A few of the men were shooting the breeze. Had they seen the third *Star Wars* movie yet or heard the Ramones' latest album? The sailors Tim knew nodded at him or gave him a clap on the arm and a quick hello, while the newer faces in the crowd dashed purposefully toward their stations. Morale was high. It always was at the start of an underway, even for the most jaded sailors among them. The ocean was in their blood, and they didn't like to be away for too long.

Tim spotted a sailor standing near the curtained entrance to a berthing area. Everyone else in the corridor was hurrying somewhere, but he was perfectly still. He was facing away, with his back to Tim, one shoulder leaning against the bulkhead as if for support.

"You okay, buddy?" Tim called as he approached.

The man didn't answer. He didn't even move.

"Hey," Tim called. "Everything all right?"

The man jumped as if Tim had startled him. He straightened up slowly, still facing away. He moved stiffly away from the bulkhead and smoothed down his uniform. He glanced over his shoulder at Tim, who recognized him as PO3 Warren Stubic. Only, he'd never seen him like this before. Stubic had always been someone who grabbed life by the horns, who liked to tell raucous stories in the mess, but today he looked distracted and out of it. His face glistened with sweat, and his eyes looked wild.

"You feeling all right, Stubic?" Tim asked, walking closer.

"Fine, fine," Stubic muttered.

"If you're not feeling well …"

"I said I'm fine, Spicer," Stubic insisted.

He bolted past, his shoulder bumping Tim's as he went by. Tim turned and watched him go, dumbfounded.

***

The bridge of a submarine was nothing like the bridge of a ship. It wasn't the room from which the sub was commanded—that was the control room on the top level—but rather a small, open observation platform at the top of the tall dorsal tower known as the sail. When the clock struck 1500 hours, Tim was already on the bridge, determined not to miss his shot. Captain Weber joined him, along with Lieutenant Commander Lee Jefferson, *Roanoke*'s six-foot-five executive officer, who had played starting linebacker for the Naval Academy and looked as though he still could. As a commissioned officer, Jefferson wore a different uniform from the blue coveralls of the enlisted men, and to Tim it looked a hell of a lot more comfortable—a starched and pressed khaki shirt and pleated khaki slacks, with the gold oak-leaf pin on his collar that marked him as a lieutenant commander.

Now that Tim was outdoors, it was appropriate for him to salute his superior officers. "Reporting as requested, Captain. Lieutenant Commander, sir."

"Good to see you, Spicer," Jefferson said with a nod.

"You too, sir," he replied.

Tim hadn't encountered a lot of black officers in the submarine service, especially senior officers, but it was the 1980s now, and it seemed things were finally changing. Here was a man who was going places. Talk among the crew was that Jefferson would have his own command within a year. Tim had served with him on previous underways and found him to be a good man with a sharp mind and a practical outlook. But more than that, Jefferson didn't mind walking among the enlisted men. He didn't keep them at arm's length or consider them beneath him the way other officers did. Even Captain Weber fell into that mind-set much of the time. Tim liked and respected the captain, but the man rarely came out of his stateroom to talk to the crew.

Standing here with the two highest-ranking officers on the boat was an enormous honor, but Tim felt distinctly out of place. Still, he refused to let it bother him. He had always wondered what it would be like to see a launch from the top of the sail, the way the captain and a few lucky officers did, and now he finally had the chance, at the captain's personal invitation. If anyone had a problem with his being here, they could take it up with Captain Weber.

The sail rose thirty feet above the water, with the observation periscope, attack periscope, and multipurpose antenna mast forming a gray metal forest overhead. From up here, Tim could see everything. It was a clear day with gentle swells in Pearl Harbor, and the Honolulu sun washed over them, bright and warm. Ever since he was assigned to Naval Station Pearl Harbor, Tim had marveled at how warm it stayed all year round, even in mid-November. Sometimes, he thought he would never get used to it. Other times, he felt that he'd rather die than go back home to Presque Isle, where everything was buried in snow, and the sun hid for months at a time.

He looked up into the sky, shielding his eyes. When Captain Weber had said it was his last chance to say goodbye to the sun, he wasn't exaggerating. The three of them—Weber, Jefferson, and himself—would be the last to see the sky. Once the submarine went under, it would be three long months before anyone saw it again.

At 1530, USS *Roanoke*, SSN-709, pulled out of port. Captain Weber and Lieutenant Commander Jefferson stared straight ahead at the lane of open water before them. But this was Tim's first time at the top of the sail, and he turned every which way, taking in the sights. He watched the braids of water twisting along the side of the hull, and the crewmen in bright green life jackets working briefly along the top of the hull, behind the sail, to secure the rigging. They were moving at about eight knots, Tim guessed, and the wind whispered in his ears.

Freighters and destroyers towered over them on either side. As they passed an oil tanker, Tim craned his neck to look up at its deck and saw the silhouettes of sailors staring down at him. He fantasized about waving at them, but that would be a costly breach of decorum. Still, the idea of one final interaction with other human beings above the surface of the ocean, one last gesture before it was just him and 139 other men in the dark water for months, was tempting.

The American flag was lowered from its pole and folded into a crisp military triangle. Their work finished, the life-vested crewmen on the hull below dropped back down into the sub, sealing the hatches behind them. Tim watched the Honolulu shoreline vanish in the distance as they moved out of the harbor and into Mamala Bay. Beyond the bay, the vast Pacific awaited, its depths as dark and quiet as a tomb.

The captain's hand fell on Tim's shoulder, pulling him from his thoughts. "Enough daydreaming, Spicer. Time to go below."

"Aye, sir," he replied.

He took one last look up at the sun, as if he could commit its light and warmth to memory. Then he followed Captain Weber and Lieutenant Commander Jefferson down the ladder into the sub. His heart sped up, and an expectant grin creased his face. He was feeling the same thrill of a new mission that he'd seen on the excited faces of the sailors in the corridor.

All except PO3 Stubic, he reminded himself. He couldn't stop puzzling over how strangely the man had behaved, and the wild, disturbing look in his eye.

Once Tim reached the bottom of the ladder, another enlisted man scrambled up and secured the hatch to the bridge with a loud clang, sealing them all inside.

CHAPTER TWO

Being in the control room of a submarine felt like being in an egg carton. Calling it close quarters didn't really convey how cramped it was. Crewmen were wedged into their seats practically on top of one another. Sailors couldn't have issues about personal space on submarines, but especially not in the control room, where they were quite literally breathing down each other's necks until the end of their watch section. When Tim, Captain Weber, and Lieutenant Commander Jefferson entered the control room, most of the men were at their stations already, including, Tim noted, the new planesman, Jerry White—the transfer Captain Weber had tasked him with keeping on the straight and narrow.

He was a couple of years younger than Tim, in his early twenties, with a skinny frame and sandy-blond hair. He sat at a control panel at the front of the room, with a yoke in front of him that he would use to steer *Roanoke* once they were underwater. As planesman, White operated the winglike horizontal hydroplanes on the boat's bow and sail, steering the submarine up or down. He also controlled the vertical rudder at the stern, to make left and right turns. Seated beside him, separated by less than a foot of space, was the helmsman, with the yoke that controlled the angle of the submarine, through the horizontal hydroplanes at the stern. For the sub to run smoothly, both the helmsman and the planesman had to work in unison, developing a wordless rapport.

The helmsman on duty was Steve Bodine, a skinny kid out of Oklahoma and the only black sailor on *Roanoke* besides Lieutenant Commander Jefferson. Like White, Bodine was in his early 20s, but he was already halfway bald. He denied it strenuously, but everyone knew it was the real reason he kept his hair stubble-short. Bodine had the most stereotypically suburban middle-class background of any sailor Tim had met: swimming pool in the backyard, newspaper delivery route as a kid, Boy Scouts—the whole nine yards. He was a nice, uncomplicated guy, the kind you could have a beer with when you had a night off at the base. Tim figured that if anyone was going to be a good influence on White, helping keep him out of trouble as the captain wanted, it was Bodine. Captain Weber should have asked him instead.

The diving officer of the launch, Lieutenant Junior Grade Charles Duncan, sat behind White and Bodine in a chair so close he could reach past them to the control panel just by leaning forward if he wanted to. A cold and distant officer, Duncan wasn't one for small talk. Indeed, he was extraordinarily strict with enlisted men. Tim had seen him ruthlessly dress down sailors for even small, easily fixed mistakes.

Ensign Mark Penwarden took his position beside the captain as the acting officer of the deck, or OOD. Sailors abbreviated everything, Tim mused. The chief of the boat was the COB. The executive officer was the XO. Petty officers were POs. The trash disposal unit was the TDU. Nothing and no one was spared the indignity of an initialism. Being OOD was a temporary station, a responsibility that passed between officers with other jobs on board. Normally, Penwarden worked in fire control, where he operated and maintained the combat and weapons direction systems, but he needed to pass his off-quals to earn his dolphins, and acting as OOD during a launch was his final test. He looked nervous but ready. Tim knew how important this was to him. Penwarden had been working to complete the extensive quals process for almost a year now. He was desperate for the dolphin badge that so many other officers on *Roanoke* proudly wore on their uniforms, not to mention the official submarine qualification that came with it. If he didn't get it right today, he would have to wait months to try again.

Senior Chief Farrington, the COB, was serving as chief of the watch for the underway. Seated in front of the ballast control panel on one side of the control room, he oversaw the moving of water in and out of the ballast tanks to control the submarine's buoyancy, as well as monitoring all hatches and hull openings. Tim suspected that Farrington wasn't all that happy to be in the control room with White after objecting to his transfer to *Roanoke*, but the COB was a good, experienced sailor. He kept his eyes on his control panel and didn't let his personal feelings distract him.

Tim crossed the control room to the enclosed space affectionately known by sonar techs like himself as the sonar shack. Inside, he sat down in front of his display console, put on his earphones, and prepared for the launch.

***

Submarines didn't launch on a single order; they launched with a dialogue. The submarine corps choreographed its procedures to the last detail. It was the officer of the deck who began the dialogue.

"Bridge rigged for dive," Penwarden reported. "Last man down."

Captain Weber stood in front of the two periscopes on the conn, the raised stand positioned a few feet back from the helm. "Rig for dive, Ensign Penwarden," he ordered.

"Rig for dive, aye," Penwarden replied. After double-checking the report that all hatches were secured, he added, "Bridge rigged for dive, aye. Last man down, aye. Two minutes to dive point, sir."

"Excellent, Ensign Penwarden," Captain Weber said. "Chief of the Watch, rig control room for red."

"Rig for red, aye," Farrington replied.

In the sonar shack, Tim sat in front of his sonar display screen and braced himself. Though he had experienced it nearly a dozen times now, when the darkness came there was always something menacing about it. The overhead lights winked out in the control room, and the red lights snapped on. The crimson hue lent the control room an eerie, other-worldly appearance, as if everyone and everything in it were covered in a haze of blood.

"Officer of the Deck, report," the captain said.

But here Penwarden, who had been doing well until now, tripped over his tongue and didn't answer quickly enough.

"Officer of the Deck, what is our status?" the captain repeated, an annoyed edge creeping into his voice.

Lieutenant Commander Jefferson came up beside Penwarden and whispered in his ear, "Take a deep breath, Ensign. You're doing fine. We haven't hit anything yet."

With Jefferson's encouragement, Penwarden pulled himself together. He called out the depth soundings, course, and speed to the captain. "Ship rigged for dive, sir. We are one minute from dive point, Captain, confirmed by navigator. We hold no surface contacts by visual or sonar. Request permission to submerge boat, sir."

"Very well, Ensign Penwarden," the captain replied. His expression gave no indication whether Penwarden had burned his chance or pulled himself out of the fire at the last moment. "Submerge boat to one-five-zero feet."

White adjusted his yoke, ready to control the dive as soon as the OOD made the necessary announcement. Penwarden picked up the phone talker of the main circuit, the submarine's PA system.

"Dive! Dive!" he shouted into the phone talker.

The high, shrill alarm sounded, and Tim braced himself. The first dive was always a tense moment. Then the floor tilted under his feet, and he could picture *Roanoke* submerging beneath the waves, engulfed in the endless dark of the ocean.

CHAPTER THREE

Fully stocked, *Roanoke's* torpedo room held 24 torpedoes, 20 of which were housed in the storage racks. The other four currently rested on a set of skids along the bulkheads—trays that were used to load live torpedoes into the tubes. The space was long and narrow, no more than eight feet across from bulkhead to bulkhead, but with the skids taking up two feet on either side, that left only four feet of width for Warren Stubic and the other sailors manning the torpedo room.

They moved about the space, double-checking that the torpedoes had been properly secured for the launch. If one came loose, it could roll out of the racks or off the trays when the submarine dived. It wouldn't explode when it hit the floor—this wasn't a *Road-Runner* cartoon—but the fall could damage it enough to render it useless as a weapon, and one dud torpedo during an exchange with a Soviet sub could mean *Roanoke's* number was up. And that wasn't even taking into account the injuries it could cause if it fell on a sailor. Torpedoes were long, heavy, and made of steel. If one got loose, it wouldn't be pretty.

Stubic knew the routine. This wasn't his first time helping secure a torpedo room, but he found it hard to concentrate. He was sluggish, groggy, and deeply worried because he couldn't remember what happened last night in Waikiki. A dull, throbbing headache had developed behind his eyes this morning, and it showed no signs of leaving.

"Look alive, pal." One of the other torpedomen grinned at him. "Plenty of time to deal with the hangover later."

Stubic smiled back weakly, blinking in the bright, painful light. If only this *were* a hangover. Then he would have an explanation for at least some of what was happening to him. But not for everything. Even if he'd had too much to drink last night, which he damn well hadn't, it wouldn't explain the marks he found this morning on the side of his neck. Two small welts like bug bites. The tropical climate made Hawaii a welcoming environment for all sorts of insects, especially the nocturnal ones. Something had bitten him, and he wondered whether his symptoms were an infection brought on by the bite. Oh, God, was this malaria? He took a deep breath and tried not to think about it.

His head throbbed as if it were being jackhammered from the inside. The waves were getting worse with each one that crashed over him. Maybe he should go see Matson, the hospital corpsman, and get himself checked out. Except that he couldn't, could he? Matson would want to know where he'd been, and Stubic couldn't tell him. If anyone knew he'd gone to a brothel, he could lose pay or get bumped down in rank. Matson would also want to know everything that had happened, and Stubic wouldn't be able to answer that, either, because there were things he simply couldn't remember.

Why couldn't he?

After he entered that dark hallway, everything was a blank until he woke up in his barracks at the naval station, feeling like shit. He couldn't remember driving home from Waikiki. He couldn't remember *anything*. Something had happened to him in that hallway …

The sharp klaxon of the dive alarm jolted Stubic from his thoughts and made his head flare with pain.

Another torpedoman shouted, "Grab hold of something, Stubic. We're about to dive!"

He held on to the steel support of the torpedo rack. A moment later, the deck tipped dizzyingly downward. He closed his eyes. This must be what it would be like to be awake when they lowered you into the grave.

CHAPTER FOUR

Tim Spicer's first watch section went smoothly, though not quickly. As one of *Roanoke's* sonar techs, his job kept him planted in front of a sonar display screen for the full six hours of his watch. It was harder work than it looked. People thought he got to just sit there, basically watching TV, goofing off until a blip appeared on his screen. But the reality was more like being a guard in a maximum-security prison. He had to be on constant alert, his mind focused and continually interpreting data. If he took his eyes off the sonar display for any extended time, he would be leaving his boat vulnerable to attack. Staring at a screen for six hours straight was enough to leave even the strongest mind feeling wrung out. But, of course, there was nothing dangerous for the sonar to pick up yet as they sailed north from the Hawaiian islands—just other friendlies sailing into and out of port.

The details of a submarine's military operations were routinely classified and were never revealed to the crew until they were underway. It was a security measure designed to prevent leaks, but it also meant Tim had no idea where they were going until Captain Weber finally got on the main circuit and announced their orders. *Roanoke* would be sailing toward Petropavlovsk on the Soviet Union's Kamchatka Peninsula. Tim recognized the name. Petropavlovsk was where the Soviets kept their biggest submarine facility, Rybachiy Nuclear Submarine Base. The news put him on edge. Not that this was an unusual op. The navy was constantly sending boats to the international waters near the Soviet Union, and besides, *Roanoke* was a fast-attack sub, a hunter-killer, she could certainly hold her own if she found herself in trouble. But the state of the world had become a lot more agitated lately, worse than Tim could remember. Earlier this year, a South Korean 747 jetliner bound for Seoul had been shot down by a MiG fighter after apparently straying into Soviet airspace. All 269 civilians aboard had died. Two months later, terrorists had blown up a US military base in Beirut, killing 227 marines. If the navy wanted to send *Roanoke* to the very edge of Soviet waters, there was surely a good reason for it, but suddenly it felt a lot more dangerous than it normally would.

When his watch was over and another tech came to relieve him, Tim left the sonar shack. Crossing the control room toward the stern, he could see that White and Bodine had already been relieved at the helm by two other sailors. He kept walking, through the attack center, which housed the equipment necessary to operate *Roanoke* as a warship, through fire control, where the combat control systems were maintained and operated, until he reached the main ladder, which led down to the middle and lower levels.

The growling of his stomach reminded him that he hadn't eaten in half a day. He climbed down the ladder to the middle level and made his way to the mess. He got in the chow line and grabbed a long foil-wrapped hoagie sandwich from the heating rack on the counter. It was supposed to be a fried-shrimp po'boy. Tim had never had such a thing before, but his hunger made him adventurous. Besides, the chow on *Roanoke* had never let him down. Holding his tray, he scanned the crowded mess deck, looking for a place to sit. The mess had six tables, each with a bench for four or five men, bolted to the floor on either side. A lot of the sailors who had been on the first watch section with Tim were eating now, so most of the tables were filled to capacity. He spotted Jerry White in the crowd and noticed a free seat at his table, right across from him. The captain had asked him to keep an eye on the new transfer, and this seemed as good an opportunity as any to get acquainted. Tim walked over to the table and put his tray down across from White.

"Mind if I join you?" It was a question one rarely had to ask in the mess, but he figured it was a good way to break the ice.

White looked up at him. "Suit yourself," he said, and took a bite of his sandwich.

Tim sat down. "White, isn't it?"

White nodded, chewing.

"Tim Spicer," Tim said, extending his hand across the table.

White shook it. His grip was strong and confident. "Call me Jerry. When I hear 'White,' I think of my father."

"Then you can call me Tim," he said. "Is your father in the navy too?"

Jerry shook his head. "He manages a used-car lot back in Idaho."

"So what brought you to the service?" Tim asked.

Jerry looked at him for a long moment, then said, "I grew up in Idaho, and the family business was used Buicks and Subarus."

"Point taken," Tim said. "Welcome to *Roanoke.*"

Jerry chuckled, his blue eyes flashing with intelligence. "A submarine with the same name as the sixteenth-century colony in North Carolina where everyone mysteriously disappeared? You can't tell me that's not a bad omen."

Tim frowned. "I don't think that's what she's named after."

"I was joking," Jerry said. "Don't people make jokes on this boat?"

"Not good ones," Tim said. He unwrapped the foil around his po'boy and took a bite. The crisp bread and battered shrimp crunched between his teeth. He chewed for a moment, enjoying the spicy, savory taste, then looked down at the sandwich in surprise.

"Something wrong?" Jerry asked.

"No, I just never had Cajun food before," Tim said. "It's damn good."

"I guess you've never been to Louisiana, huh?"

"Nah," Tim said. "Before they sent me to Pearl, I was stationed in San Diego and Tudor Hill."

"Tudor Hill?" Jerry said, growing more animated. "The listening post in Bermuda?"

Tim smiled. "I know. I was lucky. I spent more time working on my tan than listening to submarine traffic."

"Damn right, you were lucky," Jerry said. "While I was freezing my tits off in Idaho, you were soaking up sun on the beach."

"Hey, now, I know a thing or two about freezing," Tim said. "I'm from Maine, a little town up north called Presque Isle. It's farther north than Nova Scotia! On good years, we saw five months of sunny days. On bad years, maybe three."

"Why the fuck would anyone live there?" Jerry asked.

Every new sailor on *Roanoke* had his guard up for a while. Even Tim had been a little prickly when he first joined the crew. But now, judging from the smile on his face, Jerry's guard was coming down. So far, he struck Tim as an all right guy. Maybe keeping an eye on him wasn't going to be so hard after all.

"Potatoes," Tim answered.

Jerry raised his eyebrows. "Come again?"

"My folks were farmers," he said. "I never really took to it the way they did, but that's not why I left. It was the damn winters. Ice and snow are one thing, but the darkness—that's what bothered me the most. Elsewhere, kids spend their free time flying kites or riding bicycles. Me, I spent my free time inside, praying for sunshine."

"Strange that you would go into the submarine service, then," Jerry said. "It's always dark down here. Permanent midnight, and no moon."

"We all have to face our fears sometime," Tim said.

"I guess so," Jerry said. "How's that working out for you?"

Tim gave a half shrug. "I'm still here, aren't I?"

***

When Jerry White had first entered the mess, he was worried, as he had been ever since his transfer orders came through, that he might never fit in on *Roanoke*. Leaving the sailors he had served with on *Philadelphia* and transferring to a boat where he didn't know anyone was hard enough, but a lot of these guys already seemed to know each other pretty well. It was easy to feel like the odd man out, as if he were still that shy high school kid worrying about who he was going to sit with in the cafeteria. He certainly hadn't expected to leave the mess thirty minutes later having made a friend. Tim Spicer seemed like an okay guy—a little stiff, maybe, but his friendliness had put Jerry at ease. Maybe this transfer wouldn't be so bad after all.

"White, hold up," someone called.

Lieutenant Junior Grade Duncan stepped out of the wardroom, where the commissioned officers took their meals.

"Yes, sir," Jerry said, pausing.

"Come here, White."

Duncan beckoned Jerry over to the side of the corridor. He wore a sullen expression, bordering on angry. Jerry walked over to him, wondering what was going on.

"I thought I should give you a heads-up, White," he said. "Your old XO, Frank Leonard, is a buddy of mine. We go way back."

Shit, Jerry thought. He had a bad feeling where this was going.

"Your little stunt on *Philadelphia* cost a good navy man his career," Duncan said. "I hope you're happy."

"Sir—"

"Save it," Duncan interrupted. "I'm watching you, White. You step out of line, you screw up, you so much as miss a button your uniform, and I will be on your ass. Don't doubt it for a second."

Duncan walked off. Jerry stayed where he was, watching him go. *Damn.* Just when things were starting to look up. He glanced nervously at the other men moving through the corridor, hoping they hadn't seen what just happened, but on a submarine, privacy was as scarce as sunshine. Everyone knew everyone's business. Of course they had seen. He could feel their eyes on him. His cheeks burned. They would talk about it too. There was no stopping it. Gossip ran through a submarine faster than beer through a sailor on shore leave.

Welcome to Roanoke, Jerry thought. *Only three months to go.*

CHAPTER FIVE

Sailing deep and slow to avoid detection, it took a week for *Roanoke* to reach the international waters south of Kamchatka Peninsula. For Warren Stubic, that week passed agonizingly slowly. The dull pain behind his eyes had stayed with him since the day of the launch. It was getting harder to concentrate on his duties, on studying for his quals, or on the "hot run" drills they ran in the torpedo room, where they practiced what to do if a torpedo blew inside the tube. Now, on top of everything else, he was feeling physically ill as well.

It had started slowly, with the glare of the boat's fluorescent lights intensifying an already blinding headache. But in the couple of hours since his watch section ended, the throbbing had worsened to the point where a mere glimpse of a light fixture felt like staring into the sun. It burned his eyes and pierced his skull like daggers.

Then there was the heat. He was sweating like a sumo wrestler, really burning up, but it didn't feel like any fever he'd ever had. It felt as if someone were stoking a coal forge in his chest.

Stubic locked himself in one of the stalls in the head. Everything in the head was stainless steel: sinks, stalls, toilets, and all of it reflecting the searing light from the overheads into his eyes. But where else could he go to be alone? He couldn't let anyone see him like this. They would make him go see Matson, the hospital corpsman, who would need to know when it started and where he'd been, and soon enough, everyone on the damn boat would know he had been to a brothel. Sailors gossiped worse than his grandmother's canasta circle, especially on a submarine, where there wasn't much else to keep them entertained. Worse, it would turn into a black mark on his record, and then he could kiss his navy career goodbye. Being a navy man like his father and grandfather before him was all he had ever wanted. He couldn't lose that. He just couldn't.

But his eyes were burning. His head was burning. His whole body was burning. He just wanted to stand under a freezing-cold shower for half an hour. Or even just 10 minutes. Hell, he'd settle for five minutes—anything to stop the feeling that he was burning up from within. But it wasn't allowed, not on a submarine. Water was too scarce. They had to distill potable water from seawater, which gave them only a limited supply for drinking, cooking, and bathing. When you took a shower on a sub, you were supposed to turn the water on and wet down, then turn the water off and soap up, then turn the water on again and rinse off. You couldn't ever leave the water running anywhere, not even while brushing your teeth. If Stubic turned on the shower and let the cold water run over him for as long as he wanted—dear God, what blessed relief that would be—it would draw attention, and that was the last thing he or his career needed.

Maybe the fever would break on its own. Maybe he could just ride it out and not have to see Matson. Yes, that was it. He just had to tough it out, soldier through it, walk it off, as his high school coach used to tell him.

But he kept having flashes of that Filipino girl with the strange jade-green eyes. Every few minutes, the memory barged into his mind, like an unwanted guest. The girl ... the hallway ... the eyes in the dark. Those eyes—what *were* they? Something had been with him in that pitch-black hallway. Something whose eyes weren't ... Weren't what? Weren't human? That was ridiculous. What else could they be?

Had those glowing eyes even been real, or were they something his feverish mind had dreamed up—a false memory?

But instead of comforting him, the thought filled him with terror.

What had happened in that hallway?

Why couldn't he *remember*?

Stubic heard someone come into the head, enter the stall next to his, and latch the door. He heard the sailor urinating, the sound amplified by the stainless steel toilet, and winced as the noise sharpened his headache. Sweat rolled down his face. God, all he wanted was to be somewhere cold. It was too hot here. Too hot everywhere aboard *Roanoke.* He wanted to be anywhere else, anywhere that was cold.

He heard the toilet flush, the stall door open, and the sailor begin washing his hands at the bank of sinks along the bulkhead. Stubic stayed still, not wanting to be noticed, just wanting to be left alone—but a scent came to him on the air. Not the usual stench of the head, but something sweet, enticing. He had never smelled anything like it before. It compelled him to stand up, unlock the stall door, and walk out into the head.

Steve Bodine, the helmsman, stood at the sink, washing his hands. He looked up when he heard Stubic approach.

"How's it going, Stubic?" he asked in his pleasant Oklahoma twang. He turned off the sink and did a double take. "Jesus, man, are you all right?"

"I'm—I'm fine," Stubic said. That scent … It was coming from Bodine, from inside him, somehow.

"You don't look fine to me," Bodine said. "In fact, you look like hammered shit."

Stubic blinked rapidly, squinting against the painful light.

Bodine moved closer. "Hey, man, you want me to get the hospital corpsman?"

"No, no, not Matson," Stubic insisted.

He stepped closer to Bodine. Somehow, he could see the network of veins and arteries running beneath Bodine's chestnut skin. He could see the blood moving through them, pushing forward in time with Bodine's pulse.

A pulse that Stubic could hear as clearly as the ticking of a grandfather clock.

"What are you doing, Stubic?" Bodine asked, taking a step back.

Bodine's blood—that was what he smelled, the source of the sweet, enticing scent. Stubic hadn't been hungry all day. Just the thought of eating had sickened him. But now, suddenly, he was hungry. So very hungry.

He reached for Bodine quickly, faster than he ever thought he could move.

CHAPTER SIX

To Lieutenant Gordon Abrams, the department head in charge of the galley, operating the mess on a submarine felt a lot like tending bar. He got to know the crew the way bartenders got to know their regulars: by listening to them talk. And boy did they love to talk. Through first meal, lunch, dinner, and midrats—those midnight meals for sailors still on duty—every day of every operation felt like a new episode in an ongoing soap opera. If a realistic movie was ever made about life on a sub, it would be a lot less *Run Silent, Run Deep* and a lot more *Peyton Place*. But you couldn't seal 140 men in a can for three months and not expect their deepest, darkest shit to come to light. If any sailor was nursing a grudge, picking fights, cheating on his girl back home, or even suspected someone of pissing in the showers, Gordon was usually the first to know.

The current topic of conversation was the tension between one of the POs, Jerry White, and Lieutenant Junior Grade Charles Duncan. Duncan had chewed White out in front of everyone over a stink White made on his last assignment. Apparently, he had lodged a career-ending complaint against his XO, who happened to be a pal of Duncan's, and now Duncan was riding White hard in the control room. Word spread through the boat quickly, as it always did, and a new and palpable tension had developed between White and the rest of the crew as well. Too bad for White. Without any friends on the boat, it was going to be a long three months. Only Tim Spicer seemed to be sticking by him.

Gordon prided himself on having his ear to the ground. Nothing happened on *Roanoke* without his knowing about it.

He left his stateroom and went to the galley early to supervise the preparations for first meal. Glancing down the corridor to the mess, he noticed Lieutenant Commander Jefferson and an auxiliary tech from Engineering standing by one of the tables and looking up at the ceiling. He walked into the mess and noticed four more crewmen sitting at one of the other tables. They had playing cards spread out in front of them, untouched as they looked up at where the XO and the tech were staring. Gordon paused when he saw it. One of the overhead fluorescent light fixtures had been smashed. Shards of glass littered the table below and the surrounding floor.

"Lieutenant Commander," Gordon said, "what happened, sir?"

"What does it look like, Abrams?" Jefferson replied. His duties as XO included being in charge of security on *Roanoke,* and he didn't look happy at having to deal with this. "We've got a goddamn vandal on the boat."

The fixture looked as though someone had put his fist through it. The glass shield that covered the fluorescent tubes had been smashed in, leaving a jagged round hole. Dried blood clung to the spiky shards and, now that he noticed, flecked the table and the floor below. The vandal had cut himself nicely breaking the light. Good. Gordon hoped it hurt like hell.

Jefferson turned to the table of crewmen. "Are you men sure you didn't see anyone when you got here?"

"Positive, sir," one of them replied. "It's like I said when I went to get you: it was like that when we found it."

Jefferson shook his head and looked up at the fixture again. "Whoever broke it must have been in and out fast."

"Fast" was an understatement. There was no place to hide in the mess, so the miscreant would have had to smash the light and run. But where? The galley? Sick bay? There wasn't much room to hide there, either. The head, maybe? But how could anyone move so fast he wouldn't be seen?

Gordon shook his head. This had come out of nowhere. He hadn't heard anyone talking about anything that might have led up to this. So much for nothing happening on *Roanoke* without his knowledge.

The auxiliary tech, Goodrich, a skinny kid with copper-red hair and a face full of freckles, pulled on a pair of thick black rubber insulating gloves. He carefully cleared the broken glass off the table and into a trash can. Gordon made a mental note to have the table thoroughly cleaned before first meal. The floor too. Goodrich stepped up onto the bench and then the tabletop for a closer look. He removed what was left of the broken glass shield. Inside, both yard-long fluorescent tubes behind the shield were shattered. The ends were still in their sockets, but the rest of the tubes had been reduced to dust and little curved splinters of razor-thin glass. The tech climbed down and dumped the remains of the shield in the trash too.

Gordon wished he had been here to catch the son of a bitch, or even stop him, but when he left the galley and hit his rack before midrats, the light had been just fine. The mess was rarely ever completely empty, even in the hours between midrats and first meal. It was where sailors tended to gather during their downtime to study, play cards, or watch a movie on the small TV and VCR setup. Whoever did this either had been very lucky to find the mess empty or had waited for a moment when no one was around.

"Any idea who would do this, Abrams?" Jefferson asked.

Gordon shook his head. "Sir, my mama worked for twelve years as a nurse in a psychiatric hospital. If there's one thing she taught me, it's that you can't understand crazy. Don't even try."

Jefferson sighed. "I was hoping for something a little more concrete than that. Like a name."

The auxiliary tech climbed back up onto the table. He pulled the broken ends of the tubes out of the fixture and dumped them in the trash. Then he took a pocket light out of his poopie suit, turned it on, and clamped one end between his teeth. He used both hands to open a little hatch in the back of the fixture, then took the light out of his mouth to check the wiring inside.

"The ballast that regulates the current is trashed, sir," Goodrich said. "You're definitely going to need a whole new fixture." He turned off his pocket light and looked down at Gordon. "Unfortunately, sir, we don't have any spares."

"What do you mean?" Gordon asked.

"If it were up to me, sir, we'd bring everything we might need on an underway, but we don't have the space. The Supply Department brings only the essentials."

"You're saying there are no spare light fixtures on board?" Gordon said.

"Sorry, sir," Goodrich said. "If you have a light fixture back there in the galley that you don't need, I could cannibalize it to replace this one. But I'm afraid that's the best I can do, Lieutenant."

"For Christ's sake," Gordon muttered.

"Can you get by with fewer lights in the galley?" Jefferson asked.

Gordon sighed. The mess was supposed to be bright, cheerful, and inviting for the crew—their home away from home. It made sense to take a light from somewhere else if it meant keeping the mess cheery and welcoming, but it felt like robbing Peter to pay Paul.

"Not the galley, sir. We need to see what we're cooking." He added reluctantly, "Maybe one from the pantry, sir."

"Do it," Jefferson told Goodrich.

Sure, do it, Gordon thought glumly. He could just use a flashlight every time he needed flour or canned goods. He was only keeping the crew fed; why should anyone care whether he tripped over something in the dark and broke his goddamn neck?

"Whoever did this won't be hard to find," Jefferson said. "He nicked his hand good."

"Everyone on *Roanoke* comes through the mess eventually," Gordon said. "All we have to do is keep an eye out for someone with cuts on his hand."

"Why wait? I'll inspect every damn sailor's hands on this boat if that's what it takes." Jefferson looked up at the broken light again and shook his head. "It's the damnedest thing. Why break a light? And why break *this* light?"

CHAPTER SEVEN

There was a gravity to being *Roanoke*'s executive officer that Lieutenant Commander Lee Jefferson gladly shouldered. As the submarine's second in command, he was the one who would step into the role of commanding officer if anything should happen to Captain Weber. He liked to think he was ready for that. Hell, he *knew* he was ready. He had heard rumors back at Pearl that the navy was thinking of giving him his own command when this underway was over. He had heard it enough times to think there might be something to it, but for a black man in the US Navy, a healthy degree of skepticism was in order. He had already lost count of how many times white officers with half his experience had been promoted over him. He knew why too, and it sure as hell wasn't about performance.

It wasn't that long ago that black sailors weren't allowed to rise above the ranks of enlisted men, and most had been restricted to steward's mates—the equivalent of seagoing bellhops. Things were different now, but Jefferson knew all too well that the ghosts of the past still haunted the navy's mind-set.

And yet, for all its frustrations, there was nowhere else he wanted to be. He had dreamed of being a navy officer with his own boat since he was a kid, agog in front of an old black-and-white TV set watching movies of pirates swashbuckling their way over the seven seas. If he had to wait longer than most to realize that dream, so be it. He would show the navy the error of its ways by being the best goddamn commanding officer in the fleet.

First, though, he had to get through this underway, and he already had the feeling this would be no easy task. Someone on *Roanoke* was already losing his shit. That smashed light fixture was no accident, and he was determined to root out the culprit as quickly as possible. If he let it go too long, well, the last thing anyone needed was another Mitch Robertson situation.

After alerting Captain Weber to what had happened and his plan to find the man responsible, Jefferson and COB Farrington spent the next few hours traversing the boat and checking the crewmen's hands for cuts. Luckily, the pool of suspects was a small one. There were 124 enlisted men and 16 commissioned officers on *Roanoke*—140 men in all, and that was counting himself, Farrington, Gordon, Captain Weber, and others who couldn't possibly be involved. He and Farrington moved methodically through the boat, level by level, space by space. They inspected the hands of men at their stations and men on their downtime, men studying for their quals, and men training and drilling. Farrington inspected the hands of the enlisted men eating first meal in the mess, while Jefferson inspected the officers dining in the wardroom. A few of the officers were surprised by his order to put out their hands for inspection, but no one argued. As XO, he outranked them all. He and Farrington even went through the head to make sure they didn't miss anyone.

And yet, neither of them found anything. The blood on the broken glass clearly indicated that the vandal had cut himself in the act, but no one had lacerations consistent with putting his fist through a light fixture. With each uninjured hand he saw, Jefferson's frustration increased. He was impatient to find the vandal and be done with it.

He and Farrington split up. While the COB searched the berthing areas, Jefferson went up the main ladder to the top level. He walked through the attack center and fire control, looking at the hands of the men at their stations. Still nothing. *Damn.* He moved on to the control room.

Captain Weber stood with the quartermaster at the plotting tables behind the periscopes, mapping the submarine's course on the charts laid out before him. He looked up when Jefferson walked in.

"How goes the search, Lieutenant Commander?" he asked. "Have you found your man?"

"Not yet, Captain," Jefferson replied. "Farrington is inspecting the men in their racks now. All that's left are the men in the control room. Permission to inspect them, sir?"

"Permission granted, Jefferson," the captain said, returning his attention to the charts. "Just be quick about it."

Jefferson inspected the quartermaster's hands, the watchstanding OOD's, and the radioman's, and then crossed the control room to the sonar shack. The space was narrow and cramped inside, forcing Jefferson to remain standing in the doorway. Along one bulkhead were four consoles, each manned by a sonar tech. Tim Spicer sat at the one nearest the door, the bright colors from his sonar screen playing across his face. Jefferson glanced at Spicer's hands, at all the techs' hands. Still nothing. Hands, hands, hands—he was getting sick of looking at everyone's damn hands, especially when it wasn't bringing him any closer to catching the vandal.

"Mr. Spicer, can I have a moment of your time?" Jefferson said.

Spicer took off his headphones. "Yes, sir. Is everything all right?"

He started to get up from his seat, but Jefferson waved at him to stay.

"This will only take a moment," he said. "At some point after midrats, someone went into the mess and smashed one of the light fixtures. I was wondering if you heard anything."

"No sir, I'm sorry," Spicer said. "I was in my rack, sawing logs. Didn't hear a thing."

"The mess is just down the hall from the berthing areas," Jefferson said. "You're sure you didn't hear *anything*? Didn't notice anyone leaving their rack?"

"I'm afraid not, sir," Spicer said. "Sir, why would somebody smash one of the lights?"

"That's what I'm trying to find out," Jefferson said. He addressed the other techs in the sonar shack. "What about the rest of you? Anyone hear anything? See anything?"

They all shook their heads.

"Either this guy's a ninja, or you're all the heaviest damn sleepers I ever met," Jefferson said.

"Sorry, sir," Spicer said.

"Carry on," Jefferson replied.

As Spicer put his earphones back on, Jefferson returned to the control room and inspected the chief of the watch's hands, and those of the diving officer, Lieutenant Junior Grade Duncan.

The watchstanding planesman, Jerry White, had his hands in plain view on the yoke, making it easy to see that he wasn't the vandal. Jefferson knew all about White's trouble with his previous XO on *Philadelphia*. Captain Weber had consulted with both him and COB Farrington before accepting the transfer. Farrington had been against it, convinced White would be a troublemaker, which meant it would fall on him as COB to keep him on a short leash. Jefferson, on the other hand, had been in favor, arguing that White deserved the benefit of the doubt, especially after his heroism in saving USS *Philadelphia* from a fire. In the end, Captain Weber had agreed with him, much to Farrington's annoyance—and, it seemed, to Duncan's as well. Everyone on board had heard about Duncan giving White an earful outside the mess. Jefferson didn't gossip with the men—as XO, it was his duty to remain aloof from all that—but he felt bad for White. It couldn't be easy having everyone snicker at your public humiliation behind your back.

Next to White was Steve Bodine, whose own clearly uninjured hands were on the helmsman's yoke. Jefferson and Bodine had become close at the naval station, though he rode Bodine hard when they were on duty— harder than he rode anyone else, because a black man in a boat that was 99 percent white had to work twice as hard as anyone else to get half the respect. But when they were off duty, Jefferson took Bodine under his wing. They often spoke in private about the issues Bodine came up against, and Jefferson tried to offer the best advice he could.

Recently, Bodine had told him about an enlisted man who called him an ugly racial slur. Bodine had gone through the proper channels, complaining to the COB. The offending sailor had been punished, but the sting of the insult had stayed with him. He was having trouble seeing the sailor again day after day—it was making him angry and unsettled. When he came to Jefferson for advice, Jefferson told him it wasn't up to the COB or the other sailor or anyone else to find a way to make it work. It was up to Bodine, and the best way to make it work was to move on. Bodine had trouble swallowing that bitter piece of advice, just as Jefferson had back when he was the same age. But if the kid wanted to make a career for himself in the navy, he was going to have to do what he had to do to get along.

But now, seated at the helm, Bodine looked distracted, unwell. His shoulders twitched, and he blinked rapidly.

"Everything all right, Bodine?" Jefferson asked.

Bodine jolted slightly in his chair, as though he hadn't been aware Jefferson was behind him. "Sir? Yes—yes, sir. Fine, sir."

But he didn't look fine. He was still blinking rapidly, and he wiped his sweat-beaded forehead with one hand. A drop of sweat rolled out of his close-cropped hairline and down his neck—past two small, red welts.

"What's that on your neck, Bodine?" Jefferson asked.

The helmsman absently rubbed the side of his neck with one hand. "I don't know, sir. I—I can't remember where they came from."

Jefferson was about to tell him to get checked out by the hospital corpsman, when Farrington burst into the control room, clearly agitated. He walked up to Captain Weber at the plotting tables.

"Captain, sir, there's been a development," he said.

"Go ahead, COB," the captain said as Jefferson walked over to them.

"I was inspecting the bunks just now and discovered one of the racks was empty, sir," Farrington said.

"Who's missing?" Captain Weber asked.

"It's Stubic, sir," Farrington said. "Petty Officer Third Class Warren Stubic."

CHAPTER EIGHT

While Lieutenant Commander Jefferson and COB Farrington were traversing the submarine inspecting the crew's hands, Lieutenant Gordon Abrams was busy with first meal, making sure the hungry sailors who weren't currently on their watch sections had something hot in their bellies.

Roanoke's galley felt like home to Gordon in a way that almost nowhere else did, except maybe the house he had grown up in. When things were going right in the galley, every day was the same. Only the menu changed. And that was how he liked it. The banging of pots, the hiss and sizzle of the deep fryer, the noise of his culinary specialists cooking an all-you-can-eat buffet for 140 men—these sounds had become his constant companions, his comfort zone. He got nervous only when the noise stopped, because that meant something was wrong. Still, he had to admit, there were times when he envied the variety he was sure the other crewmen experienced each day. Keeping watch for Soviet boats, steering *Roanoke* through deep and enemy-infested waters, manning the torpedoes. But he knew he didn't really have the temperament for it. This was where he belonged, amid the noise and controlled chaos of the galley, supervising the culinary specialists who cooked chow for the men; the bakers who were responsible for making fresh muffins, dinner rolls, and desserts; the dishwashers; and the team of stewards who brought the chow to the wardroom on one side of the galley and the mess on the other. Gordon took pride in his contribution, making sure his galley produced the finest food in the fleet.

But then some asshole had put his fist through a light in the mess, and now everything felt off-kilter. He couldn't help taking it personally. That was *his* mess the culprit had vandalized. As much as he tried not to let it distract him from his duties, it was never far from his mind. He hoped they found the bastard soon and gave him a captain's mast. Or better yet, left him on an iceberg somewhere and told him to go to hell.

Accompanying Gordon in the galley, at this moment cooking eggs, sausage, and hot cereal for the crew, were two of his newest culinary specialists: Seaman Apprentices Oran and LeMon Guidry. When the brothers had arrived for their section, they ribbed each other over the broken light fixture, blaming each other's cooking for being so bad it drove someone over the edge. Annoyed, Gordon had put a stop to it right away and put them to work scrubbing dried blood off the table and floor. They were too young to understand how serious this was, and still too new to the navy to grasp how dangerous the urge for destruction could be on a submarine.

They hailed from someplace called Bayou Bartholomew—a couple of easygoing good old boys who grew up in the marshes on a diet of catfish, alligator, and dirty rice. Their hair was so blond it almost looked white, and they both had a deep tan that spoke of a youth spent outside in the sun. The first time Gordon met them, he thought they were twins, but Oran was actually two years older than LeMon. With a nose that had obviously been broken and reset at least once, he looked like a scrapper who had seen his share of fights. According to the story they told Gordon, right after both boys had graduated from high school they hitchhiked to Baton Rouge together and signed up with their local navy recruiter.

Even though their thick Cajun accents made them sound like a couple of backwoods stump jumpers whenever they opened their mouths, according to Oran's personnel file he had scored a perfect 300 on the Armed Services Vocational Aptitude Battery. That qualified him for *any* job in the Navy. LeMon had scored 283—too low to be an electrician's mate or a machinist, but high enough to qualify him for pretty much any other enlisted man's occupational specialty. The brothers weren't exactly Naval Academy material, but they were prime candidates for the enlisted ranks.

As the story went, they had asked only two things of their navy recruiters. The first was that they stay together. LeMon had always wanted to travel the world, and Oran just wanted to look after his little brother. The second thing they asked for, even though they could have had just about any navy enlistment classification they wanted, was to be made culinary specialists. And Gordon thanked his stars that the navy had agreed to both requests, because the Guidry brothers could *cook*. Apparently, it had been a big part of their lives back home. They used spices in ways Gordon had never seen before, and earlier in the underway they had whipped up a special seasoning of paprika, pepper, salt, and dried herbs that could be rubbed on meat to make it both sweet and spicy. The crew had gone nuts for it. The Guidry brothers made an effortless team in his galley, and if they kept it up, Gordon was certain they had it in them to be culinary rock stars. That would take them far in the navy.

"Lieutenant, suh," Oran said, standing in front of the burner and working a big pan of scrambled eggs with a steel spatula, "we got roas' beef on the menu for tomorrow, but we best take it out of the freezer to thaw. You want, I'll go get it, suh."

"No, Guidry, I'll take care of it. You two stay put. When the stewards come back, I want another platter of sausages sent to the mess, okay? They're running low."

"Yessuh," Oran said. He nudged LeMon, who was minding the sausages while they roasted in the oven. "You hear that, Monje? Get your head out the clouds and make sure them sausages ready."

LeMon sucked his teeth and said, "I ain't Grandpa Zephirin. I hear just fine." Then, to Gordon, "Sausages be ready in two shakes, suh."

"Good," Gordon said. The two of them could be a couple of clowns sometimes, but he didn't mind so long as they continued to perform their duties well. In addition to their culinary skills, they handled the galley like pros. The other day a grease fire had started on the burners, and the Guidrys had calmly and quickly smothered it with a sack of flour before Gordon even noticed. He would have been tempted to call them old hands at this if they weren't so young.

He went to the pantry and glanced up at the bare spot on the ceiling, where one of the two light fixtures had been removed to replace the broken one in the mess. It rankled him how much of the room was in shadow.

The walk-in freezer was at the far end of the pantry. He put on the jacket, wool cap, and thick gloves that hung from a peg on the stainless-steel door. The freezer was kept at a steady minus-five degrees, cold enough to suck away a man's body heat awfully fast if he wasn't wearing protection.

He went in and let the door close again behind him. For safety, the door wasn't lockable and had a handle on the inside as well as the outside. The twenty-by-six room reminded him of an old narrow-gauge boxcar, with inventory packed as tight as books on a library shelf. The metal shelves were sturdy as hell; they had never once buckled on him, even loaded with hundreds of pounds of food. It was a tight squeeze between those shelves. He had to turn sideways to make his way down the length of the freezer, picking through the shelves as he looked for the roast, already feeling the subzero chill. He found it ironic that so much energy went into warming a submarine when they were running at five hundred feet below, while even more energy was spent keeping the freezer below zero.

Other than the soft noise of frigid air coming in through the vents, the room was as silent as the Arctic tundra in midwinter. His breath clouded in front of him. He had been inside less than a minute, but the cold was already turning his nose numb and stinging his sinuses as he inhaled.

He turned his head to the rear of the freezer, alerted by something he had noticed out of the corner of his eye. Something on the floor that looked out of place. It took him a second to register what he was seeing.

"What the hell?" he gasped, the words coming out in a puff of condensation.

A dead man lay on the freezer floor.

Gordon rushed over to him. He was curled in the fetal position, hands tucked between his legs as if he were trying to keep them warm. *Jesus God,* Gordon thought. *How did this happen?* Had the man gotten trapped in the freezer somehow? But the door didn't lock. There was no way to be accidentally stranded inside. Gordon shook his head in horror. He couldn't think of many worse ways to go than freezing to death in this tiny, cramped space. How had it happened? *When* had it happened? Oran had done a routine inventory check in the freezer just yesterday, and there sure as hell hadn't been a corpse in here then.

The man's face didn't ring a bell, but he was dressed in the same blue coveralls that all the enlisted men wore. The body was covered head to toe with white, crystalline frost. He was pale, as if all the color had drained out of him, except for the dark semicircles below his eyes—eyes still open and staring at Gordon. No, not at him, he realized, but at the freezer door behind him. The man had died only twenty feet from safety. Had he fallen and been unable to move? Had someone trapped him in the freezer on purpose, blocking the door from the outside to keep him there until he succumbed to hypothermia?

The thought was so horrible, Gordon tried not to think it. He grabbed the dead man by the rigid, icy legs and tried to drag him out of the freezer, but he had frozen to the floor. Gordon rocked the corpse back and forth until it broke free with a sickening pop. Then he pulled the body again, stiff as a board, to the freezer door. He used his elbow to knock the door open, then pulled the body out of the freezer and into the pantry.

"Get the corpsman!" he yelled. "Somebody get the goddamn corpsman!"

He pulled the dead man away from the freezer and left him there, dropping his legs—they made a loud *crack* as they hit the floor—and slamming the freezer door shut. In the dim light of the one remaining pantry fixture, the crewman's body looked even more horrible. The dark circles around his eyes became black pits, the empty sockets of a death's head.

Oran and LeMon came running into the pantry. As soon as he saw the body, Oran pushed LeMon back out, shouting, "Monje, go get the corpsman! Now!"

Gordon yanked off his protective gloves and jacket and crouched down over the body. "He ... he was in the freezer—I don't know for how long."

Oran shook his head. "Poor fella. How he get in there?"

"No idea," Gordon said. "Do you recognize him?"

Oran shook his head again. "No, suh. Seen a lot of faces in the mess, but they don' all stick. But looka this, suh." He pointed to one frozen hand.

Gordon leaned forward for a closer look. There was frozen blood on the dead man's hand—dark red icicles from the lacerations in his skin.

"The light fixture, suh?" Oran asked.

"Jesus," Gordon said. "A smashed light, a dead body in the freezer— what the hell is going on?"

Sick bay abutted the mess, so it didn't take long for LeMon to run back with help. *Roanoke's* hospital corpsman, Senior Chief Sherman Matson, hurried into the pantry with LeMon. Like most corpsmen, Matson wasn't a doctor, but he was the only medically trained sailor on the boat. He could tend a broken arm, take care of a crewman with the flu, hand out painkillers, or run a physical, but if something life-threatening occurred, his job was to stabilize the sailor as best he could until they reached the closest medical facility. Not that there was anything even the most gifted doc could do for the poor frozen son of a bitch at this point except lay him to rest.

Gordon and Oran backed away while Matson knelt down to inspect the corpse. He felt for a pulse in the dead man's neck, then yanked his hand back from the frozen flesh. He listened for breath passing between the icy blue lips, but the look in his eye said he knew it was futile.

"What happened here, Lieutenant?" Matson asked, straightening again.

"I found him in the freezer," Gordon said. "He was just lying there."

"How long was he in there, sir?"

"Hard to say, but it can't have been more than a few hours. Do you know who he is?"

Matson looked down at the frozen corpse and sighed. "Yes, sir, I know him. His name was Stubic. Warren Stubic."

Gordon heard a sudden murmur of shocked voices and looked up. Over Matson's shoulder, he saw the faces of every sailor in the mess, crowding in the pantry doorway. *Damn.* Now there was no way to keep word from spreading to the rest of crew, along with all the rumors and innuendo that sprang up whenever two sailors spoke.

"What are we going to do with him?" Gordon asked. There was no morgue on board, no medical ward. Even sick bay was little more than a supply closet full of bandages, medicine, and a few basic surgical instruments.

"I'm afraid we don't have a lot of options, sir," Matson replied. "It's recommended that a dead body be kept on ice until we reach the closest medical facility."

"He's already frozen solid," Gordon said. "Besides, I don't want to put him back in the freezer if that's where he died. It doesn't seem right, you know? There's got to be someplace else we can put him."

Matson thought for a moment. "It would have to be someplace private, sir. Someplace removed from the rest of the crew. The problem is, there's no place private on a submarine. The only place that even comes close is the torpedo room. No one goes in there except the torpedomen. Stubic was one, you know—a torpedoman. Maybe the others would be willing to have one of their own down there until we reach the nearest base."

Gordon nodded. "Okay, Matson, sounds good. Go get a body bag out of sick bay, and we'll take him down there ourselves."

"Aye, sir." Matson stood up and left the pantry, squeezing past the crowd that had gathered in the doorway.

"Suh, we can take him down ourselves," Oran said. "You don' have to—"

"No. I'm the one who found him. I should go with him." He looked at the sailors crowding the doorway. "Now, get those people out of here. Then one of you go get Lieutenant Commander Jefferson. He has to be informed."

Oran Guidry went to the doorway. "You heard the lieutenant, now. All y'all go on back to the mess. Galley personnel only."

Gordon looked down at the corpse again. His gaze went to the injured, bloody hand, then the staring eyes that held an expression somewhere between terror and madness. Why would a torpedoman break a light fixture in the mess? How had he wound up in the freezer? What the hell was going on?

CHAPTER NINE

When Petty Officer Tim Spicer's watch in the sonar shack was over, he left the control room and headed for the main ladder. Being on a submarine sometimes felt like being on another planet, one with a different orbit and spin. While everyone on land enjoyed 24-hour days, submariners made do with 18-hour ones. They slept six hours, worked six, had six off to unwind—eat, do laundry, study for their off-quals, read, or listen to cassettes on their yellow Walkman headphones—and then the cycle began over again.

After living in the 24-hour world, the 18-hour world could mess with a man's inner clock. It didn't help that on a sub there was no discernible difference between day and night. Sunlight didn't penetrate this deep, and it wasn't as if they had windows to enjoy the view, anyway. The lights stayed on permanently everywhere but the berthing areas, where the crewmen slept. For some, it all could be very disorienting. Tim had certainly had trouble with it on his first underway, and he was certain it had contributed to Mitch Robertson's breakdown. And now it looked as though someone else was losing it.

He spotted Jerry White stepping off the ladder on the middle level and called down for him to wait. Jerry stopped and waited for him, and they moved to one side of the corridor to let others pass by on their way to the mess, the berthing areas, or the head.

"Did you hear, someone smashed a light in the mess?" Tim asked.

"I heard the XO asking you about it," Jerry replied. "There's a rumor making the rounds that whoever did it used his bare hands. You'd have to be crazy to do something like that."

"Not everyone's cut out for living in a tin can," Tim said. "It's rare, but sometimes people snap."

"So I've heard. Something like that happened on the last underway, didn't it?" Jerry pressed himself against the bulkhead to let a group of sailors by on their way to the mess. "I heard my predecessor tried to kill himself. They say he cut his wrists in the head. They also say you're the one who found him and saved his life."

"I think it was more of a cry for help than a real attempt to kill himself," Tim said. "Matson told me afterward that Robertson had cut his wrists crosswise instead of lengthwise. Makes it a lot harder to bleed out that way. Who told you about him?"

"Pearl's not that big a station," Jerry said. "Word gets around. As soon as I got there and people heard which boat I was assigned to, they fell all over themselves telling me the sordid details. I think they were trying to spook me, but I was excited for the transfer, to be honest. After being in a Sturgeon-class sub, being in a Los Angeles class feels like moving into a bigger house. *Philadelphia* was a short-hull; there was even less room in her than there is in *Roanoke*."

"I'm glad to hear the transfer's working out," Tim said.

"Well, I wouldn't go *that* far," Jerry said. "Lieutenant Duncan's been riding my ass so hard, the other men have started giving me a wide berth. It's like they don't want to draw my fire." Jerry looked up the main ladder and then both ways down the corridor. "The other day in the mess, I asked some of the guys I know from the control room if I could join their card game. You know what they said? They said I was putting Duncan in a bad mood and he was taking it out on all of them. They told me if it stopped I could join the game. Can you believe that? Even Bodine's giving me the cold shoulder, and he's my helmsman. We're supposed to work together—although he's been a little weird too. Today he was distracted. He couldn't seem to concentrate, and he was sweating like he was in a sauna. Of course, that put Duncan in an even pissier mood." He glanced down the corridor. "Ah, shit. Weather's about to change."

Tim turned and saw Lieutenant Junior Grade Duncan walking toward them out of the wardroom.

"Just be cool," Tim said.

"White!" Duncan called. He stopped in front of them. "You were too slow at the yoke today, White. Maybe on *Philadelphia* they let air-breathing nubs like you slack off, but you're on *Roanoke* now. When you're given an order, you don't hesitate; you execute it. Am I clear, sailor?"

"Yes, sir," Jerry said. But Tim saw a hint of confusion in his eyes, as if he didn't know what the lieutenant was talking about.

Duncan raised his eyebrows. "What was that, sailor? Did you say something?"

Jerry straightened his shoulders and stood at parade rest—feet apart and hands clasped behind him at the small of the back. "I said aye, sir."

"That's what I thought. Watch where you step, White. You're on mighty thin ice—wouldn't take much for you to fall through."

With a steely parting glare, Duncan turned and continued toward the officers' staterooms.

"What was that about?" Tim asked once Duncan was out of earshot.

"He thinks I killed his friend's navy career."

"Your former XO?" Tim asked. Jerry looked at him in surprise, and Tim shrugged. "Like you said, word gets around. So did you really hesitate, or was the lieutenant just looking for an excuse to bust your balls?"

Jerry didn't meet his eye. He glanced sharply down the corridor in the direction Duncan had gone. "He's my diving officer. If he says I hesitated, then I must have hesitated. That's just the way it is."

"Bullshit," Tim said. "We could talk to the COB, maybe get Lieutenant Duncan to back off."

"Forget it," Jerry said. "It's nothing."

"You sure about that? Because I don't see him easing up on his own, and you're going to be stuck on this boat with him for three months."

"Just let it go, okay, Tim?"

Jerry headed off toward the mess. Tim hung back a moment, then followed. From what he had seen so far, Jerry seemed like a solid guy who took pride in his work. So why was he content to let Duncan keep hassling him? Was he just a masochist, or did he maybe feel guilty about something? What went down on *Philadelphia* that made Jerry file that complaint?

Up ahead, Tim spotted Lieutenant Commander Jefferson coming out of the mess, followed by Senior Chief Matson, Lieutenant Abrams, and one of the new culinary specialists, Oran Guidry. They were carrying a heavy bundle between them. It took Tim a second to register that it was a black body bag, zipped shut and bulging from the rigid, asymmetrical mass inside. He ran over to them, pushing past the knot of curious sailors that was forming around them. Jerry was right behind him.

"Sir, what happened?" Tim asked just as Abrams lost his grip on the bag for a moment and nearly dropped it.

"Spicer, White, give us a hand with this," Jefferson said.

Jerry got his hands under one side of the body bag, and Tim lifted from the other side. He winced in surprise. Whoever was inside the bag was so cold, Tim's hands started to ache. He kept his grip, though, and helped the other five men carry it to the main ladder. Maneuvering the load down the ladder to the bottom level without dropping it was difficult, but between the six of them they managed.

There were only two enlisted men inside the long, narrow torpedo room, a skeleton crew that mostly did maintenance while the boat was still in friendly waters. Both looked surprised to see Lieutenant Commander Jefferson's imposing bulk in the doorway.

"Clear the room," Jefferson ordered.

The two torpedomen hustled out into the corridor, gawking in shock at the body bag. Jefferson led Tim and the others in, then ordered them to lay the body bag on the floor in back, near the torpedo tubes. When Tim straightened again, he stuck his freezing hands under his armpits to warm them.

Oran Guidry turned to his boss. "Suh, permission to return to the galley? Best not leave Monje alone up there or he start screwin' thangs up."

"Yes, that's fine, Guidry, thank you," Abrams replied, and Oran hurried out of the torpedo room.

Tim watched him leave and saw the two torpedomen reappear in the doorway. Tim had the same questions they did, but his experience with officers told him this was something they would prefer to handle without him and Jerry getting in the way. He expected Abrams or Jefferson to dismiss them both, but they seemed too focused on the dead man to care about their presence.

"How the hell did he get inside your freezer, Lieutenant?" Jefferson asked.

Gordon wiped one arm across his forehead. "I don't have an answer for that yet, sir, but I plan to. All I know is, he was dead when I found him."

"How long was he in there?" Jefferson asked.

"Couldn't have been more than a few hours, sir."

"It wouldn't take long to freeze to death in there," Matson added. "The freezer is kept at subzero temperatures, and depending on any number of factors, he would have been dead of exposure anywhere between 15 and 45 minutes."

"Was he trapped inside?"

"Not possible, sir," Gordon replied. "The freezer opens from the inside, and you can't lock it. He couldn't have been trapped."

Jefferson looked down at the body bag with a grimace. "I hate to ask this, Matson, but is it possible someone killed him first and then put him in the deep freeze?"

"I didn't see any signs of trauma, sir," Matson said. "Nothing to indicate he was strangled, stabbed, shot …"

Jefferson shook his head in bewilderment. "When you showed me those cuts on his hands, I almost couldn't believe it. First he breaks the light fixture in the mess; then he turns up dead?"

Tim glanced at Jerry, but Jerry looked deep in thought.

"We have to bring the body to a medical facility where they can perform a proper autopsy on him and find out what happened," Jefferson continued. "Right now, the closest base is still Pearl Harbor. It's a straight shot down the Pacific, and if we turn around now we can be there in a week. I'll inform Captain Weber, but that's one hell of a detour. He's not going to be happy." He called one of the torpedomen watching from the doorway back into the room. "Your name's Cameron, isn't it?"

"Aye, sir," the sailor replied. He looked to be early 30s—older than most of the enlisted men aboard.

"You and the other torpedomen will be assigned to new stations until we reach the base and the body can be removed," Jefferson said. "I'll inform the weapons officer. But until we get to Pearl, this room is now officially the morgue."

Cameron eyed the body bag nervously. "Aye, sir."

"Dismissed, Cameron," Jefferson said.

"Aye-aye, sir," the torpedoman replied. He turned around and started to leave.

"Cameron, hold on," Jefferson called after him.

The sailor turned back to him. "Sir?"

"You worked with the deceased, Warren Stubic. What can you tell me about him? Did you notice anything unusual lately? Anything off?"

Stubic? Tim thought back to the strange encounter he'd had with the man on the day of the launch—that wild, almost panicked look in his eye. After that, it almost didn't come as a surprise to hear that Stubic had smashed the light fixture. But frozen to death in the galley's freezer? That was a shock.

Cameron glanced at the bag again, a sadness in his eyes. Tim wondered whether they had been close. "Stubic is—was—a good torpedoman, sir. At least, he used to be. He was different this time, sir."

"What do you mean?" Jefferson asked.

"He wasn't acting like himself, sir," Cameron said. "He wasn't focusing on his duties. Kept complaining about headaches, and the lights hurting his eyes. Last time I saw him, he was sweating something awful. I mean *drenched*. I worked with him on two previous underways, sir. This definitely wasn't like him. Something must have happened to him."

"Sir, if I may?" Tim said.

"You have something to add, Spicer?" Jefferson asked.

"Yes, sir. I noticed the same things about Stubic that Cameron did. I ran into him on the first day of the underway. Something was definitely wrong with him, sir. He said he was fine, but he didn't look it. He just seemed … out of it."

Jefferson nodded. "Thank you. You're dismissed, Cameron. Spicer, White, you too. Get back to your duties."

"Aye, sir," Tim said.

The three enlisted men left the room. Cameron joined his colleague from the torpedo room, while Tim and Jerry went back up the main ladder to the middle level. They entered the mess, but Tim wasn't hungry anymore. Just a week into the underway, and a crewman was already dead. Everyone in the mess was already talking about it. The rumors were flying. Stubic was on drugs. Stubic sneaked alcohol aboard. Stubic was poisoned in Hawaii by a jealous husband using a slow-acting toxin that drove him insane. It all sounded like nonsense to Tim, but how plausible an explanation could you expect for a man putting his fist through a glass light fixture and winding up frozen solid? Nothing sounded right.

"Tim, hold up a second," Jerry said.

He stopped. "Yeah, what is it?"

"I'm worried," Jerry said.

Tim nodded. "Me too. It's nuts what happened to Stubic. I can't get my mind around it."

"It's not just that," Jerry said. "You heard what Cameron said. Stubic couldn't focus, and he was sweating like a whore in church. Sound familiar? It's just like what's happening to Bodine."

CHAPTER TEN

Jefferson crouched down beside the body bag on the floor of the torpedo room. He was tempted to unzip it and take another look at the man inside, but that first look had been enough. Face covered in white crystals of frost, eyes open and staring blankly.

"Do you think he was sick?" he asked Senior Chief Matson.

Matson frowned. "It's possible. From what the crewmen told us—inability to focus, his persistent sweating—it sounds like he might have had a serious fever."

"Right," Lieutenant Abrams muttered with a mirthless chuckle. "And maybe he was looking for someplace to cool off."

"As strange as it may sound, sir, you might not be wrong about that," Matson said. "If Stubic's fever was high enough, he could have been delirious, even hallucinating. In that state of mind, he might not have understood what he was doing."

"Are you saying he could have shut himself in the freezer *on purpose?*" Jefferson said.

Matson sighed. "I don't know, sir. It's just conjecture right now, but I'm saying it's not impossible."

Jefferson stood and rubbed a hand over his short, tightly curled hair in exasperation. "Let me get this straight. Sometime between midrats and first meal, Stubic entered the mess during a rare moment when it was empty, smashed one of the lights, and then walked into the freezer and shut himself in. All because he was delirious. That's what you're saying?"

"It does sound pretty far-fetched, sir," Matson admitted. "The only other explanation I can think of is that he just snapped."

"But supposing that's true, why snap *now*?" Jefferson asked. "He's no first-timer. He's an experienced submariner who's been on a couple of underways with us already."

Neither Matson nor Abrams had an answer.

Jefferson sighed. "I'd better go inform the captain."

***

On the top level, Jefferson found the door to Captain Weber's stateroom closed. He knocked.

"Who is it?" The captain's voice sounded terse and preoccupied.

"Lieutenant Commander Jefferson, sir."

"Come in."

Jefferson opened the door and hunched over to step inside. There were no height restrictions for officers in the submarine service, but anyone over six feet risked bumping his head in the cramped staterooms, which didn't seem designed so much as carved out of available space as an afterthought. And the marine architect certainly wasn't thinking of a six-and-a-half-foot linebacker. Captain Weber was poring over a map spread across his fold-down desk. He didn't look up.

"Close the door behind you, Lieutenant Commander," the captain said, drawing lines across the map with a pencil and ruler. "I'll be right with you."

Jefferson could see the coast of Alaska on one side of the map, and the Siberian coast directly across. The Kamchatka Peninsula jutted down from the eastern end of the Soviet Union like a whale's fin, with the Sea of Okhotsk on one side, and on the other, the Pacific Ocean and the Rybachiy Nuclear Submarine Base. Captain Weber had circled the location of the base and was currently drawing several lines between *Roanoke*'s current position and the peninsula, plotting possible courses. And from where Jefferson stood, a lot of those lines looked as though they reached significantly closer to the shoreline than international maritime law allowed.

"What can I do for you, Jefferson?" Captain Weber finally asked, looking up from his work.

Jefferson pulled his gaze away from the map. "Sir, I'm sorry to say I have bad news. There's been a death among the crew."

The captain straightened in his chair. "My God. Who?"

"PO3 Warren Stubic, a torpedoman, sir. We believe he's responsible for that broken light in the mess, as well."

Captain Weber sat back and stared past his XO. "Jesus! What happened?"

"We're not sure yet, sir. Matson's working theory is that Stubic might have been sick, possibly delirious with fever. We won't know for certain until there's an autopsy."

"I see. Where is the body now?"

"I've authorized that it be stored in the torpedo room, sir. Senior Chief Matson is with the body now."

Captain Weber nodded. "Thank you for bringing this to my attention, Jefferson. As soon as we can, we'll radio back and make sure his family is informed."

"Sir, the nearest medical facility—"

"It's going to have to wait," the captain said, cutting him off. "I can't take the time now."

"Sir, I mean no disrespect, but this is protocol. The navy expects us to bring dead sailors to the nearest medical facility without delay, sir."

"It's going to have to wait!" the captain repeated, a notch louder.

"Aye, sir," Jefferson said, coming to attention. "Understood, sir."

Captain Weber took a deep breath. "I'm well aware of navy protocol, Lieutenant Commander. But if you knew how important this operation is, how much is riding on it …"

"Sir, I thought this was just a reconnaissance op," Jefferson said.

The captain picked up his pencil and a divider and returned his attention to the map, ignoring Jefferson's statement. "I need you to keep this boat running smoothly, Lieutenant Commander. I need the crew focused and ready. It won't be much farther now."

What wouldn't be much farther now? Jefferson's eyes darted to the map again, but it offered no answers, and the captain's expression invited no questions. There were things about this op he was keeping close to the vest. Of course, that was a captain's prerogative. Jefferson didn't have to like it; he only had to accept it.

"Dismissed," Captain Weber told him.

***

Back in the torpedo room, Jefferson found Matson alone, attending the body. Lieutenant Abrams had returned to the galley. The hospital corpsman wasn't happy to hear that the captain wouldn't be turning back to Pearl.

"So what are we supposed to do, sir, just keep him down here?" the corpsman asked.

"Captain's orders," Jefferson told him. He didn't like it any more than Matson did, but the captain had made his decision. And judging from the way he had snapped at Jefferson, there would be no changing his mind. It had something to do with the op; that much was clear.

"I suppose you want me to stay down here with him, sir?" Matson asked. He didn't sound happy with the idea.

"No, there's no need. Stubic's not going anywhere, and I've informed the weapons officer that the torpedo room is to remain off-limits until I say otherwise. We'll keep the hatch closed in the meantime."

"Thank you, sir," Matson said, relieved. "I was worried I'd go stir crazy if I had to stay down here for an entire section. I don't know how the torpedomen do it, sir. This has got to be the loneliest place on the sub."

Jefferson looked around. Matson wasn't wrong. The torpedo room was cramped and unfriendly, full of metal and machinery and hard edges, with torpedoes resting in their steel trays along the bulkhead, and only a narrow corridor from the doorway to the torpedo tubes. It had an isolated, inhospitable feel.

"I suppose that's why it makes a good morgue," Jefferson said. "Nobody wants to be here."

They left the torpedo room. Matson climbed the main ladder to the middle level while Jefferson secured the hatch. When he was finished, he walked the length of the corridor to the main ladder and was about to start climbing when he heard a loud metallic bang come from the auxiliary engine room at the aft end of the bottom level, followed by a loud, frustrated curse.

The auxiliary engine, also known as the Big Red Machine, had gotten its nickname from its bright red color, although some swore it was in honor of the Cincinnati Reds, who had dominated the National League all throughout the 1970s. An enormous diesel generator, the Big Red Machine was designed to power the boat if the nuclear reactor ever shut down. Jefferson entered the auxiliary engine room and found three sailors from Engineering standing in front of the engine, a scattering of tools at their feet.

"Everything all right in here?" he asked.

"Aye, sir," one of the sailors replied. "Just doing our weekly maintenance check, sir."

"Carry on," Jefferson told them.

Along one bulkhead, he saw the stack of food crates the engineers had allowed Lieutenant Abrams to store here while his pantry was full. In a few more weeks, once more of the food had been consumed and shelf space became available, the crates of big number 10 cans of vegetables, coffee, fruit, and soup would go up to the pantry for unpacking. Jefferson had been in the navy a long time now, and in submarines for most of it, but every once in a while it still amazed him how well things ran, how efficient it was when everyone pulled together. If duties were performed properly and everything was where it was supposed to be, an underway could run as smoothly as clockwork.

But it was a delicate balance. It didn't take much for things to go

FUBAR on a sub, and Warren Stubic had damn well turned things FUBAR for *Roanoke*. But why? He still couldn't puzzle it out. The theory that Stubic had snapped didn't fly. He had to pass a psych eval when he first joined the navy, and they certainly would have spotted any potential for a psychotic break. An illness, then? Possibly, but that opened a whole other can of worms. Where had Stubic picked it up? Was it contagious?

Jefferson had always tried to keep the boat running smoothly, but now everything seemed to be careening out of control, falling apart at exactly the wrong time. Not only did they have an op to complete, but his chances for getting his own command were riding on how well it went. It had been a long, hard slog over many years to convince the navy that he deserved his own boat. It was within his grasp now, but he knew they would be looking for any reason to say no. Any reason at all to keep him down, keep him in his place. And damned if he was going to give them one. Whatever was happening on *Roanoke*, he intended to get to the bottom of it.

Jefferson left the auxiliary engine room and was returning to the main ladder when he noticed that a section of corridor closer to the torpedo room had gone dark. *Strange.* It hadn't been dark a minute ago. As he drew closer, he saw shards of glass glittering on the floor. Someone had broken a light fixture down here too.

His jaw tightened. How was this possible? Stubic had broken the light up in the mess, but Stubic was dead. There were flecks of blood amid the shards on the floor. Fresh blood.

He looked up from the floor and froze where he was. A silhouette hugged the bulkhead within the patch of darkness. In the ambient light from the other fixtures, he could make out Steve Bodine's features, wet with sweat.

"Bodine?" Jefferson said.

"Sir." Bodine's voice was raspy. He was cradling one hand in the other, and Jefferson could see dark blood oozing across the knuckles. "Don't come any closer, sir."

"Bodine, what have you done?" Jefferson asked.

"I—I couldn't," he stammered. "The light … I had to …" From the shadows, Bodine's glistening eyes regarded him with undisguised terror. "It hurt my eyes. The light hurts so much. You can't understand how much."

"I don't know what's going on, but let me help you," Jefferson said, trying to put him at ease.

"You can't help me, sir. No one can." Bodine slumped against the bulkhead, clutching the wounded hand closer to his chest. "Oh, God, Lieutenant Commander, I'm burning up. I feel like my whole body's on fire."

"Bodine, you're sick. I think you've got the same thing Stubic had. Report to sick bay right now. Matson can take care of you."

"Stay back," Bodine insisted. His voice broke, and he started sobbing. "I—I don't remember what happened, sir. Something took my memories away. Something is taking *me* away!"

"I don't understand," Jefferson said.

Bodine rubbed his neck. "These welts, sir. I don't remember how I got them. I don't even remember breaking this light, but I know I did it. I know it was me, but it's like I'm not me anymore."

"That's it, you're coming with me to sick bay, Bodine," Jefferson said, moving toward him. "That's an order."

"I said stay away from me!" Bodine shouted.

Another metallic bang sounded from the auxiliary engine room behind him, followed by raised voices arguing. Jefferson turned away from Bodine for only a moment. While he was distracted, Bodine made a break for the ladder. Jefferson chased after him. He was still in good shape from his football days, in better shape than Bodine, he thought, and yet Bodine, despite his illness, was moving too fast for Jefferson to catch. He hadn't seen anyone run this fast since his days on the field. It didn't seem possible, and yet Bodine was scrambling up before Jefferson even reached the first rung.

He followed Bodine up to the middle level, emerging next to the mess, but the corridor was so crowded with sailors he didn't see Bodine anywhere. Jefferson was tall enough to look over most of the sailors' heads, but there was no sign of the helmsman. How the hell had he moved so quickly?

"Bodine?" he called. "Bodine, get your ass back here, that's an order!"

Crewmen in the mess and the corridor stared at him, wondering what was going on and murmuring among themselves, but the helmsman didn't appear. Jefferson cursed under his breath. Bodine was gone.

CHAPTER ELEVEN

Still groggy after a restless sleep, Jerry White brushed his teeth over one of the stainless steel sinks in the head. He studied his reflection in the mirror. There were heavy bags under his eyes—evidence for all to see that he hadn't slept well. He had gotten only an hour or two during his sleep section. His last encounter with Lieutenant Duncan had kept playing in his mind, keeping him awake. He hadn't hesitated to follow an order in the control room, not even for a second. He was sure of it. He was a better planesman than that. But Duncan had it in for him, and he was going to see flaws in everything Jerry did, no matter what, because he blamed Jerry for the end of Lieutenant Commander Leonard's navy career.

You're on mighty thin ice—wouldn't take much for you to fall through.

Christ, would he ever get to put USS *Philadelphia* behind him? That was why he had turned down Tim's suggestion to go to the COB about Duncan. He just wanted a fresh start, a clean slate, but it seemed the universe had other ideas. Charles Duncan and Frank Leonard were buddies? What were the odds?

In his mind, he saw Lieutenant Commander Leonard's face again, red with rage, spittle flying as he yelled at Jerry.

It was you *who filed that complaint, White? You stupid son of a bitch. It's going to hurt your buddy MacLeod a lot worse than it hurts me!*

Jerry tried to shake the image out of his head.

He had spent the section before his rack time as part of a search party scouring the submarine for Steve Bodine. Lieutenant Commander Jefferson had put every available sailor on the job, letting them know Bodine was sick and possibly delirious. They had searched *Roanoke* from top level to bottom—even the nuclear reactor compartment and the maneuvering room in the aft section—but they hadn't found him. It was clear that Bodine, in his delirium, was hiding from them, moving from space to space to avoid being found. But how could someone that sick move around quickly enough not to be discovered? And how could he stay hidden for so long on a vessel with so few places to hide?

But the worst part was that Jerry's suspicions had been confirmed. First Stubic was sick, now Bodine. Something bad was going around—something that made men lose their minds and act erratically, even violently. How many other men on *Roanoke* had caught it? How many of his fellow sailors were ticking time bombs waiting to go off? That thought had kept him awake too.

He stowed his toothbrush and toothpaste away in his dopp kit, checked his coveralls in the mirror, and left the head, exiting through the hatch into his berthing area. Whereas the officers had their own staterooms, where most of them slept three to a room, the enlisted men had expansive spaces at the center of the middle level that were closed off with curtained doorways and filled with triple-decker bunks. Because a third of the enlisted men were asleep at any given hour, the only lights in the berthing areas were small red fluorescents near the doorways. Inside, the berthing area held four rows of bunks, with two rows built directly into the bulkheads, and another two rows bolted to the deck between them. Several sailors were milling about near the bunks, some getting ready to turn in for their six-hour sleep sections, others vacating their racks and preparing for their watches. Standing beside his bunk, Jerry opened the coffin locker under his rack, stowed his kit, and checked the time. His watch section started in nine minutes. Plenty of time to get to the control room.

Behind him, one of the sailors hissed a sharp, angry whisper and banged his fist on his bunk. Jerry turned around and saw a broad-shouldered machinist's mate wearing a T-shirt and sweats. He pounded on the metal frame of the top rack, where the curtain was still closed.

"Come on, asshole!" the sailor said.

"Is everything all right?" Jerry asked.

"Mind your business, White," the sailor snapped.

Fine, fuck you, Jerry thought, turning away again. He had enough on his mind already.

The sailor banged on the bunk again. Jerry tried to ignore it.

"Rise and shine, lazy-ass," the machinist's mate said. "It's my turn to sleep, so get your dead ass up." There was no answer from the rack. "Okay, you asked for it. I'm opening the curtain. If you're pullin' your pud in there, get ready to say 'cheese'!"

Jerry heard the rustling of the curtain being pushed aside, then a shocked gasp from the machinist's mate. He spun around and saw the man take a step back from the bunk and cross himself. Jerry went over and looked inside the narrow rack.

Steve Bodine stared back at him. His face glistened with sweat, and the flesh under his bloodshot eyes was puffy and dark. Bodine didn't say anything. He stared back, slack-jawed and dull-eyed, as though he didn't recognize Jerry, despite having sat next to him in the control room during every one of his watch sections. Big drops of sweat ran down his forehead. In the red light of the berthing area, it looked almost like blood.

"Jesus," Jerry murmured. Then, louder, to the machinist's mate, "Get Matson!"

The sailor ran off. Crewmen in their racks pulled aside their curtains to see what all the noise was about. Several enlisted men gathered around the bunk, gawking.

"Careful," Jerry told them. "We don't know if he's contagious."

That was enough to draw them all back a few paces. Jerry took a step back too, just in case.

"Bodine, you all right, man?" Jerry asked. "Where have you been? We've been turning the boat inside out looking for you."

But the helmsman continued to stare right through him, his breath coming short and fast.

Matson and the machinist's mate came running into the berthing area. Matson, medical kit in hand, pushed his way through the gawkers, ordering them to get back. Jerry stepped aside to let him get closer to Bodine.

"He's hyperventilating," Matson said. "Bodine, can you hear me? How are you feeling?"

Bodine didn't respond or even show any indication he knew that Matson was there. Matson pulled a penlight from his medical kit and shined it in Bodine's eyes.

Bodine erupted, screaming and thrashing in his rack. He slapped at Matson, trying to knock the light away. When Matson turned off the light again, Bodine whimpered and calmed down.

"What the hell was *that*?" Jerry asked.

"I don't know," Matson said. "Extreme light sensitivity? An involuntary reaction to stimulus? He's obviously got a fever, so it could be delirium from that."

Bodine's arm shot out of the rack, and he seized Matson by the wrist. The corpsman yelped in alarm and pain. The sailors surrounding them gasped, and some jumped back.

"Get him off me!" Matson yelled.

Jerry grabbed Bodine's arm and jerked his hands back in surprise. Bodine's skin was hot, much hotter than any fever Jerry had ever known. He took hold of Bodine's arm again and pulled. Bodine's grip on Matson's wrist was like iron, and it took several tries to pry him loose. When Matson was free, he stepped back, rubbing his wrist and staring in shock at Bodine. The helmsman started to slide forward out of the rack, a strange, predatory grin on his face.

"Hold him!" Matson shouted, and started fishing through his medical bag.

Jerry grabbed Bodine, but the helmsman was far stronger than Jerry would have guessed. He almost knocked Jerry aside, until the machinist's mate leaped forward and helped Jerry keep Bodine in his rack.

Matson felt in his kit and took out a hypodermic syringe, already filled with a clear liquid. He pulled the cap off with his teeth, then sank the needle into the flesh of Bodine's arm. He pushed the plunger all the way down, but whatever was in the syringe seemed to have no effect. Bodine squirmed and kicked and tried to break free.

"Shit!" Matson growled. He pulled a second, identical hypodermic out of his kit and injected its contents in Bodine's other arm. This time, Bodine went slack. Jerry let go, and the machinist's mate stepped back, wide-eyed with shock, wiping Bodine's sweat from his palms onto his T-shirt.

"I don't understand," Matson said, dropping the syringes back in his kit. "There was enough sedative in the first shot to knock out a sailor twice his size."

He shined his penlight into the rack again. Despite Bodine's display of almost superhuman strength, he was in bad shape. His face was an ashen gray, and he was as drenched as if he had just been fished out of the ocean. His pulse throbbed weakly under the glistening skin of his neck.

"Is he going to be all right?" Jerry asked.

Matson didn't answer him. He grabbed a stethoscope from his kit, put the eartips in his ears, and held the diaphragm to Bodine's chest. He listened for several seconds.

"The heartbeat is weak. His breathing is fast and erratic." Matson pulled the eartips out of his ears and draped the stethoscope over his neck. "It's definitely a fever. I can tell that much, at least."

He held up each of Bodine's limp hands. On the knuckles and back of his right hand were several dark-red cuts. Just like how Jefferson had described Stubic's hand, Jerry realized. Matson gently lowered Bodine's hand again.

"I heard about the broken light in the bottom-level corridor," Matson said. "I suppose that was Bodine's handiwork."

"So he's got the same thing Stubic did?" Jerry asked.

"Almost certainly. I can't leave him here with the other crewmen. He'll have to be quarantined. I'll talk to Lieutenant Commander Jefferson about setting up a suitable space."

Jerry looked at the time and realized he was about to be late for his watch section. *Damn.* Lieutenant Duncan was the watchstanding diving officer, and the last thing Jerry needed was to give the man more ammunition against him.

"I've got to report to the control room," he told Matson.

"Thanks for your help, White," Matson said. "I've got it from here. With luck, we may have just saved this man's life."

Jerry glanced at Bodine again. The helmsman's chest was rising and falling rapidly. Sweat pooled in the hollow of his throat. Jerry hoped Matson was right, because Bodine looked to be at death's door.

CHAPTER TWELVE

By the time Jerry got to the control room, Duncan was already fuming.

"You're late, White," he snarled. "They let you get away with murder on your previous boat, but I assure you I won't tolerate any such nonsense here."

"Sorry, sir," Jerry said. "I was with the hospital corpsman—"

"I'm not interested in your excuses," Duncan interrupted. "Take your seat."

Jerry relieved the planesman of the previous watch, who fled the control room as if he couldn't stand to be around Duncan another minute. Jerry didn't blame him. The helmsman beside him was new—the sailor assigned to be Bodine's replacement when Bodine went missing.

Duncan didn't bother asking why Jerry had been with the hospital corpsman. If he had shown even a glimmer of concern or humanity, Jerry's disdain for him might have lessened. Instead, Duncan likely assumed Jerry was sick or injured, and despised him too much to give a damn. Jerry swallowed the loathing he felt before it made him say something he would regret. He was already on thin ice—best not to hop.

The watch progressed routinely until an hour in, when the officer of the deck announced, "Captain on deck!"

Jerry looked up as Captain Weber entered the control room from the captain's egress. He hadn't seen the captain outside his stateroom since the launch. What brought him out of his cocoon now?

"The captain has the conn," Captain Weber said, formally announcing his intention to take control of the boat. "Officer of the Deck, take us to periscope depth."

"Periscope depth, aye," the OOD replied. "Lieutenant Duncan, periscope depth."

"Make our depth one-six-zero feet," Duncan said.

"One-six-zero, aye," Jerry replied. Periscope depth was actually 65 feet, but because planes and surface ships could spot a sub at that depth, submarines in hostile waters had to pause partway up while the sonar techs listened for signs of activity in the surrounding area. As soon as the report came back that they were alone, Captain Weber ordered the sub taken up the rest of the way to 65 feet. Jerry complied, using the hand wheel to adjust the hydroplanes.

The captain raised the observation periscope out of the floor, an action that raised the periscope head above the surface. Taking the handles, he brought his face up to the eyepiece. He turned 360 degrees, making one final sweep of the surface for any hostiles. Satisfied, he lowered the periscope again.

"Communications officer, I need to reach SUBPAC," Captain Weber said. SUBPAC was the Pacific Submarine Force, overseen by the four-star admiral who commanded all the US Pacific Fleet. "Route communications through to my stateroom."

"Radioing SUBPAC, aye," the radioman replied, pulling on his bulky headphones in the radio room at the rear of the control room. He began fussing with the bank of switches and knobs in front of him, adjusting frequencies to find an open channel.

Now Jerry understood why they had come so close to the surface. There was no radio contact below the thermocline, the thin layer of water that separated the warmer surface waters from the cold depths. The thermocline played havoc with sound waves—a good thing when the sub needed to hide from surface traffic, but not so great when they needed to radio fleet headquarters.

Still, it was unusual—not to mention risky—to break radio silence this close to Soviet waters. He wondered whether it had anything to do with Stubic's death and Bodine's illness. If it turned out that a contagious disease was working its way through the submarine, they might be ordered back to port. Or would they be quarantined, left to float in their tin can until the disease had run its course? He forced the unpleasant thought out of his head and tried not to worry. The best he could do was accept that he didn't know anything, and not give his imagination too much running room.

"Officer of the Deck, you have the conn," Captain Weber said.

He started walking back to his stateroom, but the radioman stopped him.

"Captain, sir, there's a problem with the radio."

Captain Weber turned around. "What kind of problem?"

The radioman pulled his headphones off. "I—I'm not sure what to make of this, sir. The radio is dead."

The captain crossed the control room to the communications station and looked over the radioman's shoulder at the equipment. "What do you mean, '*dead*'?"

"It was fully operational yesterday, sir," the radioman said. "But now ... Look, sir, it's not even lighting up."

He flicked a few switches but got no signal.

Jerry and the helmsman beside him exchanged a worried glance. There were a few things no sailor wanted to hear on a submarine: that the boat was approaching crush depth, that there was a leak or a fire—or that the radio was down. A dead radio on a submarine so close to Soviet waters was more than a problem; it was potentially deadly. If the Soviets spotted them, *Roanoke* wouldn't be able to call for help, and at a maximum speed of 32 knots, it sure as hell wouldn't be able to outrun airplanes or destroyers. They would be sitting ducks, stranded with no chance of help on the way.

A contagious disease incapacitating crewmen, a dead radio—Jerry wondered what else could go wrong on this underway.

"Captain," a voice called.

Tim stood in the doorway of the sonar shack. He looked worried in a way Jerry hadn't seen before.

"Go ahead, Spicer," the captain replied.

"I'm picking something up on the sonar, sir. It's another submarine."

CHAPTER THIRTEEN

Tim knew well enough that if a Soviet boat spotted them this close, even in international waters, there would be trouble. The line that separated international waters from Soviet territory was a well-established boundary to everyone except the Soviets themselves. They patrolled the waters outside their territory like their own. Publicly they insisted that it was necessary to defend themselves against American and Western European aggression, but in truth it was their way of claiming those waters for themselves, expanding the borders of their empire one nautical mile at a time. If *Roanoke* was caught even close to the international boundary, it would be forced to surface, and the crew would be arrested and tried for espionage in front of the whole world. Soviet engineers would strip-search the submarine for any technology they might reverse-engineer, while their diplomats made the usual complaints to the United Nations about cynical US imperialism.

He had known from the start that their route to the Kamchatka Peninsula would take them close to the boundary, but he hadn't expected to run into the Soviets so soon. He had assumed that *Roanoke* was still a few hundred miles away from territorial waters, but it occurred to him now that he didn't know where he was, exactly.

Tim's sonar display utilized spectrograms, which looked like waterfalls of random, colored lights if you didn't know how to read them. They didn't work like radar, though. They couldn't pinpoint and identify enemy boats. Instead, the spectrograms picked up anomalies—noises in the water that could be engines, torpedoes being loaded into tubes, even someone on another boat dropping a pair of pliers on the deck. They were that sensitive. The readings came from the TB-23, the underwater ear that *Roanoke* was towing—a half-mile-long sonar array that trailed from the stern like the tail of a kite.

The submarine Tim's sonar had picked up sounded like a Victor. The Soviets had been producing Victor-class subs since the mid-1960s and had been stuck with them ever since. Now they were old and obsolete. Tim could tell it was a Victor from the way it rattled like an old car. He only wished he could nail down its proximity. Passive sonar was good for detecting objects, but terrible for judging how close they were. Active sonar identified everything, practically delivering a Polaroid snapshot, but to engage active sonar now would be the equivalent of sending up a flare. It would alert the Victor to their location immediately, and there was still a chance it hadn't spotted them yet.

The good news was that Victors didn't have anything even half as good as *Roanoke*'s TB-23, although this didn't mean they were deaf. And their torpedoes worked just as well as *Roanoke*'s.

"Has it picked us up yet?" Captain Weber asked, leaning into the sonar shack.

Tim said, "It's hard to say, sir. The Victor is matching our speed and course, but it's not taking any action to intercept us."

"Looks to me like we've got ourselves a shadow," the captain said. "Officer of the Deck, rig for ultraquiet."

Tim held his breath for a moment, something he instinctively did when they went to silent running, even though he knew full well that the Victor's sonar couldn't pick up breathing. It couldn't pick up voices, either, so long as they were kept to a reasonable volume, but other sounds, such as the propeller screw and the nuclear reactor's active cooling system, could give them away. In ultraquiet mode, the screw would be slowed and the reactor's cooling system would be switched off, leaving it to be cooled instead by the natural flow of water through the pipes. That was the big stuff. Smaller unnecessary noises would have to be eliminated too—in the quiet ocean, it didn't take much for a submarine to give away its position. From now on, the galley would switch from preparing hot meals to serving cold sandwiches. The mechanics had to stop whatever they were working on—even the tap of a hammer would be like setting off fireworks. Submarines sailed blind. If a sonar tech heard something, he could track it. If it stopped making noise, he lost it. It was that simple.

Being rigged for ultraquiet made everyone tense, but as a defensive tactic, it worked. One moment, the Victor's sonar could hear *Roanoke*; the next, it would hear nothing. It would look to the Soviet boat as if *Roanoke* had vanished. So long as they didn't make any sudden turns or pick up speed to more than five knots, they were invisible.

Tim had seen ultraquiet from the other side too. A few underways back, while they were shadowing a Victor, the Soviet sub had dropped off his sonar like a ghost. It was disconcerting, even frightening. He had known that the sub was out there, possibly loading its torpedoes while they scrambled to find it, but it was completely invisible to him. The only way to locate the Victor would have been to use active sonar, but that would effectively have handed them a target to lock on to. It had turned into a waiting game to see who blinked first. In the end, the Victor had chosen to slip away rather than attack. Tim could only hope for a similarly peaceful outcome now.

"Diving Officer, prepare for deep submergence," the captain said. "Make our depth seven-five-zero."

"Seven-five-zero, aye," Lieutenant Duncan replied. "Make our depth seven-five-zero."

"Seven-five-zero, aye, sir," Jerry replied. "Making our depth seven-five-zero, aye."

With *Roanoke* on alert, it looked as though the animosity between Lieutenant Duncan and Jerry had been shelved for the moment. They were working together seamlessly now. Tim wished it could stay that way, but he knew Duncan well—the harping and picking would start up again at the first opportunity. A tiger didn't change its stripes, and a bully didn't suddenly lose the urge to shit on everyone below him.

The dive alarm didn't sound when they were rigged for ultraquiet, but Tim braced in his seat as the deck tilted beneath him.

"We have to go deep," Captain Weber said. "Let her follow if she dares."

"And if that doesn't work, sir?" the officer of the deck asked.

"Then we'll still have the advantage. They can't radio back to their command center about us without rising to periscope depth, and if they do that, we'll just slip away right under them. If they stay the course at their current depth and keep following us, the thermocline will cut them off from communicating. Spicer, I want a close eye on that boat. If she so much as twitches in our direction, I want to know about it."

"Aye, sir," Tim said.

Roanoke descended quickly to 500 feet, then 600, and finally 750. Captain Weber ordered their speed cut to three knots, which would let them run so quietly, the Victor would have no choice but to ping them with active sonar if it wanted to find them.

"Spicer, what's their position?" the captain called into the sonar shack.

Tim relayed the latest reading to him. "They're moving slow and quiet, sir, just like us. They might be searching for us."

"Are they still using passive sonar?" he asked.

"Aye, sir," Tim said. "They think it's keeping them undetected, but I've got them on the sonar. Just barely, but they are there."

"Good," the captain said. "Keep watching them, Spicer. I want regular updates. Helmsman, left full rudder. Steady course three-zero-zero."

The helmsman replied, "Left full rudder, aye, sir. Making our course three-zero-zero, aye."

Watching the cascade of colors on his display screen, Tim felt his back and shoulders tensing. He told himself the Victors were obsolete, decaying submarines with antiquated sonar equipment that couldn't find a honking car in an empty parking lot. He told himself that even if the Victor did find them, it wouldn't fire on *Roanoke* unless they had trespassed into Soviet waters. He tried hard not to think about the

South Korean jetliner the Soviets had shot down earlier this year, and all the subsequent news reports that questioned whether it had actually been in Soviet airspace. Had that Soviet pilot simply been trigger happy, or had word come down from the Kremlin ordering their military to shoot first and ask questions later? Tim prayed they weren't about to find out.

CHAPTER FOURTEEN

It was Murphy's Law: whatever could go wrong would go wrong, and at the worst possible time. As far as Lieutenant Commander Jefferson was concerned, this whole damn underway was Murphy's Law in operation, with all its corollaries. One dead crewman, one sick crewman, a couple of smashed lights, a dead radio, and now there was a Soviet bear on their tail. Not even two weeks into the op, and Jefferson had already given up waiting for something to go right.

Where had the Victor come from? How had they run into one so soon? He thought back to the map on the captain's desk, the lines he was drawing that extended into Soviet territory. Was it possible they had crossed the border without a heads-up from Captain Weber? What would make the captain keep something that important from the crew?

If this was more than reconnaissance, if this was a spy mission, the navy shouldn't have sent a submarine. They should have taken a page from the KGB playbook and sent a spy boat disguised as a trawler. That would have served the Soviets right, considering that was what they always did. Everyone knew that the Russian trawlers were spy ships, of course, but if the US Navy so much as touched one of them, the Soviets started screaming in the UN assemblies about American imperialists encroaching on civilian fishing boats.

What a mess. Sometimes he wondered whether the Cold War would ever end, or whether the two superpowers would be stuck playing out the same scenarios until the end of time—advance and retreat, advance and retreat, like an unending global-scale game of Stratego. Except that the whole world was at stake.

Jefferson paused outside the closed hatch to the torpedo room. No longer just a makeshift morgue, the torpedo room was now quarantine too. There was nowhere else on *Roanoke* to keep the sick and possibly contagious Steve Bodine safely away from the rest of the crew. Matson had to be stationed there with him; it was the only way the hospital corpsman could continue to treat Bodine and respond quickly to any sudden changes in his health. Jefferson could tell Matson hadn't been thrilled with the idea of staying in the torpedo room, but the corpsman knew what was at stake and kept his opinion to himself.

Jefferson had seen with his own eyes what bad shape Bodine was in. He was clearly sick with the same thing that had made Warren Stubic delirious enough to shut himself in the freezer. The thought of losing Bodine put a knot in his gut. He couldn't help thinking of all the conversations they'd had, all the times Bodine had sought him out for advice. Jefferson felt like a mentor to him.

Bodine had been reluctant to open up at first. He had trouble trusting anyone after his experience at Navy Boot Camp, where several of his white classmates had treated him like a pariah, as though he didn't belong there. Their contempt had been plain even though strictly enforced navy rules prevented them from perpetrating outright abuse or harassment. But through it all, Bodine never buckled. He pushed forward, he did the work, and he graduated to the submarine service.

Bodine had come to trust Jefferson eventually, and soon enough he began confiding all his hopes and fears for his life, his career—everything. During their off hours, Bodine often came to him to ask how he managed life on a submarine with so many men whose only knowledge of black men was gleaned from TV shows or movies—or, worse, from news reports about drug dealers and gang violence. Jefferson taught him to keep his cool when dealing with the tyranny of small minds. They both had seen their share of adversity, almost all of it aimed squarely at the color of their skin. It had brought them together, and he hoped his advice had made Bodine stronger. But now Bodine was deathly sick, and Jefferson didn't know how to handle that.

He took a deep breath and opened the hatch. The first thing he noticed when he stepped into the torpedo room was the hammock they had set up for Bodine, where he now lay with a cold compress on his forehead. He was asleep, but the way his facial muscles and eyelids kept twitching told Jefferson he wasn't sleeping peacefully. Jefferson's gaze tracked to Stubic's body bag on the floor, just a few feet from the hammock. It seemed wrong to keep the two of them together in such a small space, the dead and the still living, but he hadn't had a choice. It would have to do until Bodine recovered.

Matson had arranged nine small ampules along the edge of an occupied torpedo tray, the glass bottles positioned against the side of the torpedo. Matson inspected each one, checking the labels that identified the inject-able liquid inside. At his feet were a small cardboard box of disposable syringes, and a trashcan designated for medical waste.

"How's he doing, Matson?" Jefferson asked. Bodine's skin was slick with sweat despite the coolness of the room. He was breathing fast and ragged, as if he had just done a mile of wind sprints. Jefferson could tell that this was no simple cold or flu. Whatever had him in its grip was killing him.

"I've been giving him antibiotics in case this is bacterial in nature, sir, but that's about all I can do for him," Matson said. He indicated the ampules lined up along the torpedo tray. "As you can see, I brought my entire supply. I wasn't sure how much it would take. But frankly, sir, it's not working. He's not getting better. I haven't had to sedate him again; he's just … out. He hasn't regained consciousness at all. Sir, if we could take him to a real medical facility, somewhere they could test his blood …"

"The captain made his decision," Jefferson said.

Matson nodded. "Yes, sir. I've given Bodine as thorough a physical as I can under the circumstances. His glands aren't swollen. There's no inflamed tissue, no extra mucus production, no rigidity in his abdomen or swelling in his liver or kidneys—at least, none that I could feel. His breathing is shallow and rapid, but there's no sign of congestion. Physically, the only abnormality I found was a couple of welts on the side of his neck that looked like they might be bug bites. If they were, I thought they might be responsible for the fever, but there's no redness or pus to indicate infection or envenomation."

"Could it be food poisoning?" Jefferson asked. "Some of the food the Guidry brothers are whipping up isn't exactly Betty Crocker."

Matson gave a thin smile. "I may not have an MD, but even I know food poisoning when I see it, sir. That's not what this is."

"Sorry," Jefferson said. "Just trying to help."

"I know, sir. I'm as frustrated as you are that we don't know what this is. Frankly, there's nothing else I can do but continue to give him antibiotics and hope for improvement. But if we don't get him to a medical facility, Bodine may die."

Jefferson met his eye. "It's up to you to make sure that doesn't happen."

"There's only so much I can do, Lieutenant Commander," Matson said.

"Keep trying, Matson. Don't give up on him."

Jefferson sighed and looked down at the patient again. He put his hand over Bodine's, but even with the blanket between them he could feel how uncannily hot the skin was. The man was burning up.

"Come on, Bodine," he said softly. "Fight this thing. That's an order."

He hadn't expected to feel this close to Bodine, but he couldn't deny his concern. They had shared a lot, and in some ways they had more in common with each other than with anyone else in the crew. Some of their conversations had gotten intense, and he recalled the one time that Bodine had actually called him "brother." Hoo boy, had that bugged Jefferson. *Brother*—as if they were supposed to raise a fist in solidarity: black power, the revolution, and all that. He had told Bodine his name was *Lieutenant Commander* and reminded him that the only political entity he belonged to was the United States Navy. He had given Bodine a hard time, reminding him that he was from Oklahoma, not Philly, and his favorite music was Hall and Oates, not Marvin Gaye. He grinned at the memory. He'd been tough on Bodine, but he always tried to be fair. And when he could, he tried to be a good teacher too.

"Sir, I don't mean to interrupt," Matson said, "but we still don't know how contagious he is. My advice would be not to stay down here too long, just to be on the safe side. It's best we contain this before it spreads any further, sir."

"What about you?"

"If this thing is airborne, I've already been exposed," Matson replied. "I have to remain quarantined too—at least until we know if I've been infected."

"Damn. The news just keeps getting better and better, doesn't it?"

Before Jefferson turned to leave, he watched the blanket on Bodine's chest rise and fall, moving in time with his shallow breaths.

"Hang in there," he said, "… brother."

CHAPTER FIFTEEN

Even with *Roanoke* rigged for ultraquiet and moving at a bare three knots, they couldn't shake the Victor off their tail. The tightness in Tim's back and shoulders matched the tension that permeated the sonar shack and control room alike. Captain Weber asked him for constant updates, but it was always the same: she was still there, still shadowing them. After a few hours of keeping his eye on the sonar screen, looking for any sign the Soviet sub was leaving the area, he was surprised to see Senior Chief Farrington, the chief of the boat, come into the sonar shack.

"Spicer, come with me," Farrington said. "Antopol will relieve you."

Tim got up from his seat, confused. His watch section wasn't over yet, but Farrington didn't seem to care. He led Tim out of the sonar shack as sonar tech Antopol arrived to take his place. Tim followed Farrington out of the control room and down the main ladder to the middle level.

"COB, where are we going?" he asked.

"Your presence has been requested," Farrington replied, and left it at that. He stopped in front of the wardroom and indicated that Tim should go inside.

Tim had never actually entered the wardroom before. It belonged to the officers, not the enlisted men. It was where they usually took their meals together and spent their downtime. The walls were wood paneled, just like the captain's stateroom, and filled with storage cabinets and shelves full of notebook binders. A rectangular table, long enough to seat twelve, ran down the center of the room. Sitting around that table were all *Roanoke's* department heads: Supply, Engineering, Navigation Operations, and Weapons. He recognized many of the faces, including Lieutenant Abrams from the galley, Lieutenant Carr from Engineering, and Lieutenant Carl French, the weapons officer. Since sonar fell under the umbrella of the Weapons Department, French was technically Tim's boss, although the two rarely interacted.

Tim paused in the doorway. There had to be some mistake. This didn't look like a meeting an enlisted sonar tech should be in, but no one looked surprised to see him. Farrington waved him inside, but remained out in the corridor, shutting the door behind Tim.

Captain Weber sat at one end of the table, with Lieutenant Commander Jefferson beside him.

"Spicer, thank you for joining us," Captain Weber said.

All eyes watched Tim expectantly. He felt his face grow hot. He wasn't used to being the center of attention, especially not in a roomful of officers. He stood straight and cleared his throat.

"You sent for me, sir?"

"I need to know if the Soviets are aware of our presence," the captain said. "Is the Victor shadowing us, or is it simply on the same course as us?"

"It's impossible to know for sure, sir," Tim said.

"Give me your best guess as an experienced sonar tech, Spicer," the captain prodded. "Do you *believe* she knows we're here?"

Tim took a deep breath and let it out slowly. "Yes, sir. I believe she does."

The officers around the table muttered in alarm.

"Sir, if I may?" Tim said over the noise.

"Go on, Spicer," Captain Weber said. The conversation died down.

"Sir, we're right at the edge of their passive sonar, but they haven't pinged us yet. I get the feeling they think they've caught us unawares, sir."

The captain sat forward in his seat. "Explain."

"They're running slow and quiet just like us, sir," Tim said. "I think right now, aboard their boat, they're having the same conversation we are. They're asking themselves if *we* know *they're* here. I'm convinced that's why they're still using passive sonar instead of active, sir. They're reluctant to give away their position, in case we haven't seen them yet."

"Captain, we should come about hard and nail her," said Lieutenant French. "They'll never see it coming."

Captain Weber glared at him. "Torpedoing a Soviet boat would be an act of war."

"But, sir, we're in international waters," French said. "Following us could be viewed as an act of aggression. We would be defending ourselves."

"Except, we won't be in international waters for much longer," the captain said.

That brought all conversation at the table to a halt. Everyone, including Tim, stared at the captain in surprise.

"Spicer, I'm going to ask you not to repeat anything you are about to hear—not to anyone. From now on, everything said in this room is classified information. The only reason I am allowing you to stay is because I need your help. Am I clear?"

"Yes, sir," Tim said. The words "classified information" gave him an uneasy feeling.

"Gentlemen," Captain Weber said, "at the start of this operation, I told you this would be a routine reconnaissance op and that we would remain in international waters off the Kamchatka Peninsula. I regret to tell you, that was a necessary half truth. I am not in the habit of keeping details from my officers, unless I believe there's a good reason for it.

"In this case, due to the sensitive nature of the operation, I was ordered to keep the information on a need-to-know basis. But now, with the Soviets on our tail, I think you need to know. You've no doubt heard rumors that the Soviets are looking to replace their outdated Victors with a better class of submarine. What you likely do not know is that there is speculation, based on reliable intelligence, that a prototype of this new submarine already exists and is being tested in the waters near the Rybachiy Nuclear Submarine Base. It's a sleeker, faster, quieter submarine with an advanced sonar system and, if the intelligence is to be believed, surface-to-air missile capability."

Tim's jaw fell in surprise as astonished murmurs went around the table.

"Our orders are to get confirmation of this submarine's existence," the captain continued. He looked at Tim. "That includes recording any sonar readings we take, Spicer."

Tim nodded. "Aye, sir."

"Gentlemen, the point is this," the captain went on. "To complete this operation, we have to enter Soviet waters."

"All the more reason to take out that Victor before it can tell Moscow we're here," Lieutenant French persisted.

"I won't take the risk of giving away our position, French," the captain replied. "Spicer, am I correct in assuming the Victor is still below the thermocline?"

"Aye, sir, it is."

"Then they can't tell Moscow anything," Captain Weber said. "They won't dare rise to periscope depth and give away their position. Aside from that, attacking a Soviet submarine would be a sure way to draw the kind of attention we're trying to avoid. I intend to slip by this Victor without leaving so much as a bubble for it to follow. For that, I will need to rely on your sonar expertise again, Spicer. I want your eyes on the Victor at all times. I don't want you to so much as blink."

"Aye, sir," Tim said.

"Dismissed, Spicer. Farrington will return you to the sonar shack. And remember, Spicer, not a word."

"Aye, sir," Tim replied.

He opened the wardroom door and stepped out. Farrington was waiting for him in the corridor and led him back up to the control room. Tim could feel Jerry's curious gaze on him when he entered, but he kept his eyes forward and went straight to the sonar shack, where he relieved Antopol and resumed his watch. The Victor was still there on the sonar screen, lagging probably four or five miles behind, just where he had left it.

The captain returned to the control room a few minutes later. "Officer of the Deck, rig for deep submergence."

The OOD picked up the phonetalker and told the crew, "Rig boat for deep submergence."

The crew had several duties to perform in preparation for deep submergence. All over *Roanoke*, the massive watertight hatches between compartments were shut and locked with clamps that sealed them tight, dividing the crew into small pockets of men throughout the sub. In the nuclear reactor compartment, engineers checked the seawater pipes for anything that looked abnormal, because if one of them broke and flooding occurred at deep-submergence depth, the intense water pressure would fill the compartment so quickly there would be no time to escape. The engineers would drown, the reactor would malfunction, and the added water weight would drag the sub down to the bottom of the ocean and either implode or trap them there.

Tim shivered at the thought. Sinking was every submariner's worst nightmare. To die in the dark silence at the ocean floor, with oxygen and food supplies dwindling, knowing you would never see the sky again, never see the sun—nothing else frightened him like that. Not even the awful dark winters off Presque Isle.

"Mark the sounding," the OOD ordered.

"Mark the sounding, aye, sir," the quartermaster replied from the navigation electronics station. "Sounding two-three-nine fathoms, sir."

Tim did the sounding calculation in his head. The ocean floor was 1,434 feet below them.

"Officer of the Deck," Captain Weber said, "make our depth one-three-zero-zero feet."

Thirteen hundred feet—*Jesus. Roanoke* was a Los Angeles–class submarine, which meant their crush depth was 1,475 feet. They would be descending dangerously close to that threshold—closer than he had ever been. Tim felt a bead of nervous sweat break free and trickle down his forehead. It was called "crush depth" for a reason. If a sub went below that depth, the pressure on the outer hull would squeeze it like a tin can, until it finally imploded. The fuel and air tanks would follow suit, as well as the inner hull. A leak on a sub was bad enough, but if the hull broke open, it wouldn't be a leak; it would be an unstoppable flood of water rushing in at horrifically high pressure. If they were lucky, the air trapped inside the sub would form bubbles at either end, where the crew could gather to slowly suffocate in the dwindling oxygen. If they weren't lucky, the trapped air would escape out of the broken hull immediately and they would all drown. Either way, everybody died, and neither way sounded pleasant.

"Captain, we're making five knots and rigged for dive," the OOD reported.

"Officer of the Deck, dive," Captain Weber ordered.

"One-three-zero-zero, aye, sir. Diving Officer, submerge to one-three-zero-zero," the OOD ordered. Then he announced into the phonetalker, "Dive! Dive!"

Once again, because they were rigged for ultraquiet, there was no dive alarm. The floor tilted precipitously as the submarine dived more steeply than before, setting Tim's nerves even more on edge.

Lieutenant Duncan updated their depth every few seconds. "Seven-seven-five feet, sir ... eight-two-five ... eight-five-zero ... nine-zero-zero ..."

At 900 feet, Tim knew, the pressure bearing down on the hull was 400 pounds per square inch. The bulkheads began to creak and squeal. He tried not to think about a beer can getting stomped.

"Nine-two-five, sir," Duncan continued. "Nine-five-zero."

"Spicer, any reaction from our friend the Victor?" Captain Weber asked.

"None, sir," Tim replied, grateful for a chance to focus on something other than the loudly groaning hull. "The Victor is holding steady."

"Excellent," the captain said. "Let me know if that changes."

Tim stared at his screen, wondering what was happening on board the Soviet sub right now. Could she no longer detect *Roanoke*, or was she just patiently watching them dive?

"One-zero-zero-zero feet, sir," Duncan reported. "One-zero-five-zero."

The bulkheads groaned as if the sub itself were in pain. The sound was loud. *Too* loud. There was no way the Victor, even with its lousy sonar equipment, could fail to hear it. And if the Victor heard them, it would come and investigate. Tim prayed Captain Weber knew what he was doing.

"One two-five-zero," Duncan reported. "Sir, we've reached one-three-zero-zero feet."

"One-three-zero-zero, aye," the OOD said.

"Officer of the Deck, make our speed two knots," Captain Weber said.

They slowed to a crawl, 1,300 feet below the surface of the ocean, just a few fathoms from the floor, in a submerged world that was as dark as a cave. For a few seconds, everything was quiet. And then, suddenly, the blip on the sonar screen began to turn.

"Captain, sir, the Victor is moving," Tim called.

Captain Weber hurried into the sonar shack. He stood directly behind Tim's chair, watching the screen.

"They've slowed to two knots and executed a turn, sir," Tim reported.

"They're trying to find us," the captain said.

The Soviet submarine moved slowly, practically at a drift. Thirty slow, tense minutes passed as it caught up to *Roanoke*'s position. Thirty minutes of Tim staring at the sonar screen and tracking the Victor's bearing. Thirty minutes during which every crewman in the control room sat silently and nervously at his station. Thirty minutes of listening to the hull's ominous creaks and rumbles.

The Victor floated right above them. Instinctively, Tim held his breath. He looked up at the ceiling as if he might see through the hull to the Soviet submarine above them. Everyone was quiet. The bulkheads groaned. Tim wished he could shut them the hell up.

The Victor passed over *Roanoke* and kept moving.

Tim let out his breath. "They don't know where we are, sir. I don't know how they didn't hear the hull, but they're still trying to find us."

"They heard us; they just can't find us," the captain explained. "We're shielded. I saw it on the charts earlier: an oceanic trench big enough for us to hide in. The only thing their sonar is going to pick up is solid rock."

Frustrated at losing them, the Victor switched to active sonar and lit up on Tim's console like a Christmas display. The Soviet sub gave off three loud pings, but the captain was right: all she could detect was the ocean floor. Rigged for ultraquiet and shielded by the trench, *Roanoke* was impossible to hear. The Victor tried again, and a third time. Still finding nothing, she finally changed course and sailed away.

Captain Weber gave it another hour, just to be on the safe side, but the Victor never came back. When he called off the ultraquiet, Tim and the other techs in the sonar shack cheered and slapped one another on the back. He could hear the sailors in the control room doing the same, and in a brief fit of optimism, he hoped this moment of triumph might make Jerry and Lieutenant Duncan put their differences aside. If anything could inspire them to bury the hatchet, successfully eluding a Soviet submarine in pursuit might be just the thing.

The captain ordered the boat back up to 600 feet, on a bearing north and west. Tim went back to watching his sonar screen, but his elation slowly gave way to worry again. Unlike most of *Roanoke*'s crew, he knew the truth about the op. The new course the captain had given would take them deep into Soviet territory. And somewhere in those unfriendly waters, a prototype of the Soviets' super sub was waiting.

CHAPTER SIXTEEN

A sudden, loud crash startled Jerry awake. He lay in the darkness of his curtained rack, heart pounding from the spike of adrenaline, and wondered whether he had really heard something or only dreamed it.

Things in the control room had been tense all through his watch—at least, until the captain finally shook the Soviet boat off their tail. After that, Jerry's mind and body had been so exhausted that when his sleep section came, he nodded right off instead of lying awake for hours as usual. But now, damn it, he was awake again. His annoyance grew as the silent minutes ticked by and he became convinced that he had dreamed the noise—woken himself up, sabotaging his own sleep section.

The rack he slept in didn't have a lot of room. Its thin foam mattress was narrower than a standard twin bed, with just enough space to sleep provided he didn't move around too much. Jerry had learned quickly not to turn over in his sleep and risk falling out of his rack. His was the topmost rack in a triple-decker berth, which meant it would be one hell of a fall. No one would call the racks comfortable, but he had managed to sleep just fine in them for years. It was only on *Roanoke* that he had trouble sleeping, and it wasn't the rack's fault. It was Lieutenant Duncan's. No, if he was going to be honest with himself, it wasn't even Duncan. It was the way Duncan reminded him every day of what happened on *Phil-delphia*. What kept him awake was his own sense of guilt, the ever-present question of whether or not he had done the right thing.

Again, he saw Lieutenant Commander Leonard's angry face in his mind, a twisted sense of triumph in his voice as he raged.

It's going to hurt your buddy MacLeod a lot worse than it hurts me!

Jerry sighed. He had brought a Stephen King novel with him for the underway, something about a haunted car, but he hadn't started it yet. There was a goosenecked reading light on the wall beside him, and with the heavy curtain closed he could turn on the light without bothering the sleeping crewmen. But he decided against it. If he started reading, he would never fall back asleep, and the last thing he needed was to be groggy in the control room tomorrow. When they lost the Victor, everyone had cheered and high-fived. Even the captain had joined in the jubilation, but more surprisingly, so had Lieutenant Duncan. He hadn't high-fived Jerry—that would be asking for too much—but he hadn't gotten in Jerry's face since then, either. Maybe after they had worked so well together getting out of a tough spot, Duncan would ease up on him. Probably not—the guy was an incurable asshole—but one could hope. Jerry planned to do his part, and being sharp and on his toes for tomorrow's watch section would be a good start.

Still optimistic that he might catch some shut-eye before he had to vacate the rack for the next sailor, Jerry was reluctant to get up at all, but the pressure of a full bladder didn't give him a choice in the matter. He pushed the curtain aside gently so the sound of its runners wouldn't disturb anyone. The red fluorescent light near the curtained doorway cast a faint crimson light through the room. The only noises were the soft rush of air from the ventilation system and a sound like dueling whipsaws from two snoring crewmates.

One benefit of the red lighting was that it didn't take long for his eyes to adjust. But in the seconds before he could see clearly, a shape moved through the berthing area. Someone in the darkness, heading toward the curtain that led to the corridor outside. The shape was dusky, purplish in the red light, and moved in a way that struck Jerry as strange. He was jerky and stiff, as if he'd forgotten how to walk and was learning all over again.

The man pushed the curtain aside and passed through the doorway. As he did, a shaft of light fell across his face for an instant before he was gone. Jerry blinked in disbelief. Though he'd only had a glimpse, he recognized the man right away. It was Steve Bodine. But short of a miraculous recovery, how was that possible? And even if Bodine had come back from having one foot in the grave, what was he doing wandering around the boat? He was supposed to be in quarantine. Matson would never have let him go this soon.

There were no ladders on the bunks, but it wasn't a far drop to the floor. Jerry landed quietly on his sock-covered feet. Boots or shoes of any kind weren't allowed in the racks, since every sailor shared his with two other men and tried to leave it as clean as possible, but keeping your smelly, sweaty feet in your socks was considered a courtesy. Jerry padded quietly across the floor and paused at the curtained doorway. When the brightness from outside had touched Bodine's face, his skin looked dry and ashen, and he had winced when the light hit him, as if it hurt his eyes. Jerry pushed the curtain aside and peered out into the corridor, but there was no sign of Bodine.

He turned back and went through the hatch that led from the berthing area to the head to empty his bladder. But when he opened the hatch, he gasped in horror. Then he turned and ran as fast as he could to get Lieutenant Commander Jefferson.

CHAPTER SEVENTEEN

Oran Guidry dropped quickly down the main ladder to the bottom level of the submarine. In preparation for first meal, Lieutenant Abrams had asked him to gather a few cans of tomatoes from the crates stored next to the Big Red Machine in the auxiliary engine room. But when he reached the bottom of the ladder, he paused, feeling a sudden coldness at his back. He turned around. The corridor behind him was empty, but he could have sworn someone had been there a moment ago, watching him. The closed hatch of the torpedo room stood at the other end of the corridor. He had heard that the captain let the hospital corpsman, Matson, use the torpedo room as quarantine for that sick crewman, Steve Bodine. But that was where they'd stored Stubic's body too, frozen in its body bag. The idea of keeping a sick patient in there with a corpse didn't sit right with him. It was creepy. And when he thought about how Matson had shut himself in there as well, it felt even creepier.

His instincts told him to stay away from that hatch, and Oran trusted his instincts. He had learned that lesson in New Orleans. Before enlisting with the navy, he hadn't strayed far from Bayou Bartholomew, except for that one trip to the Big Easy with LeMon and a few of their friends from high school over Christmas break. After a long night of drinking, he had gotten separated from the others and found himself walking down a dark street he wasn't familiar with. A strange feeling had come over him then, one he had never forgotten. Maybe it was instinct, or maybe it was some kind of sixth sense—his grandmother had always claimed it ran in the family—but something told him to turn around and go back. No, not just go back—*run* back. He listened to that feeling, something he might not have done had he been with the others, and ran away from that dark street. He paused only once to look back, and that was when he saw them, a group of men emerging from the darkness at the other end of the street, knives glinting in their hands. He ran all the way back to the hotel and waited for his brother and their friends there, certain in the knowledge that if he had kept walking down that street, those men would have done a lot worse than just rob him. He was alive today only because he had listened.

He got the same feeling looking at that torpedo-room hatch. He turned away from it and hurried into the auxiliary engine room—and was surprised to find it dark. The light fixtures had been broken. Two auxiliary techs were already there, standing in front of the Big Red Machine and sweeping up the shattered glass from the floor. They had square, bulky battle lanterns with them to see by, and one turned his beam on Oran.

"What are you doing down here?" the tech asked.

With the light in his eyes, Oran couldn't see their faces. "Gettin' some o' these cans out your way," Oran replied, nodding at the stacked boxes.

"Halle-fuckin'-lujah," the tech said. He lowered his lantern and went back to cleaning up the mess. "Damn stuff's been in the way since we launched."

"It hasn't been *that* bad," the other tech joked. "They've made it real easy to grab a snack whenever we're hungry."

Oran walked over to the boxes, chuckling. "Better not of. Lieutenant Abrams finds out, he'll cut you off. All you'll get's bread and water for a week." By the ambient light of the techs' lanterns, he broke open one of the cartons. "Someone knock out these lights too, eh?"

"Someone on this boat's a real head case," the second tech said. "How is it they haven't caught the son of a bitch yet?"

"Thought they did when Stubic died," Oran said. "Maybe there's more than one of 'em."

"Christ," the second tech said. "Maybe the whole crew is bat-shit crazy."

"So, what's that make you?" said the first tech, grinning.

Oran collected an armful of the torn-open cardboard and plastic and carried it down the corridor to the garbage disposal room, where it would be compacted, then ejected into the ocean at the soonest opportunity. As he was walking back to the auxiliary engine room, he paused again. He could have sworn he heard someone walking up behind him, but when he turned, the corridor was as empty as before.

The closed hatch of the torpedo room seemed to stare back at him. He shivered.

Maybe there's more than one of 'em.

He returned to the auxiliary engine room and started gathering together the armful of cans he needed. He heard footsteps again, but this time when he looked up, he saw someone silhouetted in the doorway, his face in darkness with the light at his back. The techs shined their lanterns on him just as they had on Oran, revealing Ensign Penwarden.

"Get those lights out of my face," Penwarden said irritably.

"Sorry, sir," the first tech replied.

"You gave us a start, sir," the second tech said. "Thought for a moment you might be the mad light-smasher. You never know where he'll strike next."

"Except that he already did," the ensign said. "I ran into the XO up on the middle level. He sent me to get you. He said you're needed in the head and the lights down here can wait."

"The head, sir?" the first tech asked. "He broke the lights there too?"

"It's a little worse than that. You'd better see for yourself."

Both techs picked up their tools and left the auxiliary engine room. They took their lanterns with them, leaving Oran in a darkened room with only the light from the corridor outside to see by. He felt a chill again, spooked by the idea of being alone in a dark room with a crazy man loose on the sub. He stooped to collect his tomato cans. He could barely see and had to feel his way. From the corridor outside, he heard Penwarden say something that didn't make any sense.

"Bodine? Is that you?"

Oran glanced up. Penwarden was just outside the doorway. Oran couldn't see who he was talking to, but he doubted it was Bodine. Wasn't he quarantined?

Penwarden said the name again. "Bodine?"

Penwarden walked away, and Oran collected his cans. Perhaps his bad feeling had been wrong after all. If Bodine was up and about already, maybe there was nothing to worry about from the disease. Matson must have cured it somehow, or maybe the quarantine had given the fever time to run its course and it turned out not to be life-threatening. After all, Stubic had died from freezing himself, not from the disease. Maybe everything was going to be all right after all.

Carrying four half-gallon cans of tomatoes, Oran left the auxiliary engine room. He glanced down the corridor, but neither Penwarden nor Bodine was there.

The torpedo-room hatch was still closed.

CHAPTER EIGHTEEN

As soon as Oran returned to the galley, Gordon Abrams put him right back to work, helping prep first meal. LeMon stood by the stove, stirring a big pot of bright yellow liquid with red flecks. The sharp, peppery fumes coming out of that pot made Gordon's eyes water. He wasn't sure what was in there, let alone whether it was fit for human consumption, but he had learned to trust the Guidry brothers' culinary skills as long as the crew was happy.

The three of them talked among themselves as they always did while the Guidrys were cracking eggs and frying bacon for first meal, but all conversation ground to a halt when Lieutenant Commander Jefferson stormed into the galley. Behind him were Jerry White and Goodrich, the copper-haired auxiliary tech who had replaced the broken light fixture in the mess. Jefferson looked angrier than Gordon had ever seen him.

"Lieutenant, did you hear anything out of the ordinary earlier?" Jefferson demanded.

"No, sir, nothing," Gordon replied. "What's going on?"

"Grab a lantern and catch up to us in the head," Jefferson said.

Then, as quickly as they had arrived, Jefferson, White, and Goodrich hurried away. LeMon shot Gordon a concerned look.

"What's goin' on, suh?" he asked.

"I don't know," Gordon said. "Stay here, both of you. I'll be right back."

He opened the galley cabinet where his battle lantern was stored. Every department had its share of the portable, battery-powered electric lights in case the power went out, which it rarely ever did, so the things tended to gather dust. They were bulky yellow waterproof cubes of molded high-impact plastic, with thick, sturdy handles on top, and bracket attachments on the back so they could be mounted on bulkheads. Gordon grabbed his lantern and ran out of the galley.

Jefferson had asked him to meet them in the crew head. Something must have happened in there. His mind was already preparing for the worst.

Someone had blown a shitter.

As funny as the expression was, the reality was no joke. Emptying toilets was a major problem on submarines. At 400 feet down, the pressure pushing in on the hull was about 300 pounds per square inch. If the boat tried to flush out its human waste with less pressure than what was pushing in, all that shit would fly right back into the boat. That was why, instead of flushing into the ocean, the toilets on *Roanoke* emptied into sanitary tanks, which Engineering purged every few days.

But purging the tanks still meant the contents had to be pressurized so that they didn't all come flying back. If the pressure on the hull was 300 pounds per square inch, the sanitary tanks had to be pressurized to more than that—a minimum of *301* pounds per square inch. Auxiliary Division posted signs all over the head before they pressurized the tanks, warning sailors not to use the facilities, but if some idiot ignored the signs and flushed the toilet while the tanks were pressurized, the poor bastard would be rewarded with a 301-psi enema. For comparison, the water in fire hydrants was pressurized to only 100 pounds per square inch. This would be three times as strong. Under that kind of pressure, the shit would quite literally fly.

But as Gordon approached the head, the first thing he noticed was that he didn't smell anything. If someone had blown a shitter, the stench of sewage would be overwhelming. Hell, now that he thought of it, he would have been able to smell it all the way back in the galley.

The second thing he noticed was the absence of any light coming out of the open hatch.

When he entered the head, he found Jefferson, Jerry White, Goodrich and two other aux techs standing in a completely dark room, pointing lanterns up at the ceiling. All the light fixtures in the head had been smashed. The floor was littered with shards of glass and pearly white dust from the fluorescent tubes.

"Oh, Christ, not again," Gordon said.

"Earlier, the son of a bitch got the lights down in the auxiliary engine room too," Jefferson said. "But this time, we have a witness. Isn't that right, White?"

"Yes, sir," White said. "I just wish I had more information to give you. The sound of it woke me up, but I didn't see it happen. At first, I thought it was a dream, so I didn't get out of my rack right away. I wish I had, sir; then I might have caught whoever did this."

Even if they did catch him, what then? *Roanoke* didn't have a brig, and they sure as hell weren't going to lock up someone who seemed compelled to destroy everything around him in one of the officer staterooms. They couldn't hand him off to a surface ship, or they'd wind up alerting the Soviets to their presence again, and as far as Gordon was concerned, one Victor shadowing them was one too many.

Back when his mother had worked in the psychiatric hospital, she taught him that people who did inexplicable or harmful things were more likely mentally ill than malicious. Whoever was breaking the lights on *Roanoke* obviously fit that bill. Stress, claustrophobia—all sorts of things could make a submariner lose his mind. This was Mitch Robertson all over again, except that the light-smasher was turning his anger outward instead of inward. He desperately needed help, but what help could they offer him? There was no shrink on board, and Matson didn't have any psychiatric meds in sick bay. Were they just going to have to tie this guy up somewhere until the op was over?

"Sir, there's more," Goodrich said, swinging his lantern over to the stainless steel sinks at the far end of the room.

The mirrors above the sinks had been shattered. Someone had put a fist through them, leaving round spiderweb fractures in the silvered glass. The sinks were filled with fallen shards and spatters of blood, and more broken glass littered the floor below.

Gordon was flummoxed. How the hell had the culprit gotten away with it? Breaking the light fixtures *and* the mirrors? That would have taken time. White had heard it, but he hadn't investigated right away. Surely, someone else must have heard the racket and come looking. Only a third of the submarine's crew was on duty at any given time. That left a third of the crew on their racks right next to the head, and another third milling around the deck. The head was never empty for long, and there was no way to lock everyone out—no sign, like those on a commercial airplane's lavatory doors, that he could turn to OCCUPIED. With no way to keep it quiet and no way to keep people out once he started making noise, how had the vandal done it? Gordon supposed that if the head's hatch to the corridor *and* its hatches to the berthing areas were shut, it was possible the noise would be dampened. Still, the vandal would have had to be fast to escape without being spotted—faster than Gordon could imagine anyone moving.

But the question of *how* paled beside the question of *why.* Why break the light fixtures *and* the mirrors?

"Sir, what do you think it all means?" he asked.

Jefferson shined his lantern at the shattered mirrors, then back up to the smashed fixtures on the ceiling.

"It means the people on this boat are losing their goddamn minds," Jefferson said. "They're breaking lights, mirrors, the radio, and God knows what else."

"Sir, do you think the captain will cut the op short?" Gordon asked.

"I doubt it," Jefferson said. "As far as the captain's concerned, this op is too important to abort. He wants to hang tight and see if the techs can fix the radio, but Coms doesn't think they can." He sighed and shook his head. "Frankly, we're hosed. We can't radio COMSUBRON for instructions, some crazy son of a bitch is breaking our lights, and we've got two sailors dead from bubonic plague or whatever the hell it is."

"Two, sir?" Gordon asked. "Someone else died?"

"Steve Bodine," Jefferson said sadly. "He passed a few hours ago."

"What, sir?" White said.

At the same time, Gordon asked, "Are you sure, sir?"

"Of course I'm sure!" Jefferson snapped, looking at them both. "What's gotten into the two of you? Matson called me himself over the circuit to inform me."

"Sir, I'm confused," White said. "I could have sworn I saw Bodine when I woke up, before I left the berthing area."

"Impossible," Jefferson replied.

"Sir, I'm not so sure about that," Gordon said. "Oran Guidry told me he saw Bodine earlier too. Ensign Penwarden was talking to him outside the auxiliary engine room. And, sir, didn't you mention the lights had been broken there too?"

Jefferson stared at Gordon. "It's impossible. Matson told me that Bodine died."

"Sir, if Bodine is dead, then who did I see?" White asked. "And who did Oran see, sir?"

"That's a damn good question," Jefferson said.

Leaving the aux techs behind to clean up the glass, Jefferson led Gordon and White back to the galley. He questioned Oran on exactly what had happened in the auxiliary engine room. LeMon watched nervously, stirring his pot as Oran related his story. Gordon listened intently too, but nothing Oran told the lieutenant commander differed from the story he had told Gordon earlier.

"So you didn't actually see Bodine yourself?" Jefferson asked.

"No, suh," Oran replied, "but Ensign Penwarden did. I heard him say Bodine's name twice, suh."

"And where is Ensign Penwarden now?" Jefferson asked.

"I don' know, suh," Oran said. "He was gone already when I come back up to the galley, suh."

"What about you, White?" Jefferson asked. "Have you seen Ensign Penwarden since you left the berthing area?"

"No, sir," he replied.

"Lieutenant Abrams?" Jefferson asked.

Gordon shook his head. "No, sir. If you like, I can keep an eye out for him during first meal."

"Please do," Jefferson said. "I want to talk to him."

"Sir," Gordon said, "two sightings of Steve Bodine alive and in places where the lights have been purposely broken—it can't be a coincidence."

"But it doesn't make sense," Jefferson said, though his words held far less conviction this time. He thought a moment, then said, "All right, Guidry, White, come with me. Lieutenant Abrams, let me know if you see Ensign Penwarden."

"Where we goin', suh?" Oran asked.

"To the torpedo room. You both think you saw Bodine, but Matson told me he's dead. I intend to put this matter to rest and, with any luck, get to the bottom of whatever the hell is happening on this boat."

CHAPTER NINETEEN

Jerry climbed down the main ladder, following Oran Guidry and Lieutenant Commander Jefferson to the bottom level. Jefferson was already walking up to the torpedo-room hatch when Jerry reached the bottom. He hurried to catch up. Oran, hanging back behind Jefferson, looked nervous. He kept chewing his lip and staring at the door as if he expected floodwaters to come surging through.

"You okay?" Jerry asked him.

Oran nodded, though not very convincingly. "It's just that I get a real bad feelin' down here. Felt it earlier this mornin', and I got it again now."

"What kind of feeling?" Jerry asked.

"Like we better off keepin' that hatch shut tight."

Ever since they found Stubic's dead body in the freezer, Jerry had felt something too: an unease lurking like a shadow in the back of his mind, making him feel like an animal that could sense a predator hiding in the tall grass but didn't know exactly where it was. After discovering the smashed lights and mirrors in the head, the feeling had only gotten worse.

Jefferson stood in front of the torpedo-room hatch. "You're both certain it was Bodine you saw?"

"Sir, I know it sounds impossible, but I would swear to it," Jerry replied. "I sat right next to the man in the control room for every one of my watch sections. I'd recognize him anywhere, sir."

"What about you, Guidry?" Jefferson asked.

Oran shrugged. "I didn't see hide nor hair, suh. Was Ensign Penwarden who saw Bodine. I only know what I heard. The ensign called out Bodine's name twice. When I left the auxiliary engine room two shakes later, they was both already gone, suh."

Jefferson shook his head. "It can't be him. There's no way." He banged his fist on the door and called, "Matson? It's Lieutenant Commander Jefferson. I have some questions I'd like to ask you."

When there was no answer, he knocked again. A few seconds later, the door opened, swinging outward. Senior Chief Sherman Matson poked his head out. He looked pale and groggy, his hair tousled and sweaty. Jerry knew that Matson had quarantined himself just to be on the safe side, but now he wondered whether prolonged exposure to Bodine had made him sick.

"Lieutenant Commander?" Matson said, squinting at Jefferson. "Sorry. I—I must have fallen asleep." He rubbed the back of his neck as if he had slept on it wrong. "What can I do for you, sir?"

"Did you or did you not inform me several hours ago that Steve Bodine had passed away from his illness?" Jefferson said. "Because I've got two men here who say they saw Bodine not long ago, up and walking."

Matson frowned. "Saw him, sir? No, not possible. His body is still here."

"Is it safe for us to come in and see for ourselves?" Jefferson asked. "I'd like to put an end to any speculation."

"See for yourselves, sir?" Matson asked. Jerry thought he seemed really out of it. "Yes, yes, of course. It should be safe, sir. With the host body deceased, the virus likely died with him."

"So you've determined it's a virus?" Jefferson asked.

"That's my best guess, sir."

Matson stepped aside so they could enter. Jefferson walked right in. Oran and Jerry paused and exchanged a worried look. Jerry knew why Oran didn't want to go in—that bad feeling of his—but Jerry had more concrete concerns. Matson claimed it was safe, but it was only speculation, and besides, Matson himself didn't look healthy. If he had contracted the virus, or whatever it was, from Bodine, would it spread to them too? Maybe they were better off staying out of the torpedo room.

"Come along, gentlemen," Jefferson called from inside.

Damn. The XO wanted him inside, so that was where he had to be. He and Oran reluctantly stepped into the torpedo room. As Matson sealed the hatch behind him again, Jerry saw a second black body bag on the floor, next to Stubic. The tag read BODINE, STEVEN.

"*Keeyaw,*" Oran muttered, crossing himself.

Jefferson stared at the bag a moment, his jaw set, his face unreadable. Finally, he said, "Open it, Matson."

"Aye, sir." Matson crouched over the body bag and slowly unzipped it. He took his time, and Jerry just wanted to grab the zipper from him, yank it down, and get this over with. When the bag was fully unzipped, Matson spread it open to reveal the head, neck, and shoulders of the body inside. Jerry's throat tightened.

Steve Bodine was pale and waxy, as ashen as he had been in the berthing area earlier—if that had indeed been Bodine creeping through the space. What the hell was going on? He approached the body for a closer look, all thoughts of contagion forgotten. Bodine's eyes were closed. He looked peaceful now after suffering through the illness that had killed him.

Jefferson's face, which had been so stoical just a second ago, was suddenly overcome with emotion, to the point where Jerry worried that he was going to break down. The XO pulled himself together quickly, though, resuming his air of professional detachment, but that fleeting moment of vulnerability stuck with Jerry. It was easy to forget sometimes that officers were human beings too, when all he'd ever seen them do was bark out orders or reprimand enlisted men for speaking without being asked or forgetting to say "sir." That was especially true of the higher-ups: the captain and the XO. As he watched Jefferson pull himself together, he thought maybe the XO wasn't such a bad guy. There was definitely more to him than Jerry first thought.

"I trust this is enough to put the matter to bed," Jefferson said.

"Yes sir," Jerry said. "I'm sorry, sir. I could have sworn it was him."

"It was dark in the berthing area," Jefferson said. "It could have been anyone."

But it hadn't been "anyone." Jerry had been certain, but how could it have been Bodine if Bodine was already dead?

"Aye, suh," Oran said. He looked as confused as Jerry felt. "Like White, I'm awful sorry for the confusion, suh. I woulda' swore on my mama's life Ensign Penwarden was talkin' to Bodine, suh."

"Penwarden?" Matson said. He blinked and rubbed his neck again. "Did you say Ensign Penwarden? He was … he was just here, wasn't he?"

"You saw him?" Jefferson asked.

"I think so, sir." Matson leaned back against the machinery. He looked dizzy and distracted. "Or maybe I dreamed it. I fell asleep for a while there. I mean, I must have. I don't remember much after calling you on the circuit, Lieutenant Commander." He frowned. "Or much of what I was doing before you knocked just now, for that matter."

Jerry, Jefferson, and Oran exchanged worried glances. Jerry knew they were thinking the same thing he was: Matson had the fever now too. But they didn't leave right away, as Jerry would have preferred. Instead, Jefferson crouched down beside the body bag. He opened it as wide as he could, and peered in, as though looking for something. Then he closed it again and zipped it up.

"Did you see Ensign Penwarden or didn't you, Matson?" Jefferson asked, straightening.

But Matson only shook his head, looking down at his feet. "I don't know, sir. I—I can't remember. I can't seem to remember anything."

"Bodine told me he was having the same problems with his memory," Jefferson said. "He couldn't even remember breaking one of the ceiling lights. He told me he felt like some part of him was slipping away."

Matson looked up at them. There was genuine terror in his eyes.

"You have to leave now, sir," he said. "It's clear to me I've contracted whatever Bodine had, which means all of you are at risk of contagion just by being here. You have to go."

"Damn it, Matson, you knew this would happen," Jefferson said softly. "You knew you'd get it if you locked yourself in here with him."

"You really should go, Lieutenant Commander," Matson insisted. "Before it's too late."

Jefferson nodded. "Take care of yourself, Matson. We can't afford to lose you too."

Jerry was all too happy to follow Jefferson out of the torpedo room, and from the look on Oran's face, so was he. When they were back in the bottom-level corridor, Jefferson closed the heavy hatch behind them.

"White, you were right," Jefferson said. "I think that was Bodine you saw in the berthing area. And I think he was in the head too."

"Sir?" Jerry asked, confused. "We just saw his body, sir, how could it be him?"

"When I looked in that body bag just now, I saw cuts on Bodine's hands," Jefferson said. "Matson had already patched up his old cuts; I saw it. These were new cuts, the kind you'd get from broken glass. There was blood on his hands too. New blood."

Oran moaned and crossed himself again. "What does it mean, suh?"

"It means Bodine was our man," the XO said. "He's the one who wrecked the head—and the one you say Penwarden was talking to earlier, Guidry. He must have died shortly after."

"But, sir, you said Matson called you *hours* ago to report Bodine's death," Jerry said.

Jefferson glanced back at the torpedo room. "He's not well. He's clearly ill and possibly delusional. In that state, he could easily have hallucinated or dreamed that Bodine was dead and called me to report it. I just hope Matson's the last one, and no one else gets sick. If we're lucky, he'll ride it out until we can get to a navy base. If we're not …" He trailed off, as if realizing he'd said more than he intended to a couple of enlisted men. "You're both dismissed."

Jerry and Oran climbed back up to the middle level while Jefferson continued up the main ladder to the top level, presumably to give the captain a report on his investigation and discuss Matson's condition. Oran pulled Jerry aside into the mess.

"Do you believe the XO?" he asked.

"What do you mean?" Jerry asked.

"His theory about when Bodine died?"

"I don't know." Jerry looked down the corridor. He saw an auxiliary tech come out of the head with a full garbage bag. Light was coming through the doorway now. Either they had taken fixtures from other parts of the sub to replace them or they were using battle lanterns as replacements. Either way, it was good to know he wouldn't have to relieve himself in pitch-black darkness. "I guess what the lieutenant commander said makes a kind of sense."

Oran shook his head. "Nothin' makes sense in this boat, White. Somethin' been wrong from the start, I can feel it. Back in the bayou, some folks still practice the old religion. They say everything's got a soul—even things that ain't alive. Sometimes I think they're right. And if *Roanoke*'s got a soul, it ain't a healthy one. Somethin' bad got inside her, and now she's rottin' away from within."

"You sure you don't have the fever too, Guidry? Because you're talking crazy."

He laughed, but Oran didn't. His eyes stayed narrow, sharp, and serious.

"Mark my words, White," Oran said. "There's somethin' very wrong in this boat."

CHAPTER TWENTY

After Lieutenant Junior Grade Charles Duncan's watch section was finished and he'd had something to eat in the wardroom, he got to thinking about Jerry White, Frank Leonard, and fate.

He had known Lieutenant Commander Leonard—or, he supposed, just Frank, now that the man's navy career was over—for four years, having served under him on the USS *Batfish*, a Sturgeon-class sub out of Charleston. This was after Operation Evening Star made *Batfish* a navy legend in 1978, when she detected a Soviet Yankee-class ballistic missile submarine in the Norwegian Sea, a couple hundred nautical miles above the Arctic Circle. *Batfish* had trailed the sub for 50 days without ever being detected, all the while gathering valuable intelligence on how Soviet subs operated. Although Duncan and Leonard hadn't been part of that op, when they were assigned to *Batfish* they found a sense of camaraderie among the crew that stemmed from the sub's impressive legacy. Everyone on *Batfish* knew it was a special boat, and as a result the crew was tighter than any other he had known.

He and Leonard remained friendly even after they were transferred to new submarines, calling each other regularly when they weren't underway. Duncan had felt terrible when he heard Leonard had been passed over for promotion a third time, thereby ending his career with the navy. But his sympathy had turned to anger when he learned *why* Leonard had been passed up. An official complaint by some pissant PO2 named Jerry White.

Did Frank Leonard have problems? Of course he did. Everyone had problems. Was it true Leonard had a weakness for nose candy and pills? Sure, but it sounded a lot worse than it was. He did it only when he was off duty and off base. And besides, he assured Duncan—one of the few people who knew about his habit—that he had cut way down and was in the process of stopping altogether. He promised he had it under control. Then Jerry White went and screwed everything up with that damn complaint. And the kicker? It hadn't even been about the drugs. It had been about the way Leonard treated some PO who shouldn't have been allowed in the navy in the first place—a faggot who'd lied about being a faggot so he could join the submarine service. Frank Leonard had been a good, loyal navy man, and the fact that he'd lost his career over the way he treated a goddamn homo had made Duncan furious.

The day he saw Jerry White's name added to the crew roster for *Roanoke*, it was as if fate had played a hand. He called Leonard from Pearl to tell him the news, and Leonard had made him promise to make White's life on the submarine a living hell. He didn't need to twist Duncan's arm. If fate was giving him a chance to avenge his friend and fellow member of the esteemed *Batfish* crew, who was he to say no? White had destroyed an executive officer's career, and yet White's rank was intact, his record unsullied. It was an injustice so outrageous, Duncan felt justified—no, *duty-bound*—to make White wish they had thrown him out on his ass. If the navy had been too much of an institutional pussy to teach him the lesson he needed, Duncan was happy to pick up the slack.

But there was only so much Duncan could do to him, especially knowing White's affinity for filing complaints about officers. If he harassed White too brazenly, Duncan would get gigged, and that demerit would stay on his record permanently. If he got violent with him, he would get thrown out of the navy faster than if he'd been caught diddling some boy during a stopover in Bangkok—and with just as much dishonor. He had to walk a fine line, which left him with only one option: dressing White down at every opportunity, preferably in front of as many other crewmen as possible. He had almost slipped up in the control room a couple of watches back, when they shook the Victor off their tail. In his jubilation, he had very nearly high-fived White along with the other men. He wouldn't make that mistake again. Before this underway was through, he intended to make White feel about as lucky to have transferred to *Roanoke* as a black cat breaking a mirror on Friday the 13th—make him think about putting in for another transfer the second his feet were back on dry land. It would be a petty victory, smaller in scale than that shit-heel White deserved, but the thought of it still felt pretty damn good.

He made his way to the officers' staterooms at the forward end of the middle-level corridor. He had some downtime ahead of him and wanted to catch up on his reading. He opened the door to his stateroom, slipped inside, and closed it behind him. A triple-decker bunk sat behind a curtain on one side of the stateroom. The other walls were taken up by a couple of dressers, a standing wardrobe, and a few built-in cubbies with pull-down doors. Remembering that he'd left his book in his rack, Duncan crossed the thin grass-green carpet to the curtain. He pulled it aside, and there on the middle rack, *his* rack, lay Ensign Penwarden, eyes closed, body curled into a fetal ball.

It took a moment for the astonished Duncan to find his voice.

"Ensign Penwarden," he said loudly. When the man didn't stir, he shook his shoulder roughly. "Penwarden."

The ensign roused himself as if from a deep sleep. He blinked up at Duncan. "Lieutenant, sir?"

"Ensign Penwarden," Duncan said, "would you mind telling me what the hell you're doing in my rack, in a stateroom that doesn't belong to you?"

"What, sir?" Penwarden looked around himself, confused. "Sir, how did I get here?"

"You don't know?"

Penwarden put up an arm to shield his eyes from the overhead lights. He sucked in a breath and grimaced in pain.

Duncan nearly gasped in shock. "Ensign, what—what's wrong with your teeth?"

Without warning, Ensign Penwarden grabbed Duncan by the collar and leaped out of the rack. Duncan fell onto his back. Penwarden straddled him, pinning him down. Duncan tried to throw him off but couldn't. Penwarden was unbelievably strong.

"Ensign, what—"

That was all Duncan had a chance to say before he got another look at Penwarden's teeth, up close.

CHAPTER TWENTY-ONE

Lieutenant Commander Jefferson sat down for dinner at the wardroom table with Captain Weber and seven other *Roanoke* officers—a touch of normality at the end of a day that had been anything but normal.

The stewards entered with platters of food fresh from the galley, but he found himself preoccupied, his mind spinning in different directions. He couldn't get the sight of Steve Bodine's dead body out of his head—or the bloody cuts on his hands. It made him think of the broken lights all over the boat. It was as if the submarine were being purposely thrown into darkness. But why? Bodine had said the lights were hurting his eyes, and Jefferson would wager that Stubic had the same complaint. It had to be a side effect of the fever—but it couldn't be *just* that. He would have bought it as an explanation if only the lights in the head had been smashed, but the mirrors had been broken too. Mirrors didn't give off light. At best, they reflected it, but why attack a reflection when you could just as easily destroy the light's true source? There was something more going on; he was sure of it. Some piece of the puzzle that he was missing.

He was distracted enough by his thoughts that he only barely registered the absence of Lieutenant Junior Grade Duncan, who normally ate with them. Maybe he was needed in the control room. No one had informed Jefferson, but he let it slide. He had enough on his mind.

The stewards served them steak, grilled to perfection by Gordon's galley staff. Jefferson cut into his and watched the juices flow from the lightly pink interior. Under normal circumstances, his mouth would have watered and his stomach would have grumbled in eager anticipation, but the mirrors kept returning to his thoughts. There was something eerie about shattering a mirror. Symbolically, it was like shattering yourself, wasn't it? All a mirror could do was show you your reflection, and to break it …

To break it meant you didn't like what you saw.

As he ate his steak, he looked across the table at Captain Weber, who was engaged in small talk with the other officers about sports, their families, their children—anything but the op itself or the strange and tragic events that had taken place. Such things were routinely avoided at dinners like this. The captain thought that a good meal and a chance for easy conversation was the best way to relieve stress among the officers, but it all felt forced. Two crewmen were dead, the hospital corpsman was sick, *Roanoke* was being further vandalized by the day, the radio wasn't working, and they were sailing deep into Soviet territory. No amount of steak dinner and chitchat would change any of that.

Earlier, he had informed Captain Weber about the fresh cuts he'd seen on Bodine's hands, and the possibility that their timeline of events was off, that the helmsman might have died *after* vandalizing the head, not before as they had thought. But the captain wanted facts, not conjecture, and had ordered Jefferson to continue his investigation until he had concrete answers. To do that, Jefferson needed confirmation of Bodine's time of death from Matson, but that was where he kept hitting a brick wall. Thanks to the fever, Matson's memory—indeed, his whole state of mind—could no longer be trusted. Hell, maybe, in his delirium, Matson had smashed up the head himself, then gone back to quarantine with a shard of glass and used it to mutilate Bodine's hands. No, that was too far-fetched. If Matson were that out of his mind with the fever, he wouldn't bother framing a dead man. And besides, though Matson had clearly been sick, he hadn't been *that* far gone when Jefferson saw him in the torpedo room.

Which meant that either Matson had prematurely hallucinated Bodine's death when he called Jefferson on the circuit to report it, as he suspected, or …

Or what? Steve Bodine had risen out of his body bag like Christ on Easter to go smash some lights and mirrors, then run like hell without being seen before anyone could investigate what all the noise was?

It didn't add up. Once again, Jefferson felt as though he was missing some important bit of information that would make it all make sense.

When the meal was over, Captain Weber dismissed everyone but asked Jefferson to stay behind for a moment. Both of them remained seated at the table.

"It's been a rough op so far, hasn't it, Jefferson?" the captain asked.

"Aye, sir," he replied. "This isn't like any underway I've ever been on."

"I take it you've never lost a man on your boat before?"

"No, sir. Have you, sir?"

Captain Weber shook his head. "Not until now. I've been in the submarine service long enough to see past crewmen die from cancer, heart attacks, car accidents, but never on the boat, never during an op. I've been lucky that way, I suppose. Did I ever tell you my father served in Korea?"

"No, sir."

"He was a navy man too. A love of the ocean runs in my family. We used to say we had salt water for blood. He was stationed on an aircraft carrier in the Sea of Japan, not far from Gangneung. He saw a lot of airmen fly off the ship and never come back. These were swaggering, cocksure pilots, the kind who thought they could never die. You know what he said about that? He said everyone is lucky—you, me, everyone— but only until the day they're not. There's no such thing as a charmed life, he said, but there's no such thing as a life wasted, either. Hold on a moment, Jefferson. I've got something for us. Get the door, would you?"

Jefferson got up and closed the wardroom door while Captain Weber went to one of the built-in cubbies in the wall. This one had a lock on it, but he took a key out of his pocket and opened it. He pulled out a bottle of Macallan twelve-year-old single-malt Scotch and two glasses, and set them on the table.

"Sir?" Jefferson asked, raising an eyebrow as he returned to his seat. He knew perfectly well that General Order 99, which had been in place for nearly 70 years, forbade liquor on naval vessels while at sea.

Captain Weber sat and uncorked the bottle. "Don't worry. A small amount of alcohol is permitted on submarines for medicinal purposes. According to regulations, it can be issued only on the authority of two men. The first is the hospital corpsman. The second, of course, is the captain."

He poured out two glasses and passed one to Jefferson, who accepted it in stunned silence.

"You lost someone important to you, Jefferson," Captain Weber said. "I would be a piss-poor captain if I didn't know what was going on with my own crew. I know you took Bodine under your wing, and I know you had high hopes for him." He raised his glass. "To Steve Bodine. Long may he sail."

With everything else that was going on, Jefferson hadn't really had time to let it sink in that Bodine was dead. Or maybe he just hadn't let it sink in. He had felt it for a moment down in the torpedo room, looking at his friend in a body bag, but now, with the captain toasting Bodine's memory, he felt himself choking up. He steeled himself against the rising tide of grief and raised his glass to the captain's.

"To Steve Bodine," he said. "I was going to encourage him to apply to Officer Candidate School, sir. I think he would have gone far in the navy."

"I don't doubt it," the captain said, "especially with a mentor like you."

They sipped their Scotch in silence for a while. It had been a long time since Jefferson had had a drink. It was smooth, tasting of wood and peat and honey. It went down warm and pleasant.

"Lieutenant Commander, I don't think I've ever told you this before, but you are, hands down, the best executive officer I have ever served with," Captain Weber said. "Everything you've had to deal with on this underway would have broken a lesser man. When we get back to Pearl Harbor, I'm going to recommend you for your own command. I know some of the higher-ups have already been thinking about it, but a recommendation from me will help kick the wheels into motion. You've earned it, Lee. You deserve it." He poured them both another glass. "However, should you tell anyone else on *Roanoke* about my secret stash of Macallan, not only will I withhold that recommendation, I'll put you in an inflatable and launch you out of a torpedo tube myself."

Jefferson laughed and lifted his glass. "You've got yourself a deal, sir."

***

As XO, Jefferson had his own stateroom in Officer Country, which also happened to be the forwardmost room on *Roanoke*. Beyond it was only the fore ladder, which led up to the captain's egress, and the bulkhead that separated the forward compartment from the submarine's water-filled nose cone, where the sonar sphere was housed.

By the time he returned to his stateroom, he was feeling happily warm from the Scotch. He took down the folding bed from the bulkhead, sat on it, and began unlacing his boots.

Damn, he was going to miss Bodine. He had the nagging sense again that he had ridden the young man too hard, been too stern with him in his effort to make him the best sailor he could be. But it had been born of good intentions, and that had to mean something, didn't it? Sometimes, it seemed as though white sailors in the US Navy were given as many second chances as they needed, but a black sailor had to mess up but once before others started talking in hushed tones about whether "his kind" belonged in the navy at all. And that was why he had been so tough on Bodine. Surely Bodine had known that and hadn't blamed him. Right?

He thought it was his own drunken imagination when he heard Bodine's voice just then, softly calling him.

"Lieutenant Commander …"

Jefferson shivered and pulled off his boots. It was just his imagination running away with him. Bodine was on his mind, after all. He was exhausted from a long day, and his mind was drifting pleasantly from the Scotch. Was it any wonder he was hearing things?

"Lieutenant Commander," came the voice again.

This time, Jefferson sat up bolt upright. That wasn't his imagination. He really had heard something, but he couldn't tell where it was coming from. Close enough to be heard clearly. Was someone hiding in his stateroom with him? But where? There was no place to hide.

"You should hear what they call you behind your back, Lieutenant Commander," Bodine's voice continued.

Jefferson stood up. "Who's there?"

"The captain, the other sailors—you should hear the names they have for you when you're not around. Jig. Sambo. Spade. Shine."

Jefferson turned in a circle, looking into the corners of the stateroom, but no one was there. He was alone.

"They can't stand you. They can't wait until this underway is over, so they can get away from your uppity black ass. It's all they talk about when you're not there."

"You're wrong," Jefferson said loudly. Was he going crazy? First, he was hearing voices, and now he was talking back to them? But Scotch had a way of replacing one's common sense with fearlessness. "I just spoke with the captain. He's not like that."

"They're *all* like that."

Jefferson put his hands over his ears and shook his head. He had to be losing his mind. Or maybe this was a delusion brought on by the fever that was going around. Damn it, had he been infected when he went down to the torpedo room earlier? Matson had warned him it could happen …

The sound of breaking glass outside his stateroom startled him out of his thoughts. One of the light fixtures outside? He turned toward the door.

"Do you know what the best thing about being on a submarine is, Lieutenant Commander?" Bodine's voice asked. "There's no sun. Down here, it's always night."

Another crash, closer now, followed by the tinkle of glass shards falling to the deck.

"Who are you?" Jefferson shouted.

"Don't you know your old friend Steve Bodine?"

No, it was impossible. He was dead. And yet, that voice …

Fuck this. Someone was playing a nasty prank on him, and he was going to have the son of a bitch's hide for it. He walked to the door and reached for the handle.

Another crash came from outside, making him pause. More glass fell tinkling to the deck. Christ, the three light fixtures in the Officer Country corridor.

"I'm just outside your door, Lieutenant Commander."

Jefferson stared at the handle.

"Why don't you come out and say hello?"

To hell with this sick bastard, whoever he was. Come out and say hello? That was exactly what Jefferson was going to do. And when he caught the son of a bitch, he would give him an ass-kicking to remember. He gripped the knob, turned it, and yanked the stateroom door open.

The corridor outside was dark. He was right: all three light fixtures had been smashed. The light from his stateroom bled out into the shadows before him, falling across bits of shattered glass on the deck. Beyond where the light reached, he saw a shape in the darkness—the silhouette of a man. It had Bodine's posture and stood at Bodine's height, but it couldn't be Bodine.

The silhouette's eyes glowed brightly out of the darkness as if they were reflecting the light, like a cat's.

In a harsh, inhuman whisper, Steve Bodine said, "Hello, brother."

CHAPTER TWENTY-TWO

When Jerry White showed up for his watch section in the control room, he was pleasantly surprised to find that Lieutenant Duncan was not on duty as the diving officer. Unsurprisingly, in Duncan's absence his watch went more smoothly than ever. The new diving officer didn't ride him the way Duncan did, didn't look for tiny things to criticize, or, worse, fabricate them as an excuse to dress him down in front of everyone. When the watch was over six hours later, Jerry left the control room actually feeling good about himself for a change, basking in the feeling of a job well done.

He climbed down the main ladder to the middle level, planning to get some chow and maybe finally start that book he had brought along. But as soon as he stepped off the ladder, Senior Chief Farrington came walking up to him and said, "White, come with me." Without breaking his stride, Farrington continued toward the mess.

Jerry hurried after him. "What's this about, COB?"

Farrington didn't answer. They entered the mess, and Farrington went to the closest table, where four enlisted men were eating a seafood gumbo that smelled tantalizingly good.

"Gentlemen, I need this table for a few minutes."

If it were anyone else below the rank of ensign, the men would have scoffed at the request, but for the chief of the boat they got up with their trays and took another table. Farrington indicated that White should sit down. Then the COB sat across from him.

"How would you describe your relationship with Lieutenant Junior Grade Charles Duncan, White?"

Jerry frowned. "I'm not sure what you mean."

"Lieutenant Duncan has vanished. Were you aware?"

"What?"

"When he didn't show up for his watch section, someone was sent to his stateroom. He wasn't there, either. The officers he shares the stateroom with say he wasn't present for his usual sleep section. I've had men searching the boat for the whole past section, and more searching now on the top level. Something tells me they won't find him there, either."

Jerry stared at the COB. How could anyone go missing on a 300-foot submarine? There was no place where you wouldn't be seen by *someone*. Hell, Jerry couldn't even take a piss in private most days. Then he remembered how Bodine had evaded them during the boatwide search for him. How had he done that?

Farrington interrupted his thoughts. "It's no secret there was friction between you and Lieutenant Duncan. How did that make you feel? Angry?"

"Hold on a minute, COB," Jerry said. "You think *I* had something to do with it?"

"I'm just asking questions, White. Did it make you angry?"

"Yes, it made me angry, but not enough to … to do something to him. Look, I never wanted any trouble. I just wanted to keep my head down and focus on my duties. I never so much as talked back to Lieutenant Duncan, even when he was treating me unfairly."

"So, you feel he was treating you unfairly," Farrington said. "Why didn't you come to me about it? That's what I'm here for."

"Tim Spicer told me I should, but like I said, I just wanted to focus on my duties. I didn't want to …" He trailed off.

"Didn't want to what?" Farrington asked.

Jerry sighed and looked around the mess to see if others were listening.

Of course they were. They stared at him like school kids watching someone being taken out of class by the principal. Jerry's cheeks flushed with humiliation. He was never going to catch a break on this damn boat.

"Didn't want to *what*, White?" Farrington pressed.

"I didn't want to become known as someone who's constantly making complaints against officers," he said. "I didn't want that reputation."

"You already have a reputation," Farrington said. "I read your file, I know all about how you got your previous XO drummed out of the navy. Did you know I was against your transfer for *Roanoke*, White? The captain thought you were worth it because you saved *Philadelphia* from a fire, and the XO backed him up, but I thought differently. I thought maybe you have a problem with authority. Do you, White?"

"No, COB, I don't," Jerry said. The accusation angered him, but he tried to keep his tone calm and even. It wasn't easy. "I took the same oath you did: to obey the orders of the officers appointed over me, according to regulations and the Uniform Code of Military Justice."

"And what about Ensign Penwarden?" Farrington continued. "Was he treating you 'unfairly,' too?"

Jerry frowned. "Ensign Penwarden? No, I barely know him. Why?"

"The ensign hasn't turned up, either," Farrington said.

"They're *both* missing? Wait a minute, couldn't they have gotten sick and reported to quarantine?"

"Matson would have informed us if they had," Farrington replied.

But Matson hadn't looked well the last time Jerry saw him. It wasn't outside the realm of possibility that Matson was too sick to remember to alert anyone when new patients showed up.

"But surely you've checked the torpedo room anyway," Jerry said.

Farrington shook his head. "Quarantined. It's off-limits."

A sailor came rushing up to their table, out of breath. The grease marks on his pants marked him as part of the Engineering Department.

"COB, it's—it's the XO," the sailor panted.

"Lieutenant Commander Jefferson? What about him?" Farrington demanded.

"He's gone," the sailor said. "No one can find him anywhere."

"Slow down," Farrington said. "What are you talking about?"

"The engineering officer sent me to fetch him so they could talk about the new broken lights in Officer Country," the sailor said, "but the lieutenant commander's stateroom is empty. The lights were broken in there too. His bed was down, but it doesn't look slept in. I searched for him all over the boat. I even had other crewmen searching too, but nobody can find him."

First, Duncan and Penwarden went missing, and now Jefferson too? At least, Farrington couldn't blame this one on Jerry.

In fact, it looked as though Farrington had forgotten all about Jerry. He told the sailor, "Take me to the XO's stateroom."

Jerry watched the two men walk off toward Officer Country. More broken lights almost certainly meant someone else had the fever now. But what about the three missing officers? It was like Bodine all over again. Had the three of them broken the lights themselves, then gone into quarantine with Matson during a lucid moment when they realized they were sick? He hoped that was the case. Nothing else made sense. You couldn't just walk off a submarine in the middle of an underway.

He left the mess, not feeling very hungry after Farrington's questions. In the corridor, he saw Oran Guidry help a very haggard-looking LeMon Guidry out of the galley. Oran had one arm around his brother's shoulders to help keep him upright. Jerry hurried over to them.

"What happened?" he asked.

"Monje's sick," Oran said. "Too sick to work in the galley. Lieutenant Abrams wants him out before he make everybody else sick too. Said he don't want a Typhoid Mary. I don't think that's very funny."

LeMon drooped in his brother's arms. He was pale and sweaty, dark around the eyes. It was the fever. There was no doubt in Jerry's mind.

"We have to bring him down to quarantine," Jerry said. "I'll help."

"No," LeMon moaned as Jerry got on his other side and helped shoulder his weight. "No doctors."

"Yes, Monje," Oran told him gently. "You need to see the corpsman. No complaining, now."

They started carrying him toward the main ladder, but LeMon resisted.

For someone weak from illness, he had a surprising amount of strength left. He planted his feet on the deck and refused to move any farther.

"No doctors, Oran," LeMon said again, his head lolling weakly on his neck. "You know what Papa always said. You either sleep it off, or you die in your sleep the way God intended."

"Then you'll sleep it off, but you'll do it down in the quarantine with Matson," Oran insisted, yanking him forward.

Jerry and Oran carried him to the ladder. That was hard enough, but getting him *down* the ladder was a lot trickier. Oran went down first. Then Jerry held LeMon under his arms and gently lowered him to Oran, who took his legs and helped ease him down to the bottom level. LeMon was weakening fast and didn't resist at all. But he did talk a lot in his delirium. While Oran kept LeMon balanced upright, Jerry came down the ladder and heard LeMon muttering.

"Penwarden—I dreamed about Ensign Penwarden," he said. "He— he was in the berthin' area with a funny look on his face. He caught me lookin' at him; then suddenly he was right in front of my rack. Moved like a flash. Then I woke up."

Jerry paused, remembering how he had seen Bodine in the berthing area.

"That's one crazy dream, Monje," Oran said. He shot Jerry a worried glance. "The fever playin' tricks on his mind. Ain't no one seen Penwarden in hours. The man's up and disappeared."

"I heard," Jerry said. "Lieutenant Duncan and Lieutenant Commander Jefferson too. Something tells me they're in quarantine with Matson."

"No," LeMon moaned. "No doctors."

They managed to maneuver LeMon to the torpedo room. Jerry held him up while Oran banged on the hatch.

"Chief Matson!" he shouted.

"Never seen anyone move so fast," LeMon said again. "He was like lightnin'."

LeMon laughed deliriously, and his head tipped forward, chin to chest. Near the back of LeMon's neck, Jerry noticed two small red welts. He was about to lean in for a closer look when the torpedo-room hatch clanked open suddenly, startling him. Matson stood in the doorway. He was still pale, but otherwise he looked strong and sturdy again—quite the opposite of how he looked last time.

"It's my brother," Oran said. "He got the fever!"

Matson stepped forward, took LeMon from them, and escorted him back into the torpedo room. It had taken two men to support LeMon's weight in his delirium, but somehow Matson managed it with no help. He must be stronger than he looked.

"You've made quite a recovery, Matson," Jerry told him. "Did you find a cure for the fever?"

In answer, Matson slammed the torpedo-room hatch.

Jerry and Oran looked at each other.

"He musta' found a cure," Oran said, more to himself than to Jerry. He nodded resolutely. "Monje gonna be okay. I know it."

CHAPTER TWENTY-THREE

When Oran returned to the galley, Lieutenant Abrams, seeing how distraught he was over his brother's illness, offered to give him the rest of the day off. Oran refused. "I want to work, suh. Cookin's what I do, and cookin's what'll take my mind off things. If I got nothin' to do, I'm liable to drive myself crazy with worry. So unless that's a direct order, suh, I'd like to stay."

Abrams nodded. "Very well, Guidry. But if it's too much …"

"Thank you, suh," he said, tying on his apron. "I'll be jus' fine once I'm back to it, suh."

He lost himself in the work, in the familiar heat and noise of the galley. Each vegetable he chopped, each bowl he stirred, each mix he poured took his mind off LeMon—but only for so long. He had never seen his brother so sick before, and with the same fever that had resulted in two sailors' deaths. What was he going to do? What *could* he do? He had always protected his little brother, but how could he protect him against this?

LeMon always hated it when Oran tried to protect him. He thought it was his older brother's way of saying he was weak or helpless, but nothing could be further from the truth. Oran protected LeMon because you were supposed to protect your loved ones. That was just the way it was.

LeMon didn't see it that way. When he was in sixth grade, he had gotten in a fight with some other kids in their parish. One afternoon, in the dry grass of the schoolyard, those kids surrounded LeMon and started throwing punches. Oran didn't remember what the fight was about— probably nothing all that important, but when you were that young everything, no matter how small, was a big deal. The kids had LeMon outnumbered, but he put up a good fight. Gave at least one of them a black eye, as Oran recalled, and was handing out fat lips like Mardi Gras beads. But the numbers weren't on his side, and soon they overpowered him. They took him down to the ground and pounded on him. That was when Oran found them.

Spotting Monje in trouble, Oran hadn't even hesitated. He jumped into the fray and started throwing elbows and knees into the other kids. He managed to make his way through the pile of squirming bodies, tossing them aside until he reached LeMon. His little brother was swollen around the eyes, and his nose and lip were bleeding. Oran helped him to his feet, then turned to the other kids with an angry war cry. They turned tail and ran, unwilling to take on both Guidry brothers.

Oran had expected at least a thank-you, but LeMon was furious. He could have handled them, he said, and he didn't need his older brother fighting his battles for him. Oran was perplexed at the time. Even now, so many years later, he remembered LeMon's righteous indignation as he scolded Oran for helping him, while the blood and tears were still streaming down his face.

"I jus' wanted to help," Oran had said in his own defense. "And look, they ran away. They gone."

"They gone *now*, but I still have to see 'em in school tomorrow," LeMon pointed out. "What you think they'll say then, Oran? That I'm a *couillon* who needs his older brother to fight for him, that's what! You can't be there to protect me all the time. You have to let me protect myself."

Oran knew that his brother was right, but that never stopped him. In the years that followed, Oran got into a lot of scrapes, about half of them in LeMon's behalf.

"Even now, we grown men and you can't stop thinkin' of me as a little brother you got to protect, can you?" LeMon had said after Oran flattened some trucker in a parking lot.

He was right. Monje would always be his little brother, and it was still an older brother's duty to protect a younger brother. But how could he protect LeMon against an illness? You couldn't whip the fire out of a fever. You couldn't bloody its nose and send it packing. He had never felt this helpless before. His little brother needed him, and there was nothing he could do.

Oran worked through lunch and then supper, and then, when the cooks and bakers came to relieve him, he insisted on staying and helping the incoming staff with preparations for midrats. It went against navy custom for someone to work two sections in a row except in an emergency, but Abrams took pity on him and let him stay.

Oran was standing at the counter, chopping carrots with a chef's knife, when he heard Lieutenant Abrams say, "Hey, Guidry, look who's here!"

Oran turned toward the galley doorway, and there was LeMon, good as new, walking into the galley as if nothing had happened.

"Monje?" Oran said, rushing over to him. "Monje, you're okay! I knew Matson could fix you. I knew it!"

He touched LeMon's arm, and LeMon turned to look at him, squinting against the bright lights. Oran backed away in horror. Those eyes. Those weren't Monje's eyes.

"No," Oran murmured. "No."

"What's the matter with you?" Abrams demanded.

Oran continued backing away, refusing to tear his gaze from the impostor in the galley. He bumped into a crewman washing dishes, who growled, "Watch it, Guidry," but Oran wasn't listening. The other two enlisted men in the galley stopped their work and stared at him in confusion.

"I thought you'd be happy to see LeMon back so soon," Abrams said. "You've been so worried about him."

"Suh," Oran said softly, "that ain't Monje."

"What are you talking about?" Abrams said.

"I know my brother, suh," Oran insisted. "That's not Monje. His eyes. Somethin' wrong with his eyes."

Abrams looked at LeMon, who stood still as a statue, glaring past the galley staff as if they didn't exist, focusing on Oran.

"*Rougarou*," Oran said in barely a whisper.

Abrams turned back to him. "What did you say?"

Oran looked down at his hand. He was still holding the chef's knife. He knew what he had to do. Gathering his courage, he walked back to the thing that wore his brother's face and drove the knife into his gut. He stabbed him just above the waistline and drove the blade upward.

"Oran, no!" Abrams cried, rushing forward. "Jesus Christ, Jesus Christ!"

He grabbed Oran and pulled him away from LeMon. Oran struggled against him, but Abrams had him in a strong bear hug from behind.

LeMon looked down curiously at the knife protruding from his gut. Then he crumpled silently to the floor, falling on his side.

"Rougarou!" Oran yelled. "Rougarou!"

He continued to struggle, but Abrams refused to let him go. Oran stared at the creature on the floor of the galley. It was pretending to be dead, but he knew full well that it wasn't. It refused to move, refused to show Gordon and the others what it really was.

"Rougarou!" Oran continued to yell until four men from the galley staff piled on him and brought him to the deck.

CHAPTER TWENTY-FOUR

A US Navy submarine didn't have a brig. There simply wasn't room. Most of the time, it wasn't a problem. The navy was an all-volunteer service, after all, and highly selective, accepting only the best. It was why fights on submarines were a rare thing. Things could get tense, sure—it was inevitable when you had over 100 men crowded together with limited space—but between all the basic requirements and the psychological profiling, the navy screened out the hotheads. Which was why, no matter how hard he tried, Lieutenant Gordon Abrams couldn't wrap his mind around the fact that Oran Guidry had killed his own brother.

LeMon hadn't survived the attack. He died right there on the galley floor. Matson, who seemed to have made as miraculous a recovery as LeMon had, came up from quarantine to pronounce him dead. The corpsman ordered LeMon's body transported to the torpedo room, where Gordon supposed he would lie in a body bag next to Warren Stubic and Steve Bodine. The thought of it made him shiver. He hadn't canceled midrats—galley rule number one was that meals for the crew went on no matter what. But it was hard. He kept staring at the spot on the floor where LeMon had died.

If it was some kind of elaborate murder plot, if Oran had planned this all along like something out of an Agatha Christie novel, stabbing his brother while they were still moored in Pearl Harbor would have been the polite thing to do. Then Lieutenant Commander Jefferson could have assigned a couple of sailors to watch him until the MPs hauled him off to a real brig. If only *Roanoke* still had a working radio, they could have signaled for a surface ship to take Oran away. Aircraft carriers and battleships were floating cities, complete with brigs.

But *Roanoke* didn't have a working radio, and even if it did, they were in Soviet waters and couldn't risk alerting the enemy to their position. No surface ship could come to take Oran away, so Captain Weber had improvised and turned Jefferson's now-empty stateroom into a makeshift brig.

Gordon decided he had to go see Oran. He had to find out why he had done such an unthinkable thing. When midrats were over, he went to Officer Country. A battle lantern had been mounted on the bulkhead to replace the broken overhead lights. Since Jefferson's stateroom locked only from the inside, an ensign named Van Lente stood sentry by the door, a pistol strapped to his belt. Oran Guidry wasn't going anywhere.

Aside from the guard and Oran, Officer Country was empty. The other officers had joined the boatwide manhunt for the three missing officers. Gordon suspected it was futile. They had already searched the submarine from bow to stern, so he didn't know what they hoped to find by doing it again. He had heard old navy men talk about cursed missions—surface ships that encountered nothing but heavy storms in otherwise calm seas, submarines that sprang fresh leaks in new places every week—but never anything like this.

One mystery at a time, though.

"How's it going, Van Lente?" Gordon asked clumsily. He didn't know what else to say.

"The prisoner's been quiet, sir," the ensign reported. "Hasn't tried to get out."

The prisoner. God, how had it come to this?

"Can I see him?" Gordon asked.

"I'm not supposed to let anyone in," Van Lente said. "Seaman Apprentice Guidry is considered dangerous."

Gordon had seen with his own eyes just how dangerous Oran was, but he was still having a hard time understanding what had happened. Taking LeMon down to quarantine earlier, he had been out of his mind with worry. There was no question how much he cared about his brother. That was what Gordon didn't get. Why would a man who loved his brother that much turn around and coldly, brutally murder him? It wasn't the fever. Oran wasn't delirious and out of control like Stubic or Bodine. So why had he done it? Gordon needed to know. He needed to understand.

"I hear you, Van Lente, but I have to see him," Gordon insisted. "Please."

Van Lente shook his head. "I'm sorry, sir. My orders are to keep everyone out for their own protection."

"Please," he said again. "I'm his DivO. I just … I need to talk to him. You know me, Van Lente. How many ops have we been on together? You know I'm no fool. I wouldn't go in there if I thought he was a danger to me. Just give me five minutes with him. That's all I ask."

It would have been so much easier if he could have simply ordered Van Lente to let him into the stateroom. He was a lieutenant, after all, well above an ensign, but security orders couldn't be countermanded by anyone outside the security division. The only way he was getting in there was if Van Lente did him a favor. Luckily, it appeared that Gordon had gotten through to him.

With a sigh, the ensign stepped aside. "You're going to get me in trouble, Lieutenant."

"This whole damn boat's already in trouble," Gordon said.

He stepped past Van Lente and opened the stateroom door, walked in, and closed it behind him. A single battle lantern hung from the bulkhead in the otherwise dark room, casting a cone of light onto the center of the floor. Oran sat on the foot of the fold-down bed, just beyond the edge of the light, half his face veiled in shadow. He didn't say anything. He didn't even look in Gordon's direction. He kept his eyes down, pensive and melancholy.

"Your brother is dead, Guidry," Gordon said. "I don't know if anyone told you yet."

Oran didn't respond.

"Did you hear me?" Gordon pressed. "LeMon is dead. You killed him."

Oran shook his head. "That wasn't my brother, suh. And I tell you now, he ain't dead. He'll still be alive long after the rest of us are gone."

Christ, he had lost his mind. From the guilt, probably. Gordon moved to stand across from Oran. He leaned back against the bulkhead and crossed his arms. "Why'd you do it? Why kill LeMon? I thought you two were close."

"Suh, I didn't kill LeMon," Oran insisted, finally looking up and meeting Gordon's eye. "I stabbed that *thing* in the galley so I could show you."

"Show me what?" Gordon asked.

"That it wasn't him," Oran said.

"By *stabbing* him?"

Oran fell silent again.

"Guidry, I'm here as your friend, all right?" Gordon said. "Not your DivO, not your boss—your *friend*. I'm trying to understand what happened, but if you're just going to give me riddles, I might as well go."

"Do you believe in God, suh?" Oran asked him. "Jesus and the Holy Mother, all that?"

Gordon hadn't expected such a question, and he didn't know how to answer it. His mother was Catholic, kind of. He didn't remember her ever taking Communion or attending mass, but she was baptized, and she'd had him baptized as a baby. She always wore a little silver cross on a silver chain around her neck, so it must have meant something to her once. Maybe it was her work at the psychiatric hospital that had put her off religion. All that suffering, all those bent and broken minds, for no reason other than that God had willed it so. Gordon's father was Jewish, but about as Jewish as his mother was Catholic. He never saw him go to synagogue. Gordon had been raised without much in the way of religion, somewhere between lapsed Catholic and lapsed Jew. No confirmation, no bar mitzvah, just the occasional Easter service with his mother's family, or Passover Seder with his father's. He gave Oran the only honest answer he could.

"I don't know," he said. "Sometimes I believe, sometimes not. I guess that's like most people."

"I'm a good Catholic, suh," Oran said. "I love the Holy Mother and the baby Jesus, and I pray to them. I wish … I wish I'd gone to church more often, suh. Gone to confession."

"Murder is a lot to confess," Gordon said.

"Do you know who Saint Bruno is, suh?"

"I've never heard of him," Gordon said.

"He's the patron saint of exorcism, suh, of ridding the world of evil spirits. I think he's the one I should pray to now."

Gordon raised his eyebrows. "*Exorcism?*"

"My family, suh, we go way back in the bayou. We come from Acadian stock, suh—Frenchmen who migrated all the way from Quebec down to Louisiana. My family were trappers, and over time they mixed with locals—Spanish colonists, escaped slaves, Tunica Indians from the surrounding territories. We're bayou through and through, suh; it's in our blood now. And in the bayou, Catholics don't just believe in what comes out of the Vatican. It's combined with stories people been tellin' in the bayou for centuries. We believe Jesus rose from the dead to forgive our sins, but we also believe there are things out in the swamps. Ghost lights, spirits, creatures, the vengeful dead. The rougarou."

Gordon straightened. "You used that word before, in the galley. What is it?"

"The rougarou is a creature from the swamp that sucks the life out of people while they sleep," Oran said.

The most astonishing part was that he said it absolutely straight-faced, just as he might say that a cat was an animal that chased mice. But on some level, Gordon knew he shouldn't be surprised. He had seen Oran stab his brother with a chef's knife. The man had obviously lost his mind. Was rambling about swamp monsters much of a stretch after that?

"I heard lots of stories about the rougarou growin' up," Oran continued. "They look like old hags. They tear off their skin and leave it in a stone bowl, then go out prowling the bayou as spirits. Some say it tears off its victim's skin too, wears it as its own so no one can tell the difference. Ain't no way to kill it except by finding its bowl and sprinkling salt on the skin it left behind."

Gordon shook his head. Clearly, Oran was too far gone for him to reach. This story that his brother had been replaced by the roving spirit of a swamp hag was stark-raving lunacy.

"I know how this must sound, suh," Oran said. "But they're here, suh, on this submarine. That thing I stabbed, it ain't LeMon. It's not my brother. It's a rougarou. And I'm tellin' you, it's still alive."

Gordon walked back toward the stateroom door.

"Where you going, Lieutenant?" Oran asked.

"We're done here, Guidry."

Oran hung his head. "You think I'm crazy, don't you?"

Gordon didn't answer. His silence was answer enough.

"Just be careful out there, suh," Oran said. "Promise me. There never is just one rougarou."

"That was your brother you stabbed," Gordon snapped. "Not some creature from your bayou folktales. Don't you understand that? Doesn't that bother you?"

"Monje was already dead," Oran said.

Gordon gave up. There was no reasoning with the man. He just wished he had spotted the warning signs sooner. If he had, maybe he could have saved LeMon's life. He went to the door, ready to leave this madhouse. More than ready.

A loud crash came from outside. Gordon stiffened. Oran stood up quickly from the bed.

"Ensign Van Lente, is everything all right out there?" he called through the door.

He heard Van Lente cry out, then a gunshot. Gordon grabbed the doorknob.

"Don't!" Oran warned.

Gordon ignored him. He opened the door slowly, just a crack. The corridor outside was pitch black.

"Ensign Van Lente?" he said. There was only silence.

He opened the door farther, and the lantern light from the stateroom spilled out into the dark corridor. It fell across the lantern mounted on the bulkhead outside, and Gordon saw that it had been smashed. He pushed the door open farther, and the light fell on Ensign Van Lente. He was lying on his back on the floor, staring at the ceiling. His pistol was on the floor beside him. Something was straddling him—a dark shape in the shadows. Gordon pushed the door open farther, until the light hit the shape. Its head was bowed, its face buried in Van Lente's neck. The shape looked up at him, leaving behind a bloody wound in Van Lente's throat. Gordon nearly screamed.

It was Ensign Penwarden. His mouth and chin were red with Van Lente's blood. Penwarden threw one arm across his eyes, shielding them from the light, and hissed angrily. Gordon had only a moment to notice the elongated teeth in the grimacing mouth. Then Penwarden sprang at him.

CHAPTER TWENTY-FIVE

Tim Spicer awoke to a loud pounding. He opened his eyes in the darkness of his rack. Confused and groggy, it took him a moment to realize that someone was pounding on the side of his bunk.

"Tim!" a voice hissed. "Tim, wake up!"

It was Jerry White's voice. Tim leaned up on one elbow and slid the heavy curtain aside. In the dim red light of the berthing area, he saw Jerry standing in front of his bunk, quickly buttoning his poopie suit. Tim rubbed his eyes.

"What the hell's going on?" he asked, his voice low and raspy with sleep.

"You've got to come with me," Jerry said breathlessly. "Right now. You have to see this!"

"Jerry, it's my rack time," he said. "Can't this wait? Shouldn't you be sleeping too?"

"Now!" Jerry hissed, keeping his voice down so he wouldn't wake everyone else.

Tim sighed. He swung his legs out of the rack and dropped to the floor. He had fallen asleep in his coveralls after an exhausting day, and suddenly he was glad for it. He quickly pulled on his shoes and followed Jerry to the curtained doorway.

"What's this about?" Tim whispered.

But Jerry just motioned for him to stay quiet.

They left the berthing area, but as soon as they were in the middle-level corridor, Jerry pushed Tim back against the bulkhead. Then he pointed silently down the corridor, past the mess. Another overhead light was out, and the deck beneath it was littered with broken glass. Then he saw what Jerry was pointing at. Someone stood with his back to them in the shadows beneath the broken light. He wasn't moving. He just stood there, staring at the bulkhead that separated the forward compartment from the nuclear reactor. Tim couldn't get a good look at him in the shadows, but he was pretty sure he saw white-blond hair.

"Who is that?" Tim whispered.

Jerry grabbed him and dragged him into the head. The auxiliary techs had mounted battle lanterns on the bulkheads and taped plastic garbage bags over the broken mirrors.

"Jerry, what's going on?" Tim demanded.

"That was LeMon Guidry."

Tim stared at him. "*What!*"

"I think he broke that light in the corridor, and now he's just standing there."

"That's impossible," Tim said. "LeMon's dead. Oran killed him in the galley. He stabbed him."

"I know," Jerry said. "But remember when I thought I saw Steve Bodine after he died? Oran said Ensign Penwarden saw him too."

"But you said Bodine was in a body bag in the torpedo room," Tim said.

"That's where LeMon should be too," Jerry said. "But he's not."

Tim blinked and rubbed his face. "Hold on. How can you be sure it's him?"

"Come on, you saw his hair. Who else has hair that white?"

"His brother, Oran," Tim said.

"Who is currently under armed guard in the XO's stateroom," Jerry pointed out. "That's not Oran out there."

Tim shook his head. It wasn't possible. He turned away from Jerry and went to the hatch.

"What are you doing?" Jerry said.

"I need another look," Tim said.

"Be careful," Jerry said. "Don't let him see you."

He opened the hatch a crack and peered out. He couldn't see the far end of the corridor from this angle, so he risked poking his head farther out of the doorway. He felt exposed leaning that far out, and spooked by what Jerry had said, but the corridor was empty.

"He's gone," Tim said, stepping out of the head.

Jerry followed him. "We need to find him."

"It can't be LeMon," Tim insisted.

"I'm telling you, it is."

"Maybe we should talk to Senior Chief Farrington," Tim said. "He'll know what's going on."

"There's no time. We have to find LeMon."

"If that even *was* LeMon."

"It was him," Jerry said, and he started down the corridor.

Tim sighed and followed him. He was awake now, anyway. He may as well see this through. As they passed the mess, he stole a glance inside. The room was empty. It was well past midrats and still hours from first meal, but it was unusual to see the mess completely deserted. Even when the galley wasn't serving, crewmen usually gathered there to talk or play cards. But there was no one. Was everyone still searching for the three missing officers?

They stopped at the main ladder. Tim looked up through the hole to the top level and saw lights, heard voices. Then he looked down through the hole to the bottom level and saw only darkness, heard only the hum of the air vents. He had a bad feeling about what Jerry was about to say.

"I think he went down."

Tim sighed. "Yeah."

Jerry went down the ladder first. Tim followed, thinking about the white-haired figure he had seen in the shadows. Even if it wasn't LeMon, something had been off about him. The way he stood so still under the freshly broken light, just staring at the bulkhead as if he could see through to the other side …

Descending to the bottom level, he felt very exposed again. He had never realized just how vulnerable he was on a ladder. His back was fully exposed, and his arms and legs were too busy with the rungs to fight anyone off. If someone came up behind him, he wouldn't even know until it was too late.

He chided himself. There was no sense spooking himself further, so he tried to put the thought out of his mind, but it clung tight. Some instinctive part of him was raising an alarm, making the hairs on the back of his neck stand up, telling him to watch his back.

When he reached the bottom level, he saw that all the ceiling lights had been broken. The whole level would have been black as India ink if battle lanterns hadn't been mounted to the bulkhead at ten-foot intervals. He scanned the ceiling, following the conduit pipes from broken light to broken light.

"What happened down here?" he asked.

"The mess, the head, Officer Country, and now the whole goddamn bottom level," Jerry said. "This isn't the work of one man. It can't be."

"Warren Stubic, Steve Bodine, and LeMon Guidry all got sick," Tim said. "We know that Stubic and Bodine became sensitive to the light. LeMon probably did too."

"Then there are more sick sailors than we thought, because LeMon didn't break all these lights himself."

"Matson got sick too," Tim said. "Maybe he helped before he got better."

"*Did* he get better?"

"That's what I heard. Matson came to retrieve LeMon's body himself and brought it back down here with a couple of POs from the mess. But everyone who saw him said he looked like he'd made a full recovery."

Jerry took a lantern off the bulkhead. It made a soft click as he pulled it free. Not a loud noise, but in the silence of the corridor it may as well have been the bang of a snare drum. He shined the light up and down the corridor. There was no sign of LeMon—or anyone else, for that matter. It was completely deserted, just like the mess deck. Where was everybody?

"So, what do we do now?" Tim asked.

Jerry trained the light on the torpedo-room hatch. "We see if LeMon Guidry is where he's supposed to be."

He walked up and banged on the hatch with his fist.

"What are you doing?" Tim demanded, coming up behind him. "It's still quarantined. No one's allowed in there."

Jerry ignored him. He pounded again and shouted, "Senior Chief Matson! We need to talk to you!"

When there was no answer, he tugged on the hatch. It unlatched and swung outward a couple of inches.

"Matson?" Jerry called again.

He pulled the hatch open. It was dark inside the torpedo room. Except for the LEDs on the equipment, the lights had been broken in there as well. Tim pulled a battle lantern off the bulkhead and nodded at Jerry. The two of them moved slowly into the shadows of the torpedo room. Tim closed the hatch behind them, sealing them in.

He had to remind himself to breathe. The darkness was suffocating, filling his lungs like water. He felt like that little kid on Presque Isle again, praying all winter long for the sun to come back and drive away the endless darkness. Their two lanterns helped illuminate the dark space, but not nearly enough. He shined his lantern all over the torpedo room, checking every corner, every patch of darkness, but there was no sign of Matson. *Strange.* As far as Tim knew, the corpsman was still supposed to be stationed in the quarantine.

Jerry approached the closest body bag lying on the deck. Its flat black finish seemed to eat the light from his lantern. Tim went over to it and read the name on the tag: GUIDRY, LEMON.

"It's him."

Every instinct told him to leave it alone and just get the hell out of here, but he had to see this through. Too many strange things had happened on *Roanoke* already. If LeMon Guidry was in his body bag, that was one thing, at least, he could take off the list.

And if LeMon *wasn't* in the bag? Tim didn't want to think about that.

But Jerry didn't appear to have any reservations. He crouched over the bag and unzipped it quickly, head to foot. Tim shined his lantern into the bag as Jerry spread it open.

"Oh, God," Jerry breathed.

There was a body in the bag, but it wasn't LeMon Guidry. It was Lieutenant Carl French, *Roanoke*'s weapons officer.

"Fuck two ducks!" Tim exclaimed. "We've got to tell the captain!"

Jerry looked up at him sharply. "Bring that light over here."

Reluctantly, Tim came closer with the lantern. As he shined the light down on French's waxy face, Jerry turned the corpse's head to one side. There on the neck were two red welts.

"What are they?" Tim asked.

"LeMon had them too. So did Bodine."

"Stubic?" Tim asked.

"I don't know, I didn't look," Jerry said. "But the last time I saw Matson he was rubbing his neck a lot. What if he has them too?"

"They look like … like *bite* marks," Tim said. A chill washed over him. "Jerry, if Lieutenant French is here, where's LeMon?"

"It *was* him we saw," Jerry said. "I knew it."

"But he's dead," Tim insisted. "That's his name on the tag."

Jerry stood up. He picked up his lantern and pointed it across the floor, until the beam found another body bag. This one was unzipped, spread open, and empty. He walked over to it and checked the tag.

"Steve Bodine," Jerry read.

"Where's the body?" Tim asked.

Jerry just looked at him.

"What the fuck?" Tim said. "Dead bodies don't just get up and walk away!"

Jerry returned to the body bag at Tim's feet and shined his light down into it. "Let's close this up again. Matson could come back any second."

They zipped up the body bag and jumped at the sound of the torpedo-room hatch being opened from outside. Matson was already back.

CHAPTER TWENTY-SIX

"The lights!" Jerry whispered.

They switched their lanterns off. Jerry turned toward the hatch. It wasn't fully open yet. He heard a muffled voice outside and glimpsed the beam of another lantern through the crack. Someone had stopped Matson to talk.

Jerry turned back to Tim. "We have to hide."

"But what if Matson can help?" Tim objected. "We should tell him what's going on."

"Tim, who do you think put Lieutenant French's body in LeMon's bag?"

In the dark, he heard Tim's breath hitch. "Shit."

"Find a place to hide, and stay quiet," Jerry told him.

The torpedo room was long, narrow, and crowded. There was only one place to hide: in the gap between the bulkheads and the torpedo tubes at the far end of the space. Jerry hurried over, listening for Tim's footsteps behind him. He heard the rustle of fabric against metal as Tim squeezed into a hiding spot. Jerry went to the opposite bulkhead and shimmied into the tight space. He could wedge himself into the gap if he exhaled first and didn't take a deep breath. Not the most comfortable place to hide, but his options were few. Until he knew otherwise, he had to assume that Matson was in on it.

But in on *what*, exactly? He still didn't understand what was going on. Corpses disappearing from their body bags and being replaced with others? Had Bodine and LeMon ever truly been dead, or was it all a colossal lie? Was there even really a fever, or was it a conspiracy with Matson at the head?

The hatch opened the rest of the way, and Matson walked into the torpedo room. Behind him came COB Farrington, holding a lantern. Jerry had a limited view from his hiding place, but the light from Farrington's lantern helped him see.

"Are you sure it's safe to come in?" Farrington asked. "I thought it was still a quarantine."

Matson didn't answer. He closed the hatch behind them. Jerry wriggled in the tight space, trying to reposition himself to see better. It wasn't easy to do. Pinned into place between the torpedo tubes and the bulkhead, he didn't have enough room to turn his head.

"You're sure you haven't seen Lieutenant French at all?" Farrington continued. "The captain said he came down to the lower level a few hours ago, but he hasn't reported back. And with everything else that's going on, this boat doesn't need *another* missing officer."

Jerry wanted to yell at Farrington to get the hell out of here, but he couldn't. It would give him away, and he was wedged in too tightly, his arms pinned to his sides. If Matson found him, he would be trapped like a rat in a rain barrel, and the next thing he knew, he would be in a body bag next to Lieutenant French, or filling in for the missing body of Steve Bodine.

Matson circled around Farrington like a hungry shark. COB Farrington was in his 50s, older than Matson by at least a decade, but he was no slouch. He was a tall man with the physique of someone who had kept fit all his life. Jerry had no doubt that if they were to square off, Farrington would reduce the corpsman to a wet smear on the deck. So when Matson put one hand on Farrington's arm and effortlessly threw him across the length of the torpedo room, Jerry had to bite his knuckle to keep from crying out in terror.

Then both men were out of his line of sight. He heard a dull clang as Farrington fell against a torpedo, followed by another thump, which must have been his dropped lantern. The beam of light juddered and bounced. Farrington shouted—a short, sharp exclamation that wasn't a word so much as a cry of pain and alarm. There was the scuffle of feet, a hand desperately slapping the side of the torpedo, and then silence.

Matson came back into view, and Jerry watched as he lowered Farrington's body to the deck. He couldn't see Farrington's face—just one arm that flopped to the floor alongside his torso. Jerry risked moving closer to the mouth of his hiding place for a better view. On the deck, Matson knelt beside Farrington and bent his head directly over Farrington's neck. What followed were soft sounds, barely audible, but in the silence of the torpedo room, Jerry could discern them. He thought he was going to be sick. They were the sounds of sucking, of drinking.

A few hellishly long seconds passed, and then Matson was finished with whatever unspeakable thing he was doing. He lifted Farrington's limp body off the deck as though it weighed no more than beach ball. Jerry got a good look at Farrington's face as Matson carried him closer to the torpedo tubes. His eyes were open, staring vacantly in terror. There was blood on the side of his neck.

There wasn't a lot of light to see by, so Jerry tried to convince himself the blood could be a shadow on Farrington's neck and nothing more. But when Matson dropped Farrington's body onto the deck, the light from the COB's fallen lantern hit his neck just right, and Jerry saw slick red blood. He wondered whether, underneath that blood, there were two raised welts, just like on Lieutenant French's neck.

Bite marks. Matson had bitten Farrington, and then … what? Drunk his blood like a vampire? But that was ridiculous. Vampires weren't real. And yet, those same welts had been on French's neck, and LeMon's …

And the dead were up and walking again.

Matson left Farrington on the deck and went to the torpedo control panel between the tubes. Jerry shrank back into the shadows. Matson fiddled with the panel, clicking buttons and throwing switches that Jerry couldn't see. Maybe he should make a break for it—slide out of his hiding place and bolt for the hatch. But it would take too long to extricate himself from this tiny space. Matson would be on him in a second, and he had already witnessed the corpsman's unnatural strength. He had thrown Farrington across the room like a football.

He heard a soft whirring that reminded him of unscrewing the lid from a jar. It was the breech door of a torpedo tube, he realized. What the hell was Matson doing opening a tube? But even as he asked himself the question, a chill swept over him. When you wanted to hide a body on a vessel as small as a submarine, where would be the best place to put it?

Matson swung the heavy breech door open, and a sound filled the air that made Jerry bite his knuckle again. He heard a deep, greedy gasp from inside the open torpedo tube, as though someone were desperate for air. He heard a cough, a desperate moan—not just one voice, but a chorus.

There were people in the tubes. Dear God, the son of a bitch had loaded *men* into the tubes! Was that where the missing sailors had gone? Duncan, Penwarden, Lieutenant Commander Jefferson—were they all just an inch away from him now, slowly asphyxiating in the tubes, desperate for air that was only replenished each time the watertight breech door was opened? Just an inch away, but an inch of thick, unyielding steel. There was nothing he could do, not unless he wanted to share Farrington's fate. He cursed himself for his cowardice, but Matson would kill him in a heartbeat.

The corpsman effortlessly lifted Farrington's dead body off the deck and carried him to the open torpedo tube. Jerry closed his eyes, knowing what was coming and not wanting to see. But he heard it all—Matson stuffing the body in, the desperate, terrified gasps for air coming from inside the tube in response, and then the heavy clank of the breech door closing again. The torpedo room fell deathly silent once more.

Now that Matson had eliminated Farrington and hidden the evidence, Jerry hoped he would leave again. He didn't. He sat cross-legged on the deck instead, half illuminated by Farrington's fallen lantern, and stared into the darkness. *Damn.* Jerry's heart beat so fast, it seemed about to break free of his rib cage. How long could he last in his tight hiding spot without giving himself away? How long could Tim?

As uncomfortable as it was in this tiny space, it was unimaginably worse for the men in the torpedo tube. There were four tubes in all, each

20 feet long. Four men could fit easily inside a single tube, but when Matson had opened one, it sounded like a lot more than four men in there. He pictured sailors crammed so tightly together they couldn't move, suffocating as the sealed breech door cut off their air. How many? Six? More? The idea made his stomach jitter.

But now he was starting to understand a few things too. When he had gone to wake Tim earlier, he noticed that several of the racks, maybe a third of them, had been empty. The mess had been empty too, and the bottom-level corridor. Were *all* those men in the tubes?

Fast-attack submarines like *Roanoke* fired Mark 48 torpedoes 21 inches in diameter. The last time Jerry bought a suit, the tailor had told him his shoulders were 18 inches wide. He would fit in a torpedo tube with three inches to spare. But if Jefferson was in there, with his build …

Jesus.

Jerry's back ached, and his shoulders were painfully tight. Still, he endured it, knowing that his only other option was to be shoved into that tube, dead or alive. He stayed put and he stayed quiet. And then, finally, Matson rose from the deck as though in response to some silent call. He walked to the hatch, opened it, and went out into the bottom-level corridor. Jerry waited until he heard the hatch close, then waited a few more seconds to make sure Matson was really gone. When the corpsman didn't return, he wrestled his way out of the tiny space.

The way out of the torpedo room was clear, but he didn't take it. The only thing he cared about was getting the men out of those tubes. Nothing else mattered. As soon as he was free of his hiding place, he went to the closest torpedo tube, grabbed the handle on the breech door, and pulled. The door didn't budge. He pulled again and again, frantic, thinking of the sailors suffocating in there. How much air did they have left? It couldn't be much. Maybe a matter of minutes …

Tim slid out from beside the bulkhead and stopped him with a hand on his shoulder. Jerry turned around to see Tim looking at him with sad, shocked eyes.

"We have to get it open!" Jerry hissed. "Help me!"

But Tim only shook his head. "Flooded," he said so softly that Jerry didn't understand at first. But the tone of his voice made him freeze in place. He followed Tim's horrified gaze to the warning lights above the tubes.

They were lit, indicating the tubes had been locked and flooded with water. Jerry stared in disbelief. Matson had filled the tubes and drowned his prisoners in the near-freezing water of the North Pacific. The inhuman bastard. When Matson came back, he would probably purge the tubes and flush the evidence out to sea.

Tim tugged at his arm. "We'd better go. We have to tell the captain."

"Wait," Jerry said.

He knew there wasn't anything he could do for those sailors anymore, but there was a way he could even the score, a way to make Matson pay for what he'd done. He snatched Farrington's lantern off the floor, then unzipped Lieutenant French's body bag once more.

CHAPTER TWENTY-SEVEN

The stateroom door shook in its frame as Ensign Penwarden—if the man with those enormous teeth and inhuman eyes was truly Penwarden—threw himself against it again and again. Luckily, Gordon had slammed the door and dogged it down seconds before Penwarden leaped at him. The door was flimsy, nothing like the thick steel of the boat's watertight hatches, and he doubted the lock was strong enough to keep Penwarden out for long. He and Oran braced the door with the metal-framed desk chair, but the way the door shook with each blow made him think that wouldn't be enough, either. Nothing would be enough to keep that thing out.

"The circuit!" Gordon shouted, pointing at the heavy phonetalker mounted on the bulkhead. "Get the captain in the control room, now!"

Oran picked up the handset and listened for a moment. He tapped the switch hook a few times, then shook his head. "There's no answer, suh. It's like no one's there." He hung up.

The door rattled from another blow. Gordon leaned with his back against the door, adding his weight to the barricade. "How can there be no one in the control room?"

Oran frowned. "Maybe they got the rest of the crew already and we the only ones still alive."

"*They?*" Gordon said. "You mean there are more of those things out there?"

"It's like I told you, there's never just one rougarou," Oran said. "They multiply like cockroaches, suh."

Gordon still wasn't ready to accept a supernatural explanation for this. Rougarou didn't exist. They were just legends of a semiliterate swamp culture. He saw Penwarden's teeth in his mind again, long and sharp, and reminded himself that vampires didn't exist, either. They were folktales, stories to scare children into eating their vegetables and going to bed on time. They were creatures in black-and-white movies he caught on TV on Saturday afternoons, played by Bela Lugosi or Lon Chaney. And yet, he'd seen the teeth, the blood on Ensign Van Lente's neck.

Penwarden threw himself into the door again, so hard this time that the impact nearly knocked Gordon forward. The door cracked. He clenched his teeth hard to keep from screaming. Oran ran over to the door and pushed against it next to him, helping to keep it braced.

Okay, so barring any rational explanations his brain was still scrambling for, what if Penwarden *was* a vampire, what then? What could kill a vampire? He went through everything he remembered from the stories. Sunlight. They hated the sun; it burned them. Well, being hundreds of feet below the surface of the ocean, they were shit out of luck.

Another blow shook the door. The crack grew deeper.

Wooden stakes would work too. Put one through a vampire's heart and it was supposed to die. But where the fuck was he going to find wood on a submarine? There wasn't even any wooden furniture they could break up into stakes. Everything was made of metal or plastic so it wouldn't weaken and rot from moisture. The wood paneling on some of the stateroom bulkheads was fake. If they were lucky, maybe they could find some genuine wooden hangers in a wardrobe, but other than that, he couldn't think of anything. He didn't even have a wooden spoon in the galley.

Penwarden's voice came from the other side of the door. It sounded like a whisper, but it carried like a shout. The sound of his voice made Gordon shiver, but it wasn't Gordon he was talking to.

"Do you miss your brother, Oran? LeMon is with us now. I made him one of us."

Oran put his hands over his ears and shook his head. "The rougarou are liars, Lieutenant. Don't listen to him. Cover your ears."

"It's no lie, Oran. I found him while he was sleeping. He thought I was just a dream until I sank my teeth into his neck. Then he knew just how real I am. Pain doesn't lie."

"No!" Oran shouted. "He had the fever—"

"We *are* the fever!" Penwarden hissed.

Gordon's breath caught in his throat. Oh, God, of course. Now it was starting to make sense. He racked his brain, trying to trace it back to the start. Warren Stubic, the petty officer who had killed himself in the freezer, was the first one they found. But Gordon already knew Stubic from previous ops—ops that had gone a lot smoother than this one. So if Stubic was the first vampire, something must have happened to him before the underway, something that changed him. Bodine had gotten sick next. Stubic must have bitten him and then, perhaps from guilt or perhaps while delirious and looking for a place to cool off from the fever, he had climbed into the freezer to die. Bodine had spread it to Penwarden, then Penwarden to LeMon. Who knew how many others were infected by now? Outbreaks were rarely linear, he knew. They tended to expand geometrically as more and more people were infected. He imagined that the spread of vampirism was no different.

"LeMon tried to call out for you as I drank his blood," Penwarden went on. "His big brother was all he thought about when he knew the end was coming. You were sleeping just a few feet away, and you didn't even know. You couldn't protect him—not from us."

Oran grimaced and pressed his hands harder against his ears.

"Don't listen to him," Gordon said. "He's trying to make you angry. He wants you to lose control and open the door."

"Yes, open the door, Oran," Penwarden said. "I want to know if your blood tastes as sweet as your brother's."

"Go to hell!" Oran shouted.

"Hell? There's no hell, Oran. After you die, there's nothing. There's only the grave … and us."

"Us?" Gordon said. "What are you?"

"Why don't you ask Lieutenant Commander Jefferson?" Penwarden replied. "He's here too. He wants to say hello."

"Bullshit!" Gordon shouted.

But then Jefferson's voice came to him from the other side of the door. "Open the door, Lieutenant Abrams. Let me in. It's my stateroom."

Gordon swallowed hard. They had gotten to Jefferson too. *Damn.* In the back of his mind, he'd been hoping all this time that Jefferson would turn up unharmed, that his disappearance was just a misunderstanding. Now he saw how naive that hope had been.

"You're not Jefferson, and you're not Penwarden!" Oran shouted. "You're rougarou!"

On the other side of the door, Jefferson and Penwarden laughed. It was a hollow, haunting, malevolent sound.

"It doesn't matter what you call us," Jefferson said. "Our only true name is 'inevitability.' There's no escape. Join us, Oran."

"Join us, Gordon," Penwarden said. "You don't know what you're missing. You'll wonder why you ever resisted. Join us in the dark. Join us in the eternal night at the bottom of the ocean."

"The only price for joining us," Jefferson said, "is your blood."

CHAPTER TWENTY-EIGHT

Tim picked up the bulkhead-mounted phonetalker of the direct circuit from the torpedo room to the control room, while Jerry poked around in Lieutenant Carl French's body bag. He had no idea what Jerry was looking for, and at the moment, he couldn't concentrate enough to care. After witnessing the murder of Senior Chief Farrington and the mass drowning of the crewmen Matson had locked in the torpedo tubes, he was operating entirely on instinct, falling back on his training, which told him he needed to alert the captain. But what was he going to tell him? *Sorry to break the news to you, Captain Weber, but our hospital corpsman is a murderer and ...*

And what? He had seen Matson bite Farrington on the neck and slurp up his blood. He had seen the corpsman throw Farrington around like a child's toy. It was clear Matson wasn't human anymore. He wasn't the same man who had started this op just a few days ago. Now he was ... something else.

Tim wanted to push the absurd thought away, but it kept forcing its way back into his mind, demanding to be taken seriously.

Matson was a vampire.

I'm sorry to break the news to you, Captain Weber, but our hospital corpsman is literally a dead man walking.

But as it turned out, Tim didn't have to worry about what to say after all, because the circuit sat silent the whole time. Finally, he hung up the handset.

"There's nobody in the control room," he told Jerry.

Jerry turned away from the body bag, pocketing something Tim couldn't see. "That can't be right. There's always somebody in the control room."

"Nobody picked up," he said.

He didn't like it. Something must have gone very wrong in the control room. It wasn't just that no one had answered. There was a row of warning lights in the control room that alerted the crew to any actions taken with the torpedo tubes. When Matson flooded the tubes, it would have tripped those lights. Someone should have seen it and called down for an explanation, but no one had.

"What the hell is going on up there?" he asked.

"We've got to go," Jerry said.

Jerry was keeping a cool head, which Tim appreciated since he himself felt on the verge of panic. He was perfectly happy to let Jerry take the lead, even though he outranked the planesman. They picked up their lanterns, switched them on, and left the torpedo room. The bottom-level corridor was dark as a tomb. All the lanterns that had been mounted to the bulkhead were smashed—Matson's handiwork, no doubt. As they walked, their footsteps echoed off the bulkheads. The only other sound was their breath. Tim suppressed a shiver and forced himself to keep following Jerry down the corridor toward the main ladder. He had no idea who or what might be hiding in the darkness mere inches from them, deftly avoiding their lantern beams. Maybe Matson, or whatever Matson had become.

Vampire. The word echoed in his mind. He did his best to ignore it, but it stuck there.

Matson would return soon—he was sure of it—to flush those drowned bodies out into the depths of the ocean. He didn't want to be anywhere near the torpedo room when that happened. He quickened his pace, but the walk to the ladder still felt like an eternity. Matson hid in every patch of shadow they passed, behind every cluster of pipes along the bulkhead, in every dark-shrouded doorway, ready to leap out and kill the two of them as quickly and easily as he had killed Farrington. And then it would be into the torpedo tubes with them.

Jesus Christ. He couldn't even grasp it. Nothing made sense anymore.

Jerry stopped at the bottom of the ladder. Tim came up behind him, expecting him to start climbing, but he was looking up at the top. Tim followed his gaze and saw only darkness in the hole above. *Shit.* Someone had smashed the lights on the middle level too. Matson and maybe others. LeMon and Bodine ... They were smashing lights all over the boat.

It was starting. Whatever their plan was, this was the first step: to kill all the lights on *Roanoke*. And what would come next? More murders, more bodies for the torpedo tubes?

"We have to get to the control room," Jerry whispered.

Tim agreed, but after receiving only silence on the circuit, he had a bad feeling about what they would find up there.

Jerry went up the ladder first, carrying his lantern so that it shone against the bulkhead as he climbed. Once he reached the middle level, he stopped, shined the lantern around to make sure the coast was clear, then continued upward. Tim started up after him. When his head passed through the hole, Tim did the same with his lantern. The corridor was empty, but that didn't make him feel any safer. There was something eerie about how utterly abandoned *Roanoke* looked. Jerry was already halfway up the ladder to the top level. Tim continued climbing. When he had his feet on the middle-level deck, the hairs on the back of his neck stood up. Someone was right behind him; he was sure of it. He spun around, shining the lantern beam down the corridor, but no one was there—only the sense that someone had been there a moment ago. He climbed farther up.

When he reached the top level, there weren't any lights by the ladder, but he could see, up ahead in the control room, the dim glow from the LEDs on the instruments. The control room was the nerve center of the submarine, but as he and Jerry approached it, they heard only silence. There was none of the usual chatter, the call-and-response of orders being given and acknowledged, the footsteps of crewmen hurrying to and fro. Just an uncanny quiet.

"Where is everyone?" Tim whispered. There was no way Matson could have fired them *all* out of the torpedo tubes.

Jerry didn't answer. He crept forward, and Tim followed, his heart pounding. When they entered the control room, he lifted his lantern, throwing a beam of light into the shadowy room, and everything came into horrific focus. The control room wasn't empty. There were crewmen everywhere, either slumped over the equipment at their stations or lying dead on the deck. The quartermaster, the navigation supervisor, the messenger of the watch, the helmsman. The officer of the deck sat at the edge of the conn with his feet dangling. He still held the handset of the phonetalker in his pale hand. Tim shined his lantern toward the sonar shack and saw the dark shapes slumped in their chairs.

"What happened?" he asked. "What the fuck happened here?"

Jerry didn't answer. He walked to the helm, where the planesman was slumped forward against his yoke. Jerry held the lantern six inches from the sailor's face. His eyes were wide, and he wore a terrified expression as if he were silently screaming. Jerry pressed two fingers to the side of the man's neck, checking for a pulse.

"Is he …?" Tim started to ask, but he knew the answer already. He could tell just by looking into those glazed, unblinking eyes.

Jerry shook his head. Then he tilted the planesman's head to one side. A chunk of flesh had been torn out of the other side of the sailor's neck, leaving a ragged, bloody hole. Jerry let go and backed away from the body quickly. Neither he nor Tim said a word, but they both understood what had happened. The vampires had stormed the control room and killed everyone there. No subtle little welts on the neck this time. The vampires had gone all out, killing the men as quickly as they could.

"Where's the captain?" Tim asked, looking around the room. Captain Weber wasn't among the dead.

"Maybe he got away," Jerry said.

Tim shined his lantern on the terrified faces of the dead all around him. The control room had been turned into an abattoir. Matson alone couldn't do that. Even he, Bodine, and LeMon together couldn't over-power this many crewmen so quickly. It had to have been a much bigger group. Jesus, was *Roanoke* swarming with vampires at this point?

They needed to get off this boat. It was the only way he could see them surviving. But they were hundreds of feet underwater, thousands of miles from port, and likely already deep in Soviet waters. Where the hell could they go?

Jerry pulled a small object out of his pocket and held it up for him to see. "I found his on the WEPS's body downstairs."

Tim recognized it as the key to the weapons lockers. So that was why Jerry had been digging around in Lieutenant French's body bag. There were only two keys to the weapons lockers. The XO had one, and Lieutenant French, the WEPS, had the other. It was a stroke of luck that Matson hadn't taken the key himself when he killed French. But then, if the slaughter all around him was any indication, vampires didn't need weapons.

Roanoke had two weapons lockers. One was in the reactor room, the other on the top level, not thirty feet from where they now stood. Tim didn't know whether a gun could kill a vampire, but he sure as hell would feel a lot less helpless with one in his hand.

A loud bang echoed from the captain's egress on the far side of the control room, the corridor where the captain's stateroom was. It sounded as if someone was coming up the fore ladder from Officer Country. No, not someone—multiple someones. He heard footsteps on the deck.

Both men switched off their lanterns, although Tim wondered why they bothered when it was obvious the vampires had no trouble seeing in the dark. They bolted back the way they came, out of the control room and into the waiting darkness.

CHAPTER TWENTY-NINE

Gordon Abrams waited in silence for a full fifteen minutes after the last time he heard either Jefferson or Penwarden speak from the other side of the stateroom door, and he gestured for Oran to do the same. The time passed excruciatingly slowly. With his ear pressed to the door, Gordon was convinced he would hear something outside that would prove they were still there—a footstep, a whisper between them, another threat to get them to open the door. But when those sounds didn't come and fifteen minutes had passed, he slowly and quietly pulled the chair away from the door.

"What are you doing, suh?" Oran asked in alarm.

"I'm going to see if they're still out there."

"Suh, don't!" Oran protested. "That's crazy!"

"We can't stay locked up in here forever," Gordon said. "We have to find Captain Weber and tell him what's going on."

"He must know by now, suh," Oran said. "If he ain't dead already, I mean."

"We don't know that. We have to assume he's still alive and still in command. Since the circuit isn't working, it's up to us to find him and warn him about what's happening on his boat. You can stay here if you want, but I'm going."

"Like hell, suh," Oran said. "I ain't stayin' here by myself!"

"Then you'll have to come with me, because I'm out of here," Gordon said.

"Suh, it's suicide!"

"Duly noted," Gordon said. "You coming?"

Oran sighed. "Aye, suh."

Gordon unlocked the door and opened it slowly, just enough to peek out into the corridor. Not only was the battle lantern on the Officer Country bulkhead out, but every other light on the middle level was as well, leaving the corridor in complete darkness except for the light from the stateroom's lantern. It was quieter than he had ever heard on *Roanoke*. Something was terribly wrong. No submarine should be this quiet.

In the light that seeped out into the corridor, Gordon could see Ensign Van Lente's body on the floor. He didn't see Jefferson or Penwarden, but that didn't mean anything. It would be easy enough for them to hide in the dark and wait for the two men to come out of the stateroom. They could be just a few feet away from him right now, cloaked in darkness, and he wouldn't know it. He and Oran could be walking into a trap. In fact, chances were good that was exactly what would happen. The vampires, rougarou, or whatever they were didn't strike him as the sort that would just give up after a short wait. But Gordon knew they had to risk it. They had to find the captain.

"Let's go," he whispered to Oran.

Gordon crept out into the dark corridor. He saw a trickle of light at the dead end of Officer Country, coming down the fore ladder from the captain's egress above. He turned the other way, toward the open corridor, and thought he saw movement in the distance. He strained, trying to focus on the black-on-black shadows in the dark. Had he really seen anything? Or was his mind playing tricks on him, showing him a bogeyman everywhere he looked? Then, like a field of stars on a moonless night, multiple pairs of eyes turned his way—glowing eyes that seemed to reflect a light that wasn't there.

"Oh, fuck," Gordon muttered. He turned, grabbed Oran by the

front of his coveralls, and swung him toward the nearby ladder. "Get moving! Go!"

Oran darted to the ladder, disappearing for a moment in a shadowy corner near the ladder's foot, then scrambled up it to the top deck. Gordon kept his gaze on those glowing eyes. How many pairs were there? Four? Five? His fear made it hard to count. All he knew was that it was more than just Jefferson and Penwarden. He felt along the floor until he found Van Lente's sidearm. Snatching it up, he aimed down the corridor at the shapes moving toward him in the dark, their eyes blazing with unearthly light. He squeezed the trigger over and over again until the slide locked open, the magazine empty.

He had to have hit them, but the shapes kept coming. He threw the gun down, turned, and ran for the fore ladder. He remembered the broken light in the mess at the start of it all, and the broken lights in the head later, and how no one had seen it happen either time. These things could move fast when they wanted to, he realized, but they were only toying with him now, letting him run, confident there was no escape. Well, fuck that. That was their mistake, not his. He grabbed the rungs and scaled the ladder faster than he ever had before. He had his back to the figures as he went up, leaving him vulnerable, but he couldn't think about that. He just kept climbing as fast as he could. He heard their footsteps behind him, but he couldn't tell how close they were. The sound was muffled by the pounding of his heart in his ears. Then he was up on the top level and in the captain's egress.

Only a single battle lantern still worked up here, taped to the bulkhead across from the captain's stateroom. The door to the stateroom was closed. Gordon saw Oran at the other end of the captain's egress, standing at the entrance to the control room, his form silhouetted by the twinkling LEDs of the instrument panels. He stood so still and so silently that he reminded Gordon of a deer in the headlights, frozen in terror.

Gordon started toward him. They didn't have any time to waste. The creatures that had come after them on the middle level would surely follow any moment now.

Something struck him hard from behind—a sharp blow just below the shoulder blades, which sent him flying face-first into the door of Captain Weber's stateroom. He didn't have time to get his hands up to protect his face before he hit. His forehead struck it, cushioned only by the paper-thin fake wood veneer that covered the door. The door hadn't been properly latched, and it swung open under the impact. Gordon half fell and half staggered into the stateroom. The lights here had been smashed too, but the light from the lantern in the corridor spilled in after him, illuminating a floor stained red. Piles of dead men in blue coveralls cluttered the center of the room. Some had a smear of blood on one side of their neck, just like Ensign Van Lente. Others were in much worse shape, with their throats ripped out completely, leaving behind only glistening meat and hanging, ragged bits of skin, as if the vampires had attacked them in a frenzy.

A shadow appeared in the light. He heard the sound of the corridor lantern being smashed and was plunged into sudden darkness. Hands pushed him forward onto the pile of bodies. He tried to scream for Oran, scream for anyone to help him, but his assailant's arm snaked around his neck—so cold, so deathly cold—and cut off his air. He struggled, but his assailant was unbelievably strong.

A moment before he lost consciousness, he felt someone's mouth against his neck. In a split second, his brain registered that no breath, warm or otherwise, came from that mouth. He felt teeth brush his skin and told himself to fight, to get up and run, that if he didn't he was going to die. He felt hot pain sink into the side of his neck, and everything faded away.

***

Gordon woke in the dark. He tried to move but couldn't. An image came to him of a fly wrapped in spider's silk, waiting to be devoured, and he pushed it away. That wasn't going to be him. He wouldn't let it be. He would fight those bastards first. He tried to move again, but he was boxed in somewhere narrow that wouldn't let him budge.

He could move his head slightly. It was resting on something cold and metallic, and when he lifted his head, he bumped into another cold metal surface. He winced in pain. His forehead was still sore from hitting the captain's stateroom door. He gently lowered his head again. The metal was rounded, he realized, and damp. In the distance, he heard dripping water. It occurred to him that he was in a pipe of some kind.

Then the panic came. There was only one kind of tube on *Roanoke* big enough for a man to fit inside.

He began kicking his feet and slapping his hands against the walls. He screamed, but his cries only rang in his ears. No one would hear him through the thick steel of the torpedo tube and the breech door. Somewhere in his mind, he knew this, but he continued screaming. He screamed until he was dizzy and out of breath, and then he stopped. Air was precious in the watertight tube. If no one opened the breech door, he would suffocate. He just didn't know how long it would take. Ten minutes? Five? Two?

He managed to work his hands up along his sides so that they were pinned against his chest, but he couldn't get them any higher. He rolled onto his side, then squirmed and wriggled and pushed himself forward with his feet. The back of his head touched the inside of the breech door. He kept pushing himself toward it until he was curled with his shoulders against it. He shoved, but the breech didn't budge. He pressed more of his weight against it, but it stayed shut.

An even more terrifying thought occurred to him. What if they didn't intend to suffocate him? What if they were going to flood the tubes with water and then shoot him out into the freezing ocean? Would he drown, or would he freeze to death while still holding his breath? Or would the pressure simply crush the air-filled cavity of his chest? What would kill him first? He remembered the feel of teeth against his skin and raised a hand to his neck. He felt sticky, coagulated blood, and two small welts. *God, no!* His heart raced, and he felt light-headed with panic. Why hadn't they drained him? Why didn't they finish him off? Christ, was this their version of a pantry? Would they come back later to feed on him again? He thought of all those teeth tearing into him …

It was too much to contemplate. The horror of it overwhelmed him, and he screamed again. He screamed until there was nothing left in his lungs. After his air left him, his mind followed. For an interminable moment in the darkness of the torpedo tube, Lieutenant Gordon Abrams went mad.

CHAPTER THIRTY

Tim ran through the dark, following Jerry down the corridor, away from the control room and through Fire Control, toward the main ladder. Jerry stopped at the ladder and waited there for him to catch up, then ushered him onto the rungs.

"Go, go, move!" Jerry whispered.

"But the weapons locker," Tim said.

"No time!"

Tim grabbed the side rails, took two rungs, and dropped the rest of the way. He landed on the middle level and spun to look down the corridor. Shapes seethed toward him in the darkness, groping, hissing like animals, their eyes glowing with an unnatural light. Jerry dropped down the ladder and landed beside him. He grabbed Tim's sleeve and pulled him away from the shadowy figures, but there was nowhere to run. Their backs were to the bulkhead. Tim saw the hatch to the reactor room at the top of a short flight of steps. He ran to it. The silhouettes in the darkness swarmed closer—so close that the hair on Tim's neck stood up. He didn't have to look back to know they were reaching for him. He bounded up the stairs to the hatch, spun the handle, and yanked it open. A sliver of light spilled out into the corridor, like a beacon promising safety. The light struck one of the shapes in the dark—it was Matson. The hospital corpsman hissed angrily, showing long, sharp teeth, and ducked quickly out of the light. The other shapes fell back.

"Come on!" Tim shouted as Jerry pounded up the steps.

Together they barreled through the hatch, and Jerry slammed it behind them.

After the darkness that had filled the rest of the submarine, coming into the brightly lit space was like staring into the sun. Tim blinked, taking a moment to let his eyes adjust, then looked around him. The reactor room. He had been here only a handful of times, during emergency drills. Other than that, there was no good reason for a sonar tech to go into the boat's reactor room, although being chased through the submarine by a horde of vampires probably qualified.

The reactor room was enormous compared to the other rooms on the boat—spacious enough to give the engineers room to maneuver without stepping on each other's toes. The reactor was a hulking cylinder of metal that spanned two of the sub's levels. Crowned with a field of activators and control rods like antennae and winged by two massive pipes, one that brought in the coolant—usually seawater—and another that expelled the superheated water into the steam generator, it looked like something out of a science-fiction movie.

They weren't alone. Six sailors—*human* sailors—stepped out from where they had been hiding on the other side of the reactor. Five of them brandished thick steel crowbars. The sixth held a two-foot spud wrench that must weigh twenty pounds. They lowered their weapons when they recognized Tim and Jerry.

"Where the hell did you come from?" the sailor with the wrench asked.

"The control room," Jerry said. "They're all dead up there."

"We know," he replied. "They've got control of the boat."

"Have you seen Farrington?" another sailor asked.

Tim shook his head. "The COB is dead. Matson killed him down in the torpedo room."

"Wait, Matson's one of them?" the wrench man asked.

"He is now," Jerry said.

The phonetalker mounted on the reactor room bulkhead rang, startling Tim. He looked at it, then back at the sailors. None of them made a move to answer it. He started toward it himself, but the man with the spud wrench put a hand on his shoulder.

"Don't," he said.

"Why?" Tim asked. "What's going on?"

The phonetalker continued to ring for a few seconds, then stopped.

"That could have been the captain," Tim said.

"It wasn't," the wrench man said. "They've been calling every few minutes for an hour now. They don't say anything."

"They're just making sure we're here," another sailor said.

"So they know you're here, but they haven't tried to get in?" Jerry asked.

"Not yet, they haven't."

"That won't last," Jerry said. "Sooner or later, they're going to get in, and when they do, you're going to need more than crowbars and wrenches." He pulled the key out of his pocket. "This opens the weapons locker."

The man with the wrench looked like a hungry dog staring at a raw steak. "If we can get to those weapons, we can take back the boat. Where'd you get it?"

"Off the WEPS," Jerry said.

"Lieutenant French? He's all right?"

"We got it off his body," Tim clarified. "He's in a body bag down in the torpedo room."

"LeMon Guidry's body bag," Jerry said.

"So Guidry's in on it too?" someone asked.

The question came from the far end of the room, from the same spot behind the reactor where the six sailors had emerged. Tim recognized the voice even before he saw Captain Weber step out. The captain's gaze met Tim's, and a flicker of a smile crossed his lips.

"Spicer, I'd almost given up on you," he said.

"Still kicking, sir," Tim replied. "Thanks to PO2 White, sir. He saw what was happening before I did."

The captain turned to Jerry. "Well done, White. I'm happy to see I made the right choice in accepting your transfer to *Roanoke*."

Jerry looked genuinely gratified to receive a compliment from the captain. "Thank you, sir."

"No doubt both of you are already aware of the grave danger we're facing," Captain Weber said.

"Yes, sir, I think so, hard as it is to believe," Tim said.

The captain sighed. "It is hard to believe, Mr. Spicer. I always thought of myself as a good commanding officer, fair and understanding and not too much of a hard-ass unless I needed to be. I never thought I'd see a violent mutiny on my own boat."

"Mutiny, sir?" Tim asked.

"Mutiny, Spicer, and the way I reckon, it's been planned from the start. Now that I have confirmation that Senior Chief Matson is involved, I can see how they managed to keep it under wraps until it was time to make their move. Once he set up the quarantine in the torpedo room, they had a place they could meet and plot their takeover of the ship without interference. I'm starting to wonder if there was ever really a fever going around the boat, or if it was all a cover."

"Sir, with all due respect, I saw how sick Steve Bodine and LeMon Guidry were," Jerry said. "They couldn't have been faking it, sir."

"Couldn't they?" the captain asked. "Only Senior Chief Matson had the medical expertise to judge whether they were sick, and you said yourself he's one of them."

Tim frowned. He had seen Matson toss Farrington like a beanbag across the torpedo room. He had seen blood, bite marks on the victims' necks, glowing eyes in the darkness. This was no ordinary mutiny. Surely he and Jerry couldn't be the only ones who saw that?

"Let me see that key to the weapons locker, White," the captain said. Jerry handed it to him. "Gentlemen, come with me."

Tim and Jerry followed him to the back of the reactor room, where several more men had congregated. Tim's quick head count came to 28, including himself and Jerry. Was this all that remained of 140 men? The men in the reactor room, combined with the dead full crew in the control room, came to only 50—a little over a third of the crew. It didn't seem possible that Matson could have flushed the rest out through the torpedo tubes, not this quickly. Were other pockets of survivors still out there? He supposed it was possible—he *hoped* it was possible—but he couldn't imagine where else on the boat they could be safe.

Captain Weber continued through a doorway into the small maneuvering room behind the reactor room. Nicknamed "the box," its walls were lined with banks of bulky gray equipment and covered in countless levers, switches, and dials, making the narrow space feel even more cramped. The captain leaned against one of the machines. When he spoke, Tim had to lean in to hear him. With the turbine generator going and the propeller shaft spinning, the aft end of the *Roanoke* was a surprisingly noisy place.

"Tell me what happened to Senior Chief Farrington," Captain Weber said.

Tim told him the story, with Jerry adding details he missed. When they got to the part about the torpedo tubes, the captain kept his expression calm and composed, but Tim could see the fury in his eyes. Drowning those men like that was callous. Soulless.

Of course it was soulless, Tim's inner voice reminded him—Matson wasn't human anymore! He pushed the thought away. If he let the idea of his crewmates turning into bloodthirsty supernatural creatures linger too long, he would lose his mind.

"Currently, *Roanoke* is running on autopilot," Captain Weber told them. "I heard you mention you were up in the control room. You saw that slaughterhouse. The mutineers came up in a swarm. They smashed every light they could find, just as they did all over the rest of the boat, to keep the crew disoriented and unable to see them. It gave them the advantage. They attacked without warning or mercy. I got lucky. I managed to get away, but I wouldn't have made it two feet if PO Antopol hadn't gotten between me and the mutineers. He gave his life so I could escape."

Ah, damn. Tim hung his head. He knew Antopol. He was a great guy and an even better poker player. Tim couldn't count how many hands of seven-card draw he had lost to his fellow sonar tech.

"These men found me and brought me to the reactor room," the captain said. "We've been safe here so far, but we can't stay. We have to take back control of *Roanoke* immediately. The only problem is, we can't go back up to the control room until we know it's safe. We can control our speed from here in the maneuvering room, but not our bearing. We'll just continue sailing in a straight line until we've got hands on the helm again, but that is unacceptable. These waters are much too dangerous to be sailing blind."

"Because we're so close to Soviet territory, sir?" Jerry asked.

"No, White, because we are *in* Soviet territory. I've already informed the other men out there, and Spicer is aware, so I suppose it's time to tell you as well. This is no run-of-the-mill reconnaissance op. Our orders have taken us directly and covertly into Soviet territory."

"Sir, you're saying we're in Soviet waters with no control of *Roanoke*?" Jerry asked. "We're sitting ducks, Captain."

"Precisely why we can't let them find us," the captain said. "And that means taking back control of the boat ASAP. The mutineers were smart; they sabotaged the radio before they made their move. We're cut off with no help on the way."

"Sir, are you sure we're safe back here?" Tim asked.

"We have been so far. But I imagine it's only a matter of time before they launch an assault."

"But, sir, don't you find it strange they haven't yet?" Jerry asked. "If they killed everyone in the control room that quickly and easily, they're not going to be afraid of a few sailors swinging crowbars."

"I'm not one for looking a gift horse in the mouth, White," the captain said.

"I understand, sir, but something doesn't feel right," Jerry said. "What if this is exactly where they want us? We're stuck in the aft compartment with only one exit, and with who knows how many of them right outside the hatch. And then there are the phone calls, sir, like they're checking to make sure we're still here."

"You think it's a trap?" the captain asked.

Jerry shrugged. "I don't know, sir, but it can't be a coincidence they're not even trying to come in. For all we know, they broke a seal on the reactor and are flooding the whole compartment with radiation. Then they wouldn't need to come after us. The radiation would kill us for them."

Captain Weber tapped a small gray plastic box clipped to his pocket. "I had the same thought, White, and took precautions. I'm wearing a Geiger, and the level is normal. Besides, half the men down here are engineers. If there were a radiation leak, they'd know about it. These guys check the equipment five times an hour."

Jerry frowned. "There must be some other reason they haven't come in here. Maybe the lights?"

"There's one reason I can think of," the captain said. "The mutineers have promised to hand me over to the Soviets, along with *Roanoke*. They want me alive. It's hard to get any sensitive information out of a dead captain."

The captain was right about one thing, Tim realized. Their enemies had used the isolation of the torpedo room to gather and plan their attack on *Roanoke*. It was where Bodine had hidden when the crew was looking for him, and probably where the other crewmen turned vampires had hidden when they went missing too. But the captain was wrong about this being anything as mundane as a mutiny. He had to get Weber to listen, to believe, or things would only get worse.

But the captain wasn't interested in further conversation. He held up the key to the weapons locker.

"If we're going to take back control of *Roanoke*, gentlemen," he said, "this key just tipped the scales in our favor."

CHAPTER THIRTY-ONE

When Jerry and Tim returned to the reactor room, Tim broke off to talk to a small group of enlisted men who had a hundred questions about what was happening on the rest of the boat, while Jerry took the opportunity to take a breather. After nearly getting caught by Matson twice, first in the torpedo room and then outside the reactor room, his heart was still pounding. He needed a minute to calm down. He sat with his back against the bulkhead and listened to the men around him as they theorized about what was going on. Some were as convinced as the captain that it was a mutiny. Others suspected something else—something they couldn't explain.

"I saw their eyes light up in the dark," one sailor told his buddies in hushed tones. "You ever seen someone's eyes glow in the dark? I sure as hell haven't. There's something not right about them."

Still others had their own outlandish theories. One sailor was convinced that Seaman Apprentice Oran Guidry and Lieutenant Abrams from the galley were in on it, having laced the soup with cyanide, and that the reason Oran had stabbed his brother was because LeMon had caught them. Jerry shook his head and looked away. Poison hadn't killed those men. Matson and the others like him had. He had seen Matson carry the much bigger

Senior Chief Farrington as if he were a CPR dummy. He had seen LeMon Guidry up and walking and Steve Bodine's body bag lying empty. They weren't human anymore. When humans died, they stayed dead.

Jerry had to find a way to convince Captain Weber of the truth. Once he did, the others would fall in line behind the captain. But how was he going to prove that this wasn't a mutiny or a Soviet plot or any of that crap? That those things out there weren't men anymore? If he so much as breathed the word *vampire*, they would tell him he'd lost his mind. And although it was starting to feel very much as if he *had* lost mental moorings, what he had seen was real. Persuading everyone else, on the other hand, was going to be difficult.

Tim extricated himself from the crowd of inquisitive sailors and came over to join Jerry.

"I just wanted to say thanks," Tim said, sitting down beside him. "I didn't get the chance before."

"For what?" Jerry said.

"You saved my ass out there. If you hadn't gotten me out of my rack when you did, I'd be as dead as the rest of them, no doubt about it. Then you did it again in the torpedo room. When Matson came back, I froze up, but you didn't. You kept us alive. Same thing in the control room. I owe you my life three times over."

"Just seven more, and I get a free sandwich," Jerry said.

Tim laughed. "Something like that."

"So you knew we were in Soviet waters, huh?" Jerry asked.

"Yeah."

"And you didn't feel like sharing that information?"

"Sorry, but I was under orders from the captain to keep it to myself. He figured the fewer people who knew it, the better."

"I guess it doesn't get much fewer than this," Jerry said, looking around at the survivors scattered throughout the room. "Do you think we're all that's left?"

"I hope not," Tim said.

"People are trying to figure out what's going on," Jerry said. "Did you hear the story about Gordon and Oran poisoning the soup?"

Tim chuckled. "That's almost as bad as one I heard, that it's all a government experiment, the CIA pumping LSD into the air supply. I don't think that's even how LSD works."

"It's amazing the bullshit people will convince themselves of when their backs are against the wall," Jerry said. "But you … you saw the same things I did, didn't you?"

Tim nodded solemnly.

"And you know …" He paused and looked around, then lowered his voice. "You know what they are?"

"Yes," Tim said. He was reluctant to say it; Jerry could tell. But Tim took a deep breath, as though speaking the word aloud took enormous effort. "Vampires."

Jerry sighed in relief. It felt as if someone had lifted a heavy weight off him. "Thank God. I was starting to wonder if maybe I was slipping a gear."

"Not unless I am too," Tim said. "Still glad you transferred to *Roanoke*?"

Jerry laughed. He couldn't help it. It was just the momentary balm he needed amid all the horror. "I'm glad I met you, Tim. But I can't say I like your boat all that much."

"Listen," Tim said, "I don't know how things are going to play out, so there's something I need to tell you. I didn't just happen to sit down with you that first day in the mess. Shortly before we left Pearl Harbor, the captain asked me to keep an eye on you."

Jerry stiffened. "Go on."

"It's not as bad as it sounds," Tim said quickly. "He just wanted to make sure everything was cool, that he hadn't made a mistake accepting your transfer after what happened on *Philadelphia*."

Jerry's eyes narrowed. "And how, exactly, is that not as bad as it sounds?"

"Ah, shit, man," Tim said, the realization coming over his face that he had botched it. "I just meant—"

"You just meant you had orders to be my friend."

"I *am* your friend," Tim said.

"Go fuck yourself, Spicer," Jerry said, standing up.

"Ah, Jerry, come on," Tim said.

Jerry ignored him and walked away. He should have known better than to think anyone in the service who knew his history would actually want to be his friend. Fuck Tim. Fuck everyone on this goddamn boat who thought they knew him. They didn't know shit.

***

Captain Weber wanted scouts to search the boat for survivors, on the theory that the more loyal crewmen they had with them, the easier it would be to retake the boat. When he asked for three volunteers, Jerry stepped up at once. He didn't necessarily see any safety in numbers against the vampires, but it was as good an excuse as any to be out of the reactor room and away from Tim, the captain, and everyone else who had bullshit opinions about him. The other two volunteers were from the group of sailors who had met them at the reactor-room hatch, including the man with the spud wrench, whose name turned out to be Ortega. The other sailor, Keene, was a balding engineer with wire-rimmed glasses.

The captain led them to the weapons locker mounted against one of the reactor room bulkheads. It was scarcely bigger than a steamer trunk, maybe three feet tall by two feet wide. Using the key Jerry had taken off the weapons officer's body, Captain Weber opened the locker. Inside was a small arsenal of Browning M1911 semiautomatic pistols, nine in all.

"Gentlemen, it's no exaggeration to say the contents of this locker could decide the future of the United States," Captain Weber told them. "The Soviets aren't good at inventing things, but they're damn good at stealing them. If they take *Roanoke*, they'll get their hands on our technology. They'll learn about US Navy sonar, our torpedoes, our radio communications, and God only knows what else. Every boat in the fleet will be in danger. So arm yourselves, gentlemen. The fate of the West depends on you."

Ortega and Keene each took a gun and stepped aside. Jerry reached in and grabbed one. The .45 caliber weapon felt solid in his hand and gave him a sense of comfort. Now, finally, he could defend himself against the vampires. He just hoped bullets would stop them. He had taken the weapons qualification course in basic, so he knew how to handle an M1911. He had fired on targets at 3 yards, 7 yards, and 15 yards, and had scored well above the minimum 180 points needed to pass. But he had never fired at a living target before—if "living" was the right word to describe these creatures—and prayed he didn't freeze up when the moment came. Any hesitation out there could get him killed.

"If you find survivors, you bring them back here, to us," Captain Weber told them. "If you find any of the mutineers, you put them down. Is that understood? They're not playing around, and goddamn it, neither are we—not anymore. They didn't show any mercy when they killed your fellow crewmen, and I don't expect you to show them any in return. We're going to take back this boat, gentlemen, and we're going to do it with extreme fucking prejudice."

Jerry loaded a full magazine into the pistol, put two extra magazines in his pockets, and followed Ortega and Keene to the hatch.

The rest of the sailors came to wish them good hunting. Tim was among them, desperate to meet Jerry's eye, but Jerry ignored him. He listened halfheartedly to the others wishing them luck or telling them to be careful. A plan was already forming in his mind—a way to show everyone what was *really* happening aboard *Roanoke*.

A sailor cracked the hatch and peeked outside. Finding no one, he signaled the three scouts to go. They slipped out into the corridor, and the hatch slammed shut behind them.

In the moment before they switched on their battle lanterns, it was so dark that Jerry felt as if he were looking down into a bottomless well. He didn't see any eyes glowing in the darkness. The vampires seemed to have fallen back, but to where was anyone's guess. Lantern in one hand and gun in the other, they inched their way to the main ladder. Ortega and Keene started climbing up toward the control room, but Jerry didn't follow them. Instead, he pocketed his gun and began descending the ladder to the bottom level.

"Hey," Ortega hissed out of the darkness. "What are you doing?"

"You keep going," Jerry whispered back. "Try to find survivors. There's something I need to do."

"We should stick together," Keene said.

"Not this time. It's better if I do this alone."

"It's your funeral," Ortega said, annoyed. "Cap's not gonna like it, though."

At that moment, Jerry didn't much care what Captain Weber thought about him—or, for that matter, what any of them thought about him. All he cared about was getting proof that the so-called mutineers weren't who—or what—everyone thought they were.

Jerry listened to them climb the rest of the way up to the top level. Then he continued down the main ladder into utter darkness, jumping his left hand from rung to rung and holding the lantern in his right. It was slow going with only one free hand, and with each step downward he felt increasingly vulnerable. The vampires liked the dark. The lights had bothered them, but like many other predators, they were made for the dark. He had no doubt they could see him just fine even if his lantern weren't giving away his position. Just because he couldn't see their glowing eyes in the places where the lantern's light couldn't reach didn't mean they weren't there, watching him from just out of sight, waiting to grab him and sink their teeth into his neck. They had murdered those crewmen in the control room in a split second, before they could even get up from their stations. They could snatch him off this ladder just as quickly if they wanted to.

He listened for anything: footsteps, the creak of a hatch, breathing—if those creatures breathed. But the darkness remained silent around him. At the bottom of the ladder, he crouched, pulled out the pistol, and trained it on the open hatch of the torpedo room. Inside, the remains of Farrington's smashed lantern littered the deck, but it appeared that nothing else had changed since he and Tim hid in there.

He spun around, in the direction of the Big Red Machine at the opposite end of the corridor, and pointed his lantern into the darkness. He couldn't make his way toward the torpedo room without exposing his back to anyone hiding aft. Had they been there a moment ago, watching him, waiting to pounce, only to sink back into the shadows when he turned the lantern their way? What would happen if he took the light off the corridor? Would they come back? Would they get him?

He had to stop thinking that way or he could freeze up. He turned back to the torpedo room, determined to see his plan though. He took a step toward it, his finger on the trigger guard of the M1911.

A dark shape seemed to fold into the shadows of the torpedo room. Jerry saw it for only a fleeting moment. Someone was in there. Had Matson come back down? Or was it Bodine? Or LeMon Guidry? Or someone else who had been turned into a vampire?

As if in answer to his question, Matson's voice floated out of the room.

"Did you really think you could hide from me in the dark, White? I can see you. I can *smell* you."

Matson appeared in the doorway, right in front of Jerry, shielding his eyes from the lantern light with one hand. Gathering his courage, Jerry raised the M1911 and aimed at Matson's center mass.

"Back away from the hatch," Jerry said.

Matson didn't move.

"I won't ask again," Jerry said.

Matson took three steps backward. Jerry followed him into the torpedo room. He thought again of the drowned men in the tubes and was tempted to shoot Matson here and now. A shot from this close would blow a nice hole his chest. Putting him down was the captain's plan, and it sure as hell sounded satisfying, but he had another idea.

"You're coming back with me," Jerry told him. "I'm going to show you to the others so they can see exactly what you are."

"And what, exactly, am I?" Matson asked.

"That's easy," Jerry said. "A bloodsucking, murdering pile of shit."

He glanced over at the torpedo tubes. The LEDs on the control panel told him they were locked but no longer flooded.

"Do you have more men in there?" he said,

"There's always room for one more," Matson said.

The son of a bitch was smiling behind the hand that shielded his eyes, as if all this amused him somehow. Jerry skirted along the far bulkhead, working his way toward the torpedo tubes. Matson pivoted to face him as he moved. Jerry didn't take his eyes off him. No more than ten feet separated them, but if Matson tried anything, Jerry would happily put a bullet through his forehead. He wouldn't feel a second of regret.

"Open the breeches," Jerry said.

"I can hear your heartbeat, White."

"Open the goddamn tubes!" Jerry shouted.

"You must be terrified for your heart to beat so fast," Matson said. "I can take that fear away for you."

Jerry raised M1911, aiming it at Matson's face.

"I can take *everything* away," Matson said.

He lunged, hissing and grabbing for Jerry. Jerry fired, hitting him full in the face. The blast knocked Matson's head back in a spray of blood. Jerry had shot him at point-blank range with a .45-caliber round, but somehow he remained standing. Matson had a dark hole in the side of his face where his right eye had been, oozing blood. He casually reached into his eye socket and pulled out the bullet. It clattered onto the deck.

Jerry stared at Matson in bewildered horror. Not only had the shot not killed him, it hadn't even inconvenienced him. The damage to his flesh seemed inconsequential to him.

Jerry only hesitated a moment as his mind tried to process what he was seeing, but that was all the time Matson needed. He grabbed the pistol by the barrel, wrenched it from Jerry's grasp, and tossed it over his shoulder. It skidded across the floor to the far bulkhead. Jerry backed away. Matson swatted the lantern out of his hand, knocking it to the deck with a thud, its beam pointing uselessly up at the ceiling. *Shit.* Whatever Matson planned to do to him was going to be far worse than getting shot with a handgun.

At that moment, he simply stopped thinking, and instinct took over. The torpedo tubes at his back, and the men who may or may not be in them, were no longer his priority. He was a gazelle in the grasp of a lion. All that mattered was escape.

He broke for the hatch, but Matson caught him and threw him backward. Jerry slammed into the bulkhead, and the back of his head banged against the breech door of a torpedo tube. Matson grabbed him again, pinning him against the tubes. Jerry was too dazed to fight back.

Matson's deathly cold fingers dug into Jerry's arms and shoulders. His mouth opened wide, revealing two long, sharp upper canine teeth. When Jerry saw them, he snapped out of his stupor and started twisting, shoving, and kicking, but it was no good. He was caught. Matson bent his head toward Jerry's neck. The sharp tip of a fang brushed his skin.

Something long and narrow burst out of Matson's chest. Jerry looked down at the crudely fashioned point of a wooden spike, red with blood. Unlike when Jerry had shot him only moments before, this time Matson cried out in agony. He fell to the deck, twitching and seizing, his remaining eye wide with disbelief and pain. He flailed and hissed and snapped his jaws at the air. He tried to roll onto his back, but the two feet of broken mop handle sticking between his shoulder blades kept him on his side.

Oran Guidry stood before Jerry, glaring down at the body. He snarled, "*Connard*."

"Holy fucking shit!" Jerry said, rubbing his neck where Matson's teeth had nearly gone in.

"You okay, White?" Oran asked.

"I shot him in the face!" Jerry babbled. "I shot him in the fucking *eye* and it didn't do anything! And then he—he was going to—to …"

"Bite you? Yeah, that's what they do. One of 'em tried to bite me up in the control room earlier, but I got away. Been hidin' ever since. That ol' mop handle's the only weapon I could find."

"Well, it worked," Jerry said in amazement. "My gun didn't do shit, but a fucking mop handle took him down."

Of course, he realized. It was the wood. Just like in the stories, a wooden stake could kill a vampire.

He looked down at Matson, who had grabbed the mop handle protruding from his chest and was trying to pull it out. But he was weakening by the moment. His hands fell limp, and he stopped squirming on the deck and lay still.

Jerry just stood there, staring down at the vampire sprawled at his feet. Oran kicked Matson in the head—whether out of hatred or to make sure he was dead, Jerry couldn't say. He was just glad that Matson didn't stir. Oran stepped over the dead vampire and approached the torpedo tubes.

He grabbed the handle of one breech door and tried to open it, but it wouldn't budge. Jerry pulled himself out of his bewilderment and went to the control panel.

"Can you unlock it?" Oran asked.

"I think so."

Normally, working the torpedo control panel would be a cinch, but his mind was still trying to adjust to all that had just happened, and it took him a moment to locate the switches that retracted the safety locks on the tubes. He flipped all four and watched the lights on the control panel change.

"They're open," he said.

Oran yanked open the breech door like a man possessed, and Jerry watched in horror as a pale hand dangled out of the tube. Another of Matson's drowning victims—one he hadn't flushed out to sea yet. Jerry picked up his lantern off the floor and shined the beam into the tube. Oran grabbed the hand and pulled until a damp sleeve appeared, followed by a head that flopped limply against a shoulder. It was Lieutenant Gordon Abrams. Jerry put the lantern down and helped Oran pull Abrams the rest of the way out of the tube. The lieutenant's clothes and hair were damp but not soaking wet. Maybe he hadn't drowned after all.

Drowned or not, Abrams showed no signs of life. They lowered him to the floor, where he drooped like a corpse. His head lolled to one side, and Jerry saw a smear of dried blood and a bite mark on the side of his neck. He shot a look of worry at Oran, who was slapping Abrams' face lightly, trying to roust him.

"Come on, Lieutenant," Oran said. "Wake up. You safe now. We got you."

While Oran was thus occupied, Jerry opened the other three torpedo tubes. Inside, he found more crewmen stuffed into the narrow space, but they were dead, their bodies twisted, their hands frozen into claws, the fingernails broken from trying to dig their way out. Some still had their eyes open, staring sightlessly back at Jerry. Matson had flooded the tubes, drowning them, but hadn't flushed them out into the ocean yet.

Jerry closed the breech doors and returned to where Oran was still trying to revive his boss. Abrams was dead, surely. Between the bite and being locked in the airless tube, he had to be.

But just then Abrams coughed and groaned, making both men jump. His eyes opened.

"Guidry?" Abrams mumbled, his voice cracking.

"He's alive!" Oran exclaimed. "We gotta get him out of here. We gotta get somewhere safe."

"The reactor room," Jerry said. "That's where everyone's holed up."

Oran got Abrams onto his feet and helped him walk, carrying the lantern in his free hand. Jerry retrieved his M1911 pistol, then walked back to Matson's body. Swallowing his fear, he forced himself to take the dead body by the legs and drag it across the deck toward the hatch. It was slow going. Matson was heavier than he looked, and the broom handle poking through his chest seemed to snag on everything. Jerry thought about pulling it out but decided against it. He needed to show the others how to kill these things, and besides, he wasn't convinced Matson would stay dead if he pulled it out. He wouldn't put it past these creatures to come back to life a second time.

"What are you doing?" Oran said. "Leave him!"

"I can't. I need him so I can convince Captain Weber of what's really going on. He thinks it's a mutiny, and if we're going to survive this, he needs to know the truth."

"Survive?" Oran laughed bitterly. "Nobody survives the rougarou, my friend. Where there's one, there's more. Too many. All you can do is try to last as long as you can, and pray that when your time comes it's quick."

CHAPTER THIRTY-TWO

Jerry dragged Matson's body across the torpedo room all the way to the hatch, before he remembered that the opening wasn't flush with the deck. Along the bottom was a three-inch-high metal lip, which you had to step over when entering or leaving the room. Matson's limp body slid over it easily enough until the mop handle jutting from his torso caught on it. Jerry tugged, but the body didn't budge.

He dropped Matson's legs. He knew what he was going to have to do. He was going to have to get closer to the body than he already was and heave it over the lip. The thought made him freeze up. Matson's eyes were still open, even the gory, ruined one. The good eye stared up at the ceiling, but Jerry half expected that to change as he reached for Matson's coveralls at his waist. How did he know that Matson was really dead and not just trying to trick him? He had survived being shot in the face. Who was to say a broken mop handle through the heart was enough to do the trick? Jerry grasped a handful of material and imagined that eye snapping toward him, the body rearing up, grabbing his hand.

But Matson stayed dead. With one hand holding the web belt at Matson's waist, Jerry hauled him over the lip. Then he resumed dragging him by the legs down the corridor toward the main ladder.

Oran Guidry and Lieutenant Abrams were ahead of him. Abrams leaned against Oran for support, listing to one side and then the other as they walked haltingly forward, reminding Jerry of a drunk who couldn't find his balance. Oran was holding the lantern now, but the beam faded into darkness in the corridor beyond. He swung the lantern so its beam hit every surface, every doorway, every corner it could reach, but no one was there. That didn't mean much, though. There were still plenty of places to hide.

Not until Jerry was dragging Matson's body down the corridor did he realize how badly the vampire had injured him. He had stinging cuts on the backs of his arms where Matson's fingers had dug into his flesh, and persistent throbbing pain in a dozen places. There was blood on the sleeves of his poopie suit, which he noticed only now that it had grown cold against his skin. He refused to let his injuries slow him down, but he felt tired, weak, and light-headed. How much blood had he lost? On second thought, he didn't want to know.

Abrams went first up the main ladder to the middle level. His grip on the rungs was wobbly, but Oran went up right behind him and kept a steadying hand on his back. Getting Matson's corpse up the ladder was a lot trickier. While Abrams slumped against the bulkhead on the middle level, Oran and Jerry worked out a system similar to how they had gotten Stubic's body bag down. On the bottom level, Jerry propped the body upright against the ladder and extended the arms upward. Oran reached down from the hole above, grabbed both arms by the wrist, and began to pull. Jerry got his shoulders under Matson's body and shoved upward, climbing the ladder as he pushed and keeping the broken mop handle from snagging on the rungs. Even with Oran's help, most of the weight was still on Jerry, and he began to feel dizzy from the exertion. It was taking longer than he had thought it would. His arms flared with pain, and he felt warm blood inside his sleeves again.

"You sure you don' wanna leave him behind?" Oran groaned, hauling the body up.

"He's our only proof," Jerry said through gritted teeth.

At last, they got Matson's body onto the middle-level deck. But Lieutenant Abrams looked worse than before. He was breathing hard, and in the lantern light, Jerry saw a glistening sheen of sweat on his face.

"Lieutenant, sir, we've got to keep moving," he said.

Abrams swallowed. "I'm burning up." He touched the welts on his neck. "One of them … one of those things bit me. Gave me the fever."

"I know, sir," Jerry said. "We're going to get you back to the others and see what we can do for you."

"Do for me? Matson was the only medical officer aboard," Abrams said, glaring at the corpse on the floor. "He couldn't do anything even before he … before he turned. No one else will be able to do anything, either."

"You don't know that, suh," Oran said. "Let 'em try."

Abrams swallowed again, his throat making a dry croaking sound. "Just promise me that if I start turning into one of them, you'll kill me first."

Oran glared at him. "No, suh!"

"You'll be saving yourselves and doing me a favor at the same time," Abrams insisted. "White—Jerry—please, I'm begging you. If I turn into one of them, kill me before it's too late. I'd rather die as me than as … as one of those things."

"Don't talk like that, suh," Oran said. "You ain't gonna die."

Abrams hung his head. "You're wrong. We're all going to die. I can hear them in my head. So many voices calling me. They're all around us, in the dark. They're here. They're already here."

Oran grabbed the lantern and twisted around, shining its beam into the corridor, when out of the darkness lurched Steve Bodine, his eyes open and glowing, and his teeth bared. But when the beam hit him in the face, he reeled back with a hiss and threw an arm across his eyes.

Jerry jumped to his feet. Oran held the lantern on Bodine, keeping him at bay, while Jerry grabbed Matson's feet and started dragging the body up the short flight of steps to the reactor-room hatch. Abrams followed him. Oran brought up the rear, keeping the light trained on Bodine.

Another dark shape emerged from the mess. Two glowing eyes burned in the darkness. Oran turned the lantern toward them, and the figure stepped back. But even half shrouded in shadow Jerry could see his features. It was LeMon, Oran's brother. He stood as silent as a ghost, not coming toward them, only watching.

"Dear God, LeMon," Abrams breathed. "Oran, you were right! He's one of them!"

LeMon smiled a terrible smile, baring his elongated upper canines.

"You stay away!" Oran yelled. "You ain't Monje!"

The lantern light spilled past LeMon and into the mess. Jerry saw two bodies slumped at one of the tables: Ortega and Keene. Their throats had been torn open, leaving behind hanging flaps of skin and a red bib of blood on the front of their poopie suits.

LeMon and Bodine watched silently, not attacking. Were the vampires just toying with them, or was something holding them back? Jerry didn't know, and he wasn't about to question his good luck. In the dark corner closest to them, he saw two more glowing eyes. Oran flicked the lantern at them, illuminating the shape in the corner. Jerry nearly dropped Matson's legs in shock.

It was Lieutenant Junior Grade Charles Duncan, the man who had made it his mission to humiliate Jerry at every opportunity. Jerry stared at him, waiting for him to make a move, but he stood as still as the others.

"Mighty thin ice, White," Duncan hissed.

Abrams reached the hatch first. He opened it, and held it open as Jerry dragged Matson's body through. Oran came last, wielding the lantern as a weapon, although Jerry was convinced that something else was keeping the vampires at bay—something about the reactor room itself.

When they all were inside, Abrams slammed the hatch shut again. The sailors guarding the hatch had pistols now from the weapons locker, trained on Jerry and the others as they turned around. Jerry didn't even flinch at the sight of them. After facing down vampires, he just didn't find guns all that threatening anymore. The worst a gun could do was kill you.

"Lower those weapons!" Captain Weber told the men. "It's them!"

As the captain walked up to them, Abrams turned toward him and then collapsed. The captain stooped to catch him under his arms before he hit the deck.

Captain Weber turned to his men. "The lieutenant needs medical attention immediately!"

Two enlisted men took Abrams from the captain and escorted him farther back into the reactor room. Oran followed them.

"What happened, White?" the captain said. "Where are Ortega and Keene?"

"They're dead, sir," Jerry said. He let go of Matson's legs, and the body rolled on its side, the mop handle still jutting from its chest.

Captain Weber looked down at the body on the deck. "I see Senior Chief Matson got what was coming to him. Good work, White, but there was no reason to bring him back with you."

"With all due respect, sir, there was," Jerry said. "There's something you need to see. This isn't a mutiny, sir. It's something else."

The captain frowned. "What are you talking about, White?"

"The fever, sir," Jerry said. "It wasn't just a virus, it was the incubation period of a—a kind of transformation. A *terrible* transformation. Bodine, Matson, and all the other infected crewmen have become something no longer human, sir. They're stronger, they're faster, they're hungry for blood, and they're damn hard to kill."

The captain listened, the look of incredulity on his face growing with each passing moment. When Jerry was finished talking, Captain Weber stared hard at him.

"Mr. White," he finally said, "I can only assume that this nonsense you're telling me is the result of either a serious blow to the head, or psychological trauma, because this is not the time for a practical joke."

"Sir, he's telling the truth." Tim Spicer stepped out of the crowd of dumbfounded sailors. "I saw the vampires too, sir."

He nodded at Jerry, and Jerry nodded back. Not quite all was forgiven, but Tim had his back, and that meant something.

"*Vampires?*" the captain said. "You seriously expect me to believe that?"

"No, sir," Jerry said. "That's why we dragged Senior Chief Matson's body all the way up from the torpedo room. I knew you wouldn't believe it unless you saw for yourself, sir. I know I wouldn't have."

They knelt over the body. Matson's ruined eye socket looked even worse in the bright light of the reactor room.

"What happened to his face?" Captain Weber asked.

"I shot him with the M1911, sir," Jerry explained. "Right in the eye at point-blank range, sir, and it didn't even slow him down. He came right back at me. Would have bitten me too, if—"

"*Bitten* you?" the captain interrupted.

"Aye, sir. He would have bitten me if Seaman Apprentice Guidry hadn't stabbed him, sir. With that." He nodded at the broken mop handle skewering Matson's chest.

"A wooden stake," Captain Weber said. "You've got to be kidding me."

"I wish I were, sir," Jerry said.

The captain turned Matson's head to the side and winced at the bite marks on the neck. "Are those …?"

"Aye, sir, but that's not all," Jerry said. "Look at this, sir."

Steeling himself with a deep breath, Jerry pushed Matson's rubbery lips apart to reveal the elongated, strangely sharp canine teeth.

Captain Weber's eyes went wide. "Holy Mother of God!"

In the bright light of the reactor room, Jerry could see the teeth more clearly. They were curved like a viper's fangs, smooth across the front but sharp as carving knives. The enamel had an iridescent sheen that looked very different from human teeth. Captain Weber stared in silence. Jerry could see him trying to think it through, trying to come up with a reasonable scientific explanation for it all, and almost felt sorry for him. It was one thing to face a mutiny. They were rare, but they were recorded in the historical archives. No one doubted that they had occurred. But *vampires?* They were the stuff of horror movies and novels and campfire tales. Until now, even Jerry would have scoffed at the idea that vampires were real. Whatever mental gymnastics were happening inside Captain Weber's head at that moment were no doubt much the same as those Jerry had gone through not so long ago—a path that had led from denial to anger and, finally, to acceptance.

The captain shook his head, obviously still in the first stage. "I don't believe this. I do not fucking believe this." The astonishment in his eyes gave way to fury. "On my submarine. On *my* goddamn submarine!"

The room tilted and spun suddenly. Jerry couldn't stay upright and fell forward onto the deck. He heard Tim cry out, "Jerry!" Someone else said, "Jesus Christ, look at his back!" And then he passed out.

When he opened his eyes again, nothing had changed. He felt as if he had been out for hours, but it may have been only a few seconds.

"Don't try to get up," someone said.

Jerry hadn't realized he was trying. He looked up and saw Tim crouched over him.

"You're ... The whole back of your uniform—it's covered in blood, Jerry."

"I'm okay," he said. "Help me get up."

"Slowly," the captain cautioned. "I need to see how bad it is, White."

When Tim had him sitting upright again, Jerry unzipped his coveralls to the waist. He pulled his arms out the sleeves, wincing in pain as he peeled the sticky, wet fabric from his skin. Then he turned around to let Captain Weber and Tim see the damage.

"Dear God," Tim murmured. "Those bruises look awful. And those cuts ... Jesus ..."

"Senior Chief Matson did this to you?" the captain asked.

"Yes, sir, when he grabbed me by the arms," Jerry said. "He was unnaturally strong. He wasn't human anymore."

A shocked murmur ran through the crowd of sailors. If any of them hadn't believed Jerry's story about vampires before, they were starting to come around now.

"Someone get me some disinfectant!" Captain Weber ordered.

An engineer scurried off, and a minute later, he was dabbing Betadine-soaked cotton balls on Jerry's wounds. At first, Jerry winced with each touch, but soon the pain passed. The engineer put bandages on his wounds, and Tim brought him a fresh uniform.

"You should rest now," Captain Weber told him after Jerry had changed coveralls. "You've lost a lot of blood."

"There's no time, sir," Jerry said. "We have to take back the boat."

The captain shook his head. "You won't be any help if you're in danger of passing out again. Now go rest, White. That's an order."

Jerry didn't argue. "Aye-aye, sir."

He found Lieutenant Abrams and Oran sitting against the bulkhead. Abrams had a blanket around his shoulders, and a white, square adhesive bandage stuck to the side of his neck. He had been treated, but it didn't seem to be helping. He looked even worse. His skin was pale, and he was soaked with sweat. He blinked rapidly and turned his head to the side, away from the bright lights above.

"How are you holding up?" Jerry asked.

"I feel like I'm on fire," Abrams said, squinting at him. "The light hurts my eyes. I know what's happening to me, White. Please, remember what I asked you to do."

"It won't come to that, suh," Oran said. "I promise you."

But Jerry knew better. Oran was trying to comfort Abrams, but down in the torpedo room, he had made his true feelings known. No one would survive this.

Tim approached and squatted down in front of Abrams. "What happened?"

"We found him locked inside one of the torpedo tubes," Jerry said. "We were lucky Matson hadn't drowned him yet."

"He should have drowned me," Abrams said. "That would have been better."

Tim turned to Jerry. "What's he talking about?"

"This!" Abrams exclaimed. He tore off the adhesive bandage on his neck to show Tim the bite marks.

"Suh, don't do that," Oran said, but Abrams ignored him.

"Matson bit you, sir?" Tim asked, taken aback.

"One of them did," Abrams said. "I didn't see who. Matson, Bodine, LeMon, Jefferson, Duncan, Penwarden—what does it matter? I'm going to be like them soon, I know it. I've got the fever; the light feels like it's stabbing into my eyes. I can … I can *hear* them in my head, calling my name. How much longer will I be me?"

"Now, Lieutenant, you got to stop talking like that," Oran said.

"Sir, you should listen to Guidry," Tim said, putting a supportive hand on Abrams' shoulder. "You're lucky to be alive. We're going to do everything we can to keep you that way."

Abrams looked up at him with dark, sunken eyes. "And when I lose control and tear into your neck with my teeth, Spicer, will you still think so?"

Tim looked at Jerry. "Can I talk to you for a second?"

"Sure," Jerry said. He got up, and they stepped a few paces away from the others. "I don't know what we can do for Lieutenant Abrams. If there's a cure, Matson never had the chance to find it."

"That's not what I wanted to talk about," Tim said. "I wanted to apologize. Again. I was stupid. I should have been straight with you from the start about the captain asking me to keep an eye on you."

"Forget it," Jerry said. "Water under the bridge. If I'd been in your shoes, I probably would've done the same thing. There are more important things to worry about."

"So we're good?" Tim asked.

"Depends," Jerry said.

"On what?"

"On whether we get out of here alive."

"Something tells me the odds aren't in our favor." Tim looked past Jerry's shoulder into the main part of the reactor room. "What the hell are they doing?"

Jerry turned around to see a group of sailors carrying Matson's corpse. Captain Weber walked in front of them.

"Putting him somewhere safe, I guess," Jerry said. "In case he's not fully dead."

"Can you really kill something like that?" Tim asked. "Aren't they supposed to be dead already, technically?"

"Who knows?" Jerry replied. "They left out the chapter on vampires in *The Bluejacket's Manual*."

The sailors carrying Matson passed in front of the reactor. Several of them cried out and dropped Matson onto the deck. One of them shouted, "Captain, look!"

Jerry and Tim hurried over. On the deck, surrounded by a circle of gawking crewmen, Senior Chief Matson's corpse had begun to smoke. A moment later, his skin started sizzling, stretching like a web over his muscles and bones as it blackened and burned away.

Jerry watched the corpse smolder. His suspicions were confirmed. There was something else besides light and wood stakes could harm the vampires. Something that was right here in the reactor room.

CHAPTER THIRTY-THREE

After seeing Matson's body burn before their eyes, any lingering doubts about the veracity of Jerry's story vanished. The elongated teeth in the blackened skull were plain to see, and they were all the proof anyone needed that *Roanoke* was facing something far more dangerous than a mutiny.

When the smoke dissipated, all that remained of Senior Chief Matson was a charred husk, like a marshmallow held too long over a campfire. With the skin of his face burned away, the horrid fangs looked even longer. Tim shivered at the sight. He couldn't imagine the pain Farrington must have felt when those teeth tore into him.

Captain Weber broke the stunned silence by voicing the question everyone was thinking. "What the hell just happened?"

"Sir, maybe they—they self-destruct after they die," one sailor suggested.

"If that's the case, why would it wait so long, sir?" Tim asked. "Matson's been dead for some time now."

"I think it's something else, sir," Jerry said. He crouched over the charred crust that had once been Matson. "If the old stories are right, only three things can destroy a vampire. You drive a wooden stake through its heart, expose it to sunlight, or chop off its head. Matson already had a stake through his heart, and his head is still attached to his body. That just leaves sunlight."

"White, in case you haven't noticed, we don't get a lot of sun down here," the captain said.

"Only, this sumbitch burned up like he was outside at high noon, suh," Oran said, coming over to them. "Now why would that be, suh?"

"Hold on," Tim said. A thought had occurred to him. It was far-fetched, but they were past all that. "They haven't come into the reactor room this whole time, right?"

"On our way back, Oran, Abrams, and I saw a few of them in the corridor," Jerry said. "They stayed away from the hatch. They didn't even try to get inside."

"And when we first saw LeMon, he was just staring at the bulkhead between the forward compartment and the reactor room, remember?" Tim added. "Like he was fascinated by something on the other side."

"What are you suggesting, Spicer?" Captain Weber asked.

"I don't know, sir. But there's something in this room."

"I had the same thought," Jerry said. "But what is it? If not sunlight, *what?*"

Lieutenant Carr, the Engineering Department head that Tim had seen with the others at the wardroom meeting, stepped over to them. His uniform collar bore the insignia of a propeller flanked by two dolphins.

"Sir, if I may," Carr said, and the captain nodded. "The only thing that's special about the reactor room is the reactor itself. Is it possible that's what's keeping them out?"

The captain tapped his Geiger. "But the radiation level is within safety limits, Lieutenant."

"Yes, sir," Carr said, "but it's still higher in here, just from proximity to the reactor. Think about it, sir. The sun gives off light and heat. Both are expressions of radiation, just at different frequencies on the same spectrum. Negligible or not, sir, there's a higher radiation level in here than on the other side of the bulkhead."

Captain Weber looked skeptical. "But we don't have any proof of that, Lieutenant. The one thing we know works, that we've *seen* work, is wooden stakes, so that's what we need. If we have enough of them, we could arm ourselves. But where are we going to find that much wood? There are only so many mop handles on board."

"Wait here, sir," Carr said. "I think I've got just the thing."

He hurried off toward the back of the reactor room and returned a minute later. With him was an enlisted man carrying a bundle of long wooden rods. The sailor placed them on the deck in front of the captain. Each rod was two feet long and tapered on one end. Not a point, exactly, but it could be sharpened into one.

"Where did you find these, Carr?" the captain asked.

"They're standard equipment, sir. They're for fixing leaks. When seawater got into the auxiliary engine room of my last sub, I used these rods to plug the holes in the hull and stop the water. I reckon they'll do just as well for killing vampires, sir."

Much to Tim's surprise, the captain smiled. Captain Weber had always been so aloof and imposing that until that moment, Tim wasn't sure the man knew *how* to smile.

"Lieutenant Carr," the captain said, "this is just what we need to take *Roanoke* back."

A cheer went up from the other sailors. Tim felt it too. They were no longer helpless against the vampires. He felt an overwhelming sense of relief, like taking a deep breath after holding it for too long. Maybe they could survive this after all.

Oran Guidry's voice broke him out of his thoughts. "Lieutenant Abrams, suh, you need to rest. Sit back down, suh, please."

Lieutenant Abrams had gotten to his feet. He was even paler than before, white as paper, with dark rings around his eyes. His skin glistened with sweat, and his hair was damp and matted. Clutching the blanket around his shoulders, he raised a hand to shield his eyes from the light and squinted at them.

"I—I can't control it anymore," Abrams said. "I'm so *hungry.* I can smell the blood from Jerry's wounds and the uniform he bled into. It's driving me crazy!"

"You need to rest, suh," Oran said again. He went over to Abrams and gently tried to guide him back to where he'd been sitting.

"No!" Abrams shouted, breaking away from him. "Don't you *understand*? Don't any of you see what I'm becoming?"

"Lieutenant," Captain Weber said sternly, starting toward him.

Abrams hissed at him, revealing two long viperine fangs. The captain froze.

"Get it now?" Abrams said. "It's too late for me. My memories are starting to go. I can't remember my brother's name anymore, or—or the name of the hospital where my mother worked. All I can think about is how much the light hurts my eyes—and how hungry I am."

"Lieutenant, you've got to calm down," Jerry said, inching toward him. "We can figure something out—"

"Stay back!" Abrams yelled. "It's too late for that!"

Jerry stopped in his tracks. Abrams spun around and faced the reactor. He looked up at it fearfully, as though he could see something they couldn't. Then his expression became one of serene determination.

"This is the only way," he said.

"Lieutenant ..." Oran started to say.

Abrams ignored him. He walked toward the reactor, throwing off the blanket and spreading his arms. As he drew closer, his body began to smoke, and his skin began to sizzle like bacon on a griddle. Undeterred, he walked up to the reactor and embraced it. His body burst into flames. Men cried out, some of them running to grab the fire extinguishers mounted on the reactor-room bulkhead. Oran was at the head of the group running toward the burning lieutenant, but they could get only so close before the flames drove them back.

Tim watched in horror. If Abrams felt any pain, he didn't show it. He didn't scream. He didn't thrash about. He just stood there, embracing the side of the reactor like a long-lost lover and burning, until finally the men brought the extinguishers and turned them on him. The flames died away, and Lieutenant Gordon Abrams' body fell backward onto the deck, a charred husk like Matson's.

Oran ran to the corpse and knelt down over it. "Oh, no, Lieutenant. Why?"

Jerry helped Oran back to his feet. "It's what he wanted: to die while he was still himself, while he was still in control."

"There should have been another way," Oran said, buckling at the knees. Jerry supported him and led him away from the blackened corpse.

Captain Weber looked down at Gordon's smoldering remains. Then he turned to Lieutenant Carr.

"Radiation," he said softly, sadly. "You were right, Carr."

Tim stared in horror at Abrams' corpse. He wished it could have happened some other way, but at least they finally had the proof they needed.

CHAPTER THIRTY-FOUR

"So how do we use radiation to kill the vampires without killing ourselves too?" Captain Weber asked.

"I've been thinking about that, sir," Lieutenant Carr said. "As you yourself saw on your Geiger, sir, the radiation level here is within safety standards, and it's very well contained by the reactor."

"And yet Matson and Abrams went up in flames," the captain said. "Why?"

"I don't know, sir. We don't know anything about what kind of changes were made to the crewmen's biology when they became, erm, vampires. The best I could guess is that they have some kind of innate sensitivity to the radiation—something inside them that is affected in a way that we're not. If I'm right, that's why they haven't entered the reactor room yet. Therefore, sir, I believe all we need is low-level radiation—enough to be dangerous to them but not to us. We can do that by taking it not from the reactor itself, but from the irradiated water that comes out of it." He pointed to the massive pipe that led from the reactor to the steam generator. "We use seawater as a coolant, so the water in that outtake pipe still carries a dangerous level of radioactive neutrons until it's recycled through a series of filters." He pointed to the three massive holding tanks beside the reactor. "If we take some from the last tank, it's still going to be radio-active, but it's going to be low dosage, barely measurable. Here, watch." He held a matchbook-size Geiger counter against the farthest tank. "See? It's within safety limits, sir."

"You're sure it'll be strong enough, Lieutenant?" Captain Weber asked.

"Aye, sir," Carr said. "Judging from what happened to Matson and Abrams, even low levels of ambient radiation seem to affect the vampires much more strongly than us."

Listening to their conversation, Tim Spicer could only shake his head in astonishment. *Vampires.* It sounded so silly, like something out of a children's Halloween special on TV. *It's the Great Pumpkin, Charlie Brown, and Oh, Yeah, Vampires Are Real.* Except that there was nothing funny or cute about the carnage he had seen in the control room, or the pitiful gasps for air he had heard from the doomed men in the torpedo tubes. He shook the terrible memories out of his head and glanced over his shoulder at Oran Guidry.

Oran hadn't budged from his spot beside Lieutenant Abrams' remains, which had been covered with the blanket Abrams had worn earlier. The two of them hadn't served together very long, but they must have bonded during that short time. It was easy enough to imagine the camaraderie between Oran, LeMon, and Abrams flourishing in the small confines of the galley over the course of their shared watch sections. The thought of LeMon put a knot in Tim's stomach. Oran hadn't had any time to mourn his brother's death before LeMon came back as one of those creatures. That had to be digging into him pretty deep. Perhaps that was why he had latched on to Abrams so tightly after rescuing him from the torpedo tube. Their bond had filled the hole left by LeMon.

"Lieutenant Carr, I need you to be sure this will fry the vampires," the captain said.

"I can't be sure, sir," Carr replied. "Nothing like this was covered in the procedures manual, sir. But I think this is our best shot."

Captain Weber blew out his breath, then nodded. "Very well, Lieutenant Carr. Let's proceed."

Carr nodded to one of his engineers, who placed a five-gallon plastic bucket under the tank's valve and turned the handle. Tim half expected something green and luminous to come oozing out, but the irradiated water looked as if it could have come straight out of the tap. Carr waved his Geiger counter over the top of the bucket.

"One-point-eight roentgens, sir. That's less radiation than your average X-ray at a dentist's office. Harmless to you and me, sir."

"But to the vampires?"

"Hopefully strong enough to burn them if it touches them, sir," Carr said. "But there's no way to test what effect it will have on a living vampire until we put your plan into action, sir."

"Understood, Lieutenant," Captain Weber said.

The plan was to send out someone who would use the coolant to clear a path from the reactor room to the control room—and maybe take out a few vampires along the way. Once the path was safe enough to proceed, the others, armed with wooden stakes, would escort the captain out of the reactor room and up to the control room. The only ones who would stay behind were the engineers, who made up about half the group and who would have to make sure the engines ran properly when Captain Weber regained control.

For the first time since this madness began, Tim was starting to feel truly optimistic. There was a chance this could work, and that was something to hold on to. In the back of his mind, he had to wonder what would happen if they did survive. Once they told their story, the navy brass would probably write them all off as delusional. But hell, even living in a mental hospital beat getting ripped apart by vampires.

When the time came for someone to volunteer to spread the coolant through the boat, Tim stepped up. Captain Weber turned him down flat.

"Request denied, Spicer," the captain said. "I need you to hang back. There's no telling how far we've sailed into Soviet territory by now. That we haven't already been spotted and attacked is nothing short of a miracle, and getting out again without being seen is going to take finesse. When we retake the control room, I'm going to need men who know what they're doing. That includes a sonar tech—and as far as I can tell you're the only one left." He turned to the rest of the men assembled in the reactor room. "Any other volunteers?"

The men shifted their weight, coughed, looked down at their shoes. They were scared to leave the safety of the reactor room. Tim understood why. He had seen firsthand what the vampires could do, but he couldn't help feeling a sting of disappointment. These were trained, professional navy men. He expected better from them. And from the angry expression on Captain Weber's face, he did too. But before the captain could say anything, Jerry White stepped forward.

"I'll go, sir."

"You should be resting, White," Captain Weber said. "Those injuries need time to heal."

"Sir, time is a luxury none of us have," Jerry said. "Send me. I've been out there already, sir. I know what to expect. I can clear a path to the control room faster than anyone else. Besides, sir, I can't just sit here while the bastards who did that to Lieutenant Abrams have control of the boat. If there's anything I can do to help take them down, I want to do it, sir."

"You sure you're feeling well enough, White?" the captain asked.

"Positive, sir. Let me do this."

Captain Weber nodded. "Fine. You're on. But if we're wrong about the coolant, you'll be alone out there with God only knows how many of those things. You won't be able to signal us if you need help. We can cover you from the hatch until you're as far as the mess, but after that, you'll be completely on your own."

"Understood, sir," Jerry said.

"Captain, sir, let me take a weapon and go with him, just in case," Tim said.

"That's a negative, Spicer," the captain said. "I told you, I'll need you in the control room when the time comes."

"I'll be fine, Tim," Jerry said. "Besides, I can move faster on my own."

Tim let it go. It was out of his hands. This, he realized, was Jerry in crisis mode. Confident, brave, capable—nothing like the circumspect newcomer Tim had met on launch day. This was the sailor who had run into *Philadelphia*'s burning auxiliary engine room while everyone else ran the other way and single-handedly saved the submarine. This was the sailor Captain Weber had hoped Jerry would prove to be when he had signed off on the transfer to *Roanoke*.

"All right, then, White," the captain said. "You'd better get out there before the coolant becomes too weak to protect you."

"Don't worry about that," Lieutenant Carr said. "This stuff's got a half-life of ninety years."

He picked up the bucket and passed it to Jerry. It was made of light-weight plastic, but filled just over halfway with three gallons of seawater it weighed twenty-five pounds. The irradiated water sloshed against the sides of pail.

Jerry looked at it skeptically. "You're sure this stuff is safe for humans, sir?"

"Well, that's the good news *and* the bad news," Lieutenant Carr said. "This coolant is low dose, which means you'll be fine. But it also means the vampires won't react to its presence as strongly as they did to the reactor itself. They won't be happy about the radiation, but it won't do them serious harm unless they touch it. If you run into trouble out there, you're going to have to splash the coolant *on* them. That means getting up close and personal. You're sure you still want to do this?"

"You know it, sir," Jerry said.

Captain Weber handed him a battle lantern to hold in his free hand.

"Be careful out there," Tim said.

Jerry nodded. "I'll see you in the control room."

"Would you like a sidearm from the weapons locker as well?" the captain asked.

"No, thank you, sir," Jerry said. "A gun won't stop the vampires."

"I didn't mean for them," Captain Weber said. "I meant for you, in case the coolant doesn't work."

Tim went cold, but he didn't say anything. Jerry swallowed hard, then shook his head.

"The coolant will work, sir," he said. "It has to."

CHAPTER THIRTY-FIVE

It was Jerry's second foray out of the reactor room and into the pitch-black submarine, and he had to wonder whether he was pushing his luck. The first time, LeMon, Bodine, and Duncan—or rather, the vampires they had become—had let him pass without attacking. He couldn't count on being so lucky this time, especially since he was carrying a bucket of radioactive holy water to kill them with. He knew now that it was the ambient radiation from the reactor room that had held them back before. It was as poisonous to them as sunlight. But he was leaving the protection of the reactor room behind, and despite what he'd said to Captain Weber, he wasn't entirely sold on Lieutenant Carr's theory about the irradiated water. He hoped to God Carr was correct, not just for his own sake but for the rest of the crew's as well. They couldn't stay in the reactor room forever with no food or water. This was their last, best hope of taking back the boat, and if Carr was wrong, *Roanoke* was doomed.

The reactor-room hatch led out directly into the mess. He stepped carefully down the short flight of stairs. The mess was the closest space to the reactor room, and the captain and those protecting him would have to pass through it to reach the main ladder up to the control room. Therefore, it was vital to the success of their plan that the mess be secured first, and any vampires hiding there eliminated.

In the light from the reactor room behind him, Jerry's shadow stretched ten feet ahead. He glanced back at the men gathered in the open doorway, covering him with their Browning M1911 pistols. Bullets wouldn't be enough to kill any vampire that attacked him, but they might slow it down until he got away.

Got away. That was wishful thinking. There wasn't far to go on a submarine, and there were few places to hide.

At the bottom of the steps, he shined his lantern into the mess—and nearly jumped out of his skin. He had forgotten about the corpses of Ortega and Keene that were slumped at one of the tables. He hadn't braced himself for the sight of them with their throats torn out, their glazed eyes staring back at him. He took a deep, shivering breath and walked into the mess. Up close, he could see the strips of muscle and skin hanging from the ragged wounds in their necks, the blood-slick meat glistening in the lantern light. Jerry kept moving.

At the service counter, he saw a spread of day-old sandwiches—the last meal Lieutenant Abrams had served. Beside the sandwiches were two bowls of yellowing mayonnaise. His stomach growled, reminding him he hadn't eaten in at least six hours, but he was nowhere near desperate enough to eat anything here, now.

Setting his lantern on the counter, he grabbed an empty plastic soup bowl and dipped it into the bucket.

He whispered to himself, "This damn well better work."

He splashed the coolant across the deck of the mess, hoping it would be enough to kill any vampire who stepped in the puddle. He took the rest of the small stack of soup bowls from the service counter and lowered them carefully into the bucket. Though Carr had assured him the water was safe, he still yanked his hand out quickly after releasing the bowls.

He decided he had better check the galley too. It was right next to the mess, and the perfect place for the vampires to hide before attacking. He picked up his lantern again, walked the few steps to the galley, and aimed the light inside. The bulkheads and deck were spattered with big plum-colored stains of dried blood. Men had been killed in here, but he didn't see any bodies. The place looked as though it had been abandoned in the middle of meal prep. Various cooking utensils lay scattered across the deck, along with several overturned pots and pans. There was no sign of the crewmen whose blood was all over the galley. Either the vampires had already taken them down to the torpedo room for disposal, or …

Jerry swallowed, and backed nervously out of the galley.

Or the bodies had gotten up on their own.

He pulled a bowl from the bucket and splashed coolant water across the deck. At least it would keep the vampires away. He turned and nodded to the men in the reactor room doorway, who closed and secured the hatch, cutting off the light from inside. He was on his own. The plan gave him thirty minutes to create a path up to the control room and secure it. Normally, thirty minutes would seem excessive to go such a short distance, but he was glad for the extra time. So far, he had been lucky and hadn't encountered any of the vampires, but he didn't expect his luck to hold out indefinitely.

He heard the scuff of a shoe on the deck farther down the corridor. He froze and aimed the lantern in the direction of the sound, looking for movement. Just another dark corridor filled with countless hiding places. *Shit.* This was starting to look like a terrible idea. Running into a burning engine room had been a lot less scary.

As soon as he moved the lantern beam away, the sound came again. This time, two glowing eyes appeared in the open doorway to the officers' wardroom. He swung the lantern around again, heart pounding. Ensign Penwarden stood in the doorway, his skin as sallow as old newspaper. The ensign hissed and shielded his eyes as the light hit his face.

"Fuck!" Jerry exclaimed. His hands were full. He couldn't grab a bowl out of the bucket without putting down the lantern, but if he put down the lantern, Penwarden would attack. "Fuck, fuck, fuck!"

He had to act fast, while Penwarden was still at a disadvantage. He dropped the heavy-duty battle lantern onto the deck and, throwing caution to the wind, plunged his hand into the irradiated water to grab a bowl.

The instant the light was out of Penwarden's face, he sprang. Jerry's fingers closed around the curved underside of a bowl, but he didn't have time to pull it out of the water before Penwarden crashed into him like a linebacker sacking a quarterback. The impact slammed him backward against the bulkhead, and the bowl and its contents went flying. The bowl clattered across the deck, the irradiated water it held splashing uselessly. The force of the impact knocked the air out of Jerry's lungs, leaving him dazed and unable to breathe. Somehow, he had managed to hold on to the bucket without letting the water slosh out.

Being this close to the bucketful of radioactive coolant slowed Penwarden down, turning him noticeably sluggish and groggy, but it wasn't enough to hurt him. If Jerry wanted Penwarden to burn, he was going to have to get the irradiated water on him. He reached blindly into the bucket, pulled out another bowl, and splashed Penwarden in the face.

The vampire released an ear-splitting howl of agony that echoed off the bulkheads. He clawed at his face as it began to blacken and burn. His skin pulled tight and melted away like wax. Little flames erupted all over his body. Then the screaming stopped with a horrible suddenness, and he collapsed onto the deck.

It worked! Jerry couldn't help it; he laughed out loud as Penwarden burned in front of him. The goddamn coolant worked!

Something heavy landed on his back, knocking him to the deck, the bucket falling out of his hand. He was pinned under the weight of another man. Rough hands yanked at the collar of his uniform, tearing it away from the skin of his neck. He heard a sharp hissing in his ear, and the brief touch of the tip of a fang.

Bracing his hands against the deck, Jerry pushed with all the strength he could muster, rolling over so his attacker's back was on the deck. He managed to turn his head enough to see Steve Bodine's face. Bodine's mouth opened wide as he shrieked in pain, fangs glistening in the lantern light. As he squirmed, his grip on Jerry loosened, and Jerry scrambled away from him. Smoke began to billow from Bodine's arm, and then blue and yellow flames. Jerry understood then what had happened. He had rolled Bodine partially into the spilled coolant water.

Still howling, Bodine jumped to his feet and ran, quick as a flash. He was so fast, Jerry didn't even see him move—only saw the hatch to the head slam open. He heard the heavy thud of a body falling to the deck inside, and the screaming stopped before the hatch swung closed again.

Jerry clambered back to his feet. He considered following Bodine into the head to make sure he was dead, then thought better of it. There wasn't enough time. If the vampire wasn't already dead, the flames on his body would likely spread and consume him soon enough. Jerry needed to clear a path to the control room ASAP.

He lifted the bucket, which, by some miracle, had landed upright. It was light, though. Much of the water had sloshed out onto the deck. He would have to be sparing with what was left.

Picking up the lantern, he returned to the main ladder. Above, the top level was in darkness. Below, the bottom level was too. He scooped out a small amount of coolant and poured it down the rungs to the bottom level. If any of the bloodsucking fiends down there tried to climb up, they would have a hot time of it.

Then, peering up into the empty blackness of the top level, where the control room waited, he gripped the lantern's handle between his teeth and began to climb. His arms were sore from the injuries Matson had given him, and his shoulder ached from carrying the bucket of water. Hauling it one-handed up the ladder only made both worse. As he brought one knee up for the next rung, he banged it against the bucket. He heard the coolant slosh inside and felt a wet splash on one hand. He paused, cursing himself for his clumsiness, and held the bucket steady to avoid losing any more of the precious, lethal seawater.

At the top of the ladder, he put the bucket down on the deck and started to pull himself up. In the darkness outside the control room, two blazing amber eyes came rushing toward him. Jerry scrambled for the bucket on his other side, but the vampire was faster. He couldn't see who it was in the dark—the lantern beam was pointing in the opposite direction. Hands grabbed his arm and tried to haul him up out of the hole.

If Jerry let the vampire pull him up, he was as good as dead. He locked his legs around the ladder and pulled back, trying to break the creature's iron grip. He strained so hard, he bit into the lantern's handle. His assailant was impossibly strong, and it felt as if his arm would be pulled out of the shoulder socket. He squirmed and twisted, and the material of his uniform tore in the vampire's fingers. Jerry started to slip. The vampire grabbed him by the hand to try again, but this time the creature howled in pain as his hands began to spark and smoke, and he let go. The coolant Jerry had spilled on his hand—the vampire must have touched it. But before Jerry could grab a rung, gravity took over, and he fell back down through the hole. He landed on his side on the middle level, much too far away from the precious bucket of irradiated water still on the level above. His only other meager defense, the lantern, slipped out of his teeth and kept tumbling down to the bottom level, where it crashed to the deck and went out.

His arm flared with pain. The wounds from the fight with Matson had torn open again, and his elbow hurt like hell. Above him, he heard the vampire shrieking in pain as the irradiated seawater burned his hand. Jerry took some satisfaction in having hurt the son of a bitch, but it didn't last long. Farther down the corridor, somewhere between the mess and Officer Country, he saw another pair of glowing eyes open in the darkness.

Shit. Without the coolant, he had nothing to defend himself with. Then he remembered: he had wet the rungs down to the bottom level with the stuff. He would be safer one more level down. He only hoped the irradiated water on the ladder rungs would be enough to kill the vampire or, at the very least, keep him back.

In a blink, the eyes crossed the corridor and stared down at him. He couldn't see the vampire's face, but he knew he had only a moment, if that, to get away.

With no time to waste, Jerry rolled and threw himself into the hole, letting himself drop straight down to the bottom level. He tried to control his landing, but the pitch darkness made it impossible. He hit the bottom-level deck with his face and left knee, both of which erupted in pain.

Through his agony, he heard footsteps coming toward him, slowly, leisurely, as if whoever was approaching had all the time in the world. It couldn't be either of the creatures from the other levels—the footsteps were coming from the wrong direction, from the torpedo room.

Two glowing eyes looked at him out of the darkness.

"Well, well, well, look who finally fell through that mighty thin ice," Lieutenant Duncan said.

CHAPTER THIRTY-SIX

"I couldn't save him," Oran said. "I pulled him out of the torpedo tube, but I still couldn't save him."

Sitting on the deck beside him, Tim nodded in sympathy. Oran was still in a wounded daze after Lieutenant Abrams' death. He didn't say much, but he didn't have to. Bonds formed quickly on a submarine. It made Tim think of Jerry again, for the hundredth time since he left the reactor room. He was out there all alone, making a path to the control room. Tim only hoped that a bucket of irradiated seawater was enough to keep his friend safe.

The atmosphere in the reactor room had been tense and silent since Jerry left. A few of the men sat on the deck and, on the captain's orders, were whittling the tapered ends of the wooden rods to points. No one spoke for long stretches of time, and when they did, it was to ask how long it had been since Jerry left the reactor room.

"LeMon, then the lieutenant. Who's next?" Oran asked, as if Tim somehow knew the answer. "Why would God take them like that? Does he really hate me so bad? Does he hate all of us?"

"I don't know," Tim said. He wasn't even sure there was a God, but if there were, he wouldn't have anything to do with the vampires.

"I shoulda gone to confession more," Oran said. "I always knew that, but there were things I didn't want the priest to know. Things I did with girls, or smokin' Mary Jane sometimes. Stupid stuff. But I skipped confession too often, and look where it got me."

"I don't think God would kill LeMon and the lieutenant and everyone else on *Roanoke* just to punish you for missing confession," Tim said.

He had meant it to be comforting, but Oran only glared at him, as if he'd said the wrong thing.

"Sorry," Tim said. "Your brother seemed like a good guy. I think if I'd gotten to know him, I would have liked him."

Oran nodded. "He was a *couillon* for sho', but he was my brother. I lost count of how many scrapes I pulled him out of over the years. But it turns out I couldn't save him, either."

"You tried," Tim said. "You tried your best to save them both."

"Except my best weren't good enough," Oran said. He lifted his chin. "If I'd been thinkin' straight, I woulda been the one to take the coolant out there, not White. I owe it to LeMon and Lieutenant Abrams to make the rougarou pay. I hope I still get my chance. I'll make them wish they never came to *Roanoke*, if it's the last thing I do. I owe 'em that."

"It's been half an hour," Captain Weber announced. "It's time."

Tim and Oran got to their feet.

"Sir, are you sure Jerry has had enough time?" Tim asked.

"Either Lieutenant Carr's idea worked, Spicer, or White is dead," the captain replied. "Either way, we'll find out soon enough, because we can't wait any longer. Gather up your stakes, gentlemen. We're heading for the control room. Let's show these bastards who *Roanoke* really belongs to."

Oran was the first to reach the pile of sharpened wooden stakes, pulling one out for himself. The other men were slower to grab theirs. They were still scared and unsure about getting close enough to the vampires to stake them. Tim took a stake and hefted it, getting a feel for its weight and balance. It was roughly a foot and a half long and an inch and a half thick. He touched the point with his fingertip. It had been whittled sharp enough to pierce flesh if he put enough weight behind it. If it came down to it, though, would he be able to thrust it through the chest of someone he had worked with, bunked with? What about someone who had been an officer? He told himself yes, he could do it, but the thought frightened and sickened him. There was a world of difference between knowing you had to kill someone to save yourself and actually doing it. If the time came, he prayed he wouldn't hesitate, because that could mean his death.

There were only ten stakes, which meant only ten men could accompany the captain outside, while the other seventeen stayed behind in the reactor room. Ten men didn't sound like much against vampires who had already wiped out most of the crew, but it would have to be enough to get them up the main ladder to the top level, via the path Jerry had theoretically cleared for them with the radioactive water. Tim didn't relish the idea of returning to the control room. He had seen the terrible carnage up there and didn't want to see it again. But there was no other way to take back *Roanoke*.

They left the reactor room, moving at a snail's pace into the mess. At the front of the group, Tim held his stake ready and kept an eye out for Jerry. The lantern beams swept over the two mauled bodies of Keene and Ortega slumped at one of the tables. He heard the captain whisper the dead sailors' names sadly, apologetically. Tim knew how seriously Captain Weber took his responsibility for what happened on his boat. The massacre of his crew had to be taking a heavy toll on him.

Then the lantern beams fell on something else: a shape sprawled on the deck a little farther down the corridor. A few men gasped in surprise. It was a corpse, as charred as Matson's and Abrams' in the reactor room. Its features were burnt beyond recognition, but its elongated upper canine teeth glistened in the light. Its hair had burned away, leaving a black and blistered scalp.

The captain paused. "Someone needs to make sure it's dead."

"I got it, suh." Oran went to the body, holding his stake ready just in case. When it didn't move, he turned down the back of the corpse's collar to reveal the name tag.

"It's Ensign Penwarden, suh," Oran said.

Captain Weber nodded. "It looks like the coolant worked after all."

Tim felt the smile grow on his face. *Son of a bitch, it actually worked!*

That meant Jerry, wherever he was, just might be safe. With that bucket of irradiated water at his side, he had to be, didn't he?

A howl came from the head, high-pitched and blood-curdling. All eyes cut toward the hatch. The howl came again, long and loud and anguished. It didn't sound human.

"What the hell is that?" the captain asked. "Guidry, check it out."

Oran approached the hatch to the head, holding his stake like a dagger. Tim didn't like it. There was something in there, and sending Oran in alone seemed a bad idea.

"Sir, permission to assist Guidry?" Tim asked the captain.

"Okay, Spicer, but be careful. Remember, I need you in that sonar shack," Captain Weber said. "The rest of you, come up with me to the control room."

While the captain and the others began to climb the main ladder to the top level, Tim moved to Oran's side.

"You ready?" he asked, lifting his stake.

Oran nodded and gritted his teeth. "More than ready, *ami*."

They opened the hatch and stepped cautiously into the head. In the light of their lanterns, they saw Steve Bodine—or what was left of him—lying on the deck. Half his body was burned to charcoal just like Penwarden, but the other half was still intact.

He was alive but unable to do anything more than swipe at them with his one good arm. Bodine spat and hissed like a cornered cat, baring his fangs. Tim surprised himself by not hesitating. He put down his lantern, knelt over Bodine, and lifted his stake with both hands over the vampire's chest.

Oran put down his lantern and grabbed Tim's wrist with his free hand. "No."

"It has to be done, Oran."

"I know. Let me. Penwarden bit LeMon and turned him into one of these things, but I didn't get to kill the *connard* for it. I can't properly avenge my brother until *I* kill one. You understand?"

Tim nodded. "Okay. Just make it quick." He stood up, and Oran knelt down in his place, stake in hand.

For a moment, Tim saw Steve Bodine not as he was now, but as he used to be, the likable kid from Oklahoma City who had an accent that could charm most any city girl, and who kept his hair stubble-short to hide the fact that he was going prematurely bald. The skilled helmsman; the driven, determined sailor that Lieutenant Commander Jefferson had taken under his wing to guide and mentor. But that wasn't who was lying on the deck in front of him. This creature had Steve Bodine's face, but in his inhumanly glowing eyes were only unrecognizable hatred and hunger.

Oran brought the stake down hard, plunging it into Bodine's chest. Blood spattered out of the wound, and the vampire let loose an ear-piercing shriek.

"*Couillon!*" Oran spat. "That's for my brother, LeMon Guidry. Remember his name when you wake up in hell!"

Bodine shrieked and flailed, and blood ran from his mouth. It lasted only a few seconds, but Tim knew the image would stick in his mind's eye, maybe forever. Finally, Bodine fell still. His eyes closed, and he looked as if he was finally at peace.

"Feel better, Guidry?" Tim asked.

Oran stood again, then turned around and vomited into the sink.

CHAPTER THIRTY-SEVEN

The lens of Jerry's battle lantern had shattered when it hit the bottom-level deck. So had his knee and, from the feel of it, the bone above his right eye. He could breathe only through his mouth. His nose felt as if someone were squeezing it shut and twisting it with pliers. Probably, it was broken too. That was what happened when you threw yourself ten feet down a dark hole onto a metal floor. Stupid thing to do. He had escaped from two vampires only to end up injured and helpless in front of a third.

He heard the other men leaving the reactor room on the level above him, but he was too weak to call out for help. Duncan dragged him by his collar across the deck and into the torpedo room. If it hurt to be hauled over the raised lip at the threshold, he barely noticed. The pain of his broken bones was far worse.

The LEDs on the equipment dimly lit parts of the long, narrow space, but their light didn't reach far into the torpedo room's inky darkness, and they didn't seem to bother Duncan in the least. He dropped Jerry on the deck and loomed over him, his eyes glowing like twin stars.

"Did you enjoy killing Matson?" Duncan asked. "It's a thrill, isn't it? To kill."

"Don't ask me," Jerry said. "I'm not the one who staked his ass, though I wish I had."

He was in bad shape. The fall had left him cotton-headed, and sucking air in through his mouth was making him dizzy. He tasted blood as it ran down his throat. The pain in his nose intensified, sharpened, as if someone had just now hit him in the face with a baseball bat. His hand was wet, but it wasn't blood. It was water from the bucket that had splashed him earlier, when he was on the ladder.

Duncan grabbed a fistful of the front of Jerry's uniform and, with one hand, hauled him up off the deck. He held Jerry aloft without seeming to exert any effort at all. Jerry's feet dangled several inches off the deck.

"I told Frank Leonard that I was going to make your life on this submarine hell," Duncan said. "Now I'm going to make your *death* hell instead."

"I killed one of your kind already, possibly two," Jerry told him. "Penwarden and Bodine. Even if you kill me now, the others will destroy the rest of you. You won't have control of *Roanoke* for long."

"Then you understand the joy of killing, as I do," Duncan said. "Tell me, how did it feel to take their lives? To ram a stake through their hearts without hesitation? Did you feel strong? Powerful, for the first time in your life?"

"I didn't use a stake," Jerry said. "I killed them with sunlight. Burned them alive."

"Impossible." Duncan's glowing eyes narrowed, and he pulled Jerry's face closer to his. His fangs glistened in the colored lights. "There is no sunlight down here. That's what makes it the perfect place to hunt."

"Liquid sunlight," Jerry said.

"There's no such thing."

"Guess again."

He wiped his wet hand across Duncan's face.

With an unearthly scream, the vampire let go, and Jerry fell to the deck, his broken knee stabbing him with agony.

There had been only a little coolant on his hands, but he was relieved to see it was still enough to hurt Duncan. Smoke drifted from his face, and in the dim light Jerry could see one of Duncan's cheeks and the side of his neck bubble and blacken.

Jerry tried to get to his feet, but the world spun around him and he fell back on his butt. He turned himself over and managed to get on all fours, but the pain to his injured knee took his breath away. He fell onto his stomach and pulled himself across the deck. When he got to the torpedo tubes, he reached up for the handle of a lower tube's breech door. He grabbed it and began to pull himself up, his head spinning from the pain. It was like climbing a ladder. Once he had pulled himself up enough to get his legs under him, he reached for the breech door handle of one of the upper tubes and hauled himself the rest of the way up. When he was standing at last, he turned and saw Duncan silhouetted against the equipment lights. He was about five feet away. Much of his cheek had burned away, exposing the teeth and jaw muscles beneath it, and the cords of muscle and tendon in the side of his neck glistened in the light of the LEDs. But he was still standing, still alive.

"You'll pay for that, White!"

Jerry's injured leg buckled under his weight. His head felt as if someone had clamped it in a vise. He shifted his weight to the other leg, but the pain made him dizzy. Knowing he would fall if he let go, he gripped the breech door handle with all his remaining strength, fighting to stay upright.

"I'm going to savor killing you," Duncan said. "I'm going to make your death last a very long time, White. And when you rise again as one of us, you'll be mine to torment for all eternity."

Duncan lurched toward him. Jerry stepped to the side and swung the breech door open with one hand. With the other, he shoved Duncan toward the tube, wedging his head against the rounded inside wall. Then he slammed the round steel door as hard as he could. It hit Duncan in the smoking, exposed meat on the side of his neck and bounced open again. Duncan howled into the tube in pain and rage. Jerry slammed the door again. Again. On the fourth try, with a loud crack of bone, the door slammed all the way shut. There was a thump as Duncan's severed head fell into the tube.

Decapitation—another way to kill a vampire.

Lieutenant Duncan's headless body dropped to the deck in front of the torpedo tubes, twitching and spurting blood from the ragged stump of his neck. After a moment, it stopped moving and went limp.

"It's been a pleasure serving with you, asshole," Jerry said.

CHAPTER THIRTY-EIGHT

When Tim and Oran returned to the main ladder, the last of the men escorting the captain were climbing up it. Tim let Oran climb ahead of him, then started up. It filled him with hope to see the men ahead of him step off the ladder safely. Maybe Jerry had completed his mission and the vampires were either dead or staying clear. Hell, they would probably find him sitting at his planesman station, wondering what had taken the rest of them so long. Then things could finally get back to normal around here.

Normal. He wasn't even sure what that word meant anymore. In a world where vampires were real, what else was "normal"? Werewolves? Dragons? Goddamn mermaids and unicorns?

He could feel his thoughts rambling and tried to refocus. He needed to keep his head in the game. Getting distracted by his own crazy thoughts was a good way to end up dead.

When he got to the top of the ladder, Oran said, "Spicer, look!"

There on the deck was the big plastic bucket, with only a small amount of irradiated seawater left inside. It was just sitting there beside the ladder. It didn't look as though Jerry had dropped it. It hadn't even spilled. It was as if he had simply left it there. But why? It couldn't have been deliberate.

Had a vampire sneaked up on him, grabbed him from behind? No, Jerry would have struggled. He would likely have dropped the bucket, spilling the coolant water everywhere. Hell, he would have splashed the vampires with it, and they would have burned just like Penwarden and Bodine. There was no blood, no body, no sign of a struggle.

The men pressed on into the control room. Tim handed his stake to Oran, who had left his in Bodine's chest, and picked up the bucket. He took it with him into the control room, just in case.

The lights twinkling from the equipment were almost enough to illuminate the space, but the captain ordered the control room rigged for red so they could see better. The red lights in the ceiling of the control room, the only fixtures that hadn't been destroyed, snapped on for the first time since the underway's very first dive. The purpose of rigging the control room for red was that it helped the eyes adjust faster to the dark when surfacing or coming to periscope depth at night. So when the red lights came on in the control room, Tim's eyes didn't need time to adjust. He could see everything right away. The bodies of the dead were still exactly as he had found them before, though the thick stench of old spilled blood in the confined space was overpowering. Tim heard a man vomit, which only made the room smell worse. There was no sign of Jerry. Had he never made it this far?

"They didn't move the bodies," Tim said. "They didn't put them in the torpedo tubes like the others. Why?"

"Maybe they were feedin' on 'em all this time," Oran said. "Maybe dead blood just as good to them as livin' blood."

"Then why don't we just let 'em have the dead?" another enlisted man asked in a shaky voice. "Maybe we can make a deal. We give 'em the dead bodies, and they leave us alone."

"Rougarou don' make deals," Oran said.

A dark shape raced out from the shadows of the captain's egress and into the control room, moving faster than Tim had ever seen anyone move before. The blur of motion resolved itself into LeMon Guidry. The red light wasn't bright enough to hurt his eyes, but one of his hands was burnt, blackened and withered as if it had come in contact with the irradiated water. Had Jerry made it up here after all? What happened to him? But there was little time to speculate before LeMon attacked.

The vampire swung his good arm, knocking two sailors back like rag dolls. Then he made a beeline for Oran. Oran saw him coming, but before he could get his stake up, LeMon grabbed him by the arm and threw him into the fire-control console that ran along one side of the control room. The wooden stake went clattering across the metal deck. Oran slid down, leaving a splotch of blood on the console.

Tim and the other sailors turned their lantern on LeMon, shining them into his face. LeMon hissed and threw a protective arm over his eyes.

Forgetting himself, Captain Weber fired three rounds into LeMon's chest. The vampire didn't even seem to notice. The enlisted man that Tim had been talking to raced forward to stake LeMon. LeMon reached out with uncanny speed and grabbed him, tearing out his throat in one swift movement. He dropped the sailor, leaving him to bleed out where he fell on the deck. LeMon hissed, his chin glistening with blood in the red light, one arm shielding his eyes again. The other sailors fell back, keeping their lanterns trained on him but not willing to risk attacking him outright after seeing the fate that befell their crewmate. Tim grabbed for one of the bowls at the bottom of the bucket, ready to splash LeMon with irradiated seawater, when another vampire came streaking out of the shadows.

Lieutenant Commander Jefferson tore through the group of sailors, knocking them aside as if he were back on the football field. The sailors panicked, taking their lanterns off LeMon to shine them on Jefferson. LeMon leaped into the crowd, but Jefferson didn't even look their way. He ran straight for Captain Weber, grabbing him by the uniform and pinning him against the bulkhead.

"Jefferson, stop!" the captain yelled.

But Jefferson wasn't taking orders from him anymore. The vampire opened his mouth and bent over Captain Weber's neck.

"No!" Tim cried.

He ran at Jefferson, lunging with the wooden stake. Jefferson twisted, and the stake's sharp point only grazed his arm. Enraged, he bounced the captain's head off the helm. Captain Weber went down, and Jefferson sprang for Tim, pulling him off his feet. The bucket fell out of his hand and landed on the deck. The coolant inside sloshed precariously against the sides.

"You shouldn't have come out of your hidey-hole, Spicer," Jefferson said. "Now your sorry ass is mine!"

CHAPTER THIRTY-NINE

Jerry hobbled slowly across the torpedo room, holding on to the torpedo trays for support. He couldn't put any weight on the smashed knee, or the excruciating pain would drop him to the deck. And if he fell again, he wasn't sure he would ever get back up. He maneuvered himself out of the torpedo-room hatch, grunting with pain as he stepped over the raised lip at the bottom. In the corridor outside, he found that leaning against the bulkhead as he walked helped some.

He paused at the foot of the main ladder. He dreaded the thought of hauling himself up with a broken knee, but he couldn't stay down here alone. He took a deep breath and put his hands on the highest rung he could reach, then pulled himself up enough to hop up with his good leg on the bottom rung. Then he repeated the process, getting both hands on the next rung and hopping up. The dragging leg hurt like hell, but by now everything did.

Normally, he would have climbed the ten-foot ladder to the middle level in a couple of seconds. Now it took him nearly three excruciating minutes. When at last he pulled himself up onto the middle level, he lay on the deck, breathing hard. He glanced up at the reactor-room hatch a few short feet away and thought about calling for help, but it was unlikely anyone who was still inside would hear him through the thick steel and over the engine noise. He was going to have to bang on the hatch if he wanted anyone to know he was out here. Gritting his teeth, he began to pull himself along the coolant-slick deck.

Shouts of alarm from the control room above made him pause. Then came a scream and the sound of someone crashing into a piece of equipment.

Shit!

He turned around and used the ladder to pull himself up onto his good leg. Bracing for more pain, he started up the rungs, using the same method as before. By now, he was perspiring heavily.

It felt like an eternity before he reached the top of the ladder. He pulled himself onto the top level and tried to stand, but with the broken knee his balance was shot. He managed to get up on his good leg while leaning against the bulkhead. At the end of the short corridor that led away from the ladder, he could see that the control room had been rigged for red. They had battle lanterns too—lots of them, from the look of it— and enough light bled into the ladder space that he should be able to find the bucket of coolant he had left there. But it was gone.

He heard three gunshots and then another scream. *Shit!* There was no time to waste. He hobbled away from the ladder, toward the control room. In the short corridor between the two, he found a dropped wooden stake on the deck. He bent down painfully and picked it up. He didn't know what he could do in his condition, except maybe die. But if he had to die, he was sure as hell going to take one of those bloodsucking assholes down with him.

CHAPTER FORTY

Alive, Lieutenant Commander Jefferson had been a strong man—big, muscular, fit—but now, after his unholy transformation, his strength was astonishing. He held Tim up off the ground as if he weighed nothing at all. Jefferson's lips peeled back to reveal long, sharp fangs that glistened in the red light. It didn't matter how much Tim struggled, punched, or kicked—Jefferson wouldn't be deterred from biting into his neck and drinking his fill.

Captain Weber, dazed but back on his feet, rushed Jefferson from behind and tried to pull him off Tim. And, of course, Jefferson didn't budge. But he did release Tim before swatting the captain away like a bothersome fly.

Tim scrambled for the bucket of radioactive water, but Jefferson was too fast. He grabbed Tim and tossed him across the room as easily as he had tossed Captain Weber.

Tim collided with the dead body in the planesman's station, then fell, banging his head on the metal base of the seat. For a moment, the whole room spun like a carousel. It took him a second to snap out of it. When he did, he saw LeMon and Jefferson moving like lightning through the red-lit control room, slaughtering sailors and smashing battle lanterns.

Terrified, Tim began to crawl along the deck on all fours. A hand grabbed him by the wrist, and he recoiled.

"It's me," Oran whispered.

Tim relaxed a degree. Earlier, LeMon had smashed Oran into the fire-control console so hard that Tim had thought the culinary specialist was down for the count. He glanced up and saw Jefferson shove a sailor against the bulkhead and tear into the screaming man's throat with his teeth.

"We gotta get back to the reactor room," Oran said. "They're killin' us, Spicer. We need a new plan!"

"The captain won't go for it, and we can't just abandon him," Tim said.

Oran's grip on Tim's wrist slipped as the Cajun was yanked roughly away. LeMon had him by the leg. Oran cried out as his brother threw him hard against the deck.

"Gonna taste your blood now, brother," LeMon said. "Better'n Ma's étouffée."

Shit. Tim stayed down, crawling across the deck on all fours toward the bucket, avoiding the fallen bodies in his way, old dead and new. He tried not to look at them. Their throats were open and bleeding, their faces locked in expressions of pain and terror. The irradiated water was their only chance. Something grabbed him in the dark, lifted him, and spun him around. Disoriented, he smacked into a bank of small, twinkling equipment lights. His face collided with a metal panel and he slid to the deck, dazed. Jefferson loomed over him. *This is it,* Tim thought. *The end.* He had tried to be a good sailor for the navy. He had tried to be a good crewman for Captain Weber. He had tried to be a good friend to men like Mitch Robertson and Jerry White. There was so much more he wished he could have done, so many more parts of the world he wished he could have seen. Now none of that was going to happen. He braced himself and waited for Jefferson's teeth to tear into him.

Jefferson bent down to bite him. Tim spotted the bucket nearby and sprang desperately for it, but Jefferson planted a foot in his back so hard he thought his spine would snap. He was pinned to the deck.

Jefferson laughed. "You've got some fight in you, Spicer. That'll make killing you all the sweeter."

Across the control room, LeMon straddled Oran on the deck while fighting off a handful of sailors who were trying to stop him from tearing into his brother's neck. Captain Weber picked up a dropped stake and lunged at LeMon. He stabbed, but LeMon twisted, and Weber missed his heart, punching through the left shoulder instead. LeMon hissed with rage and pulled the stake out, but it was enough of a distraction for Oran to struggle free. LeMon rose to his feet and tossed the stake aside. Oran grabbed Captain Weber and pulled him away, then ran for the bucket. He snatched it up by the bail and spun around with it.

LeMon sprang as Oran flung the contents of the bucket onto him, water and plastic soup bowls alike. The bowls bounced and clattered to the deck as the coolant splashed over him in a wave.

"I'm sorry, Monje," he said. "I couldn't save you this time."

LeMon screamed and burst into flames. He collapsed to the deck, convulsing as he burned, and then lay still. Oran dropped the empty bucket, which made a hollow thud.

Jefferson grabbed Tim and lifted him off the deck.

"Let go of him, Jefferson!" the captain yelled.

Oran grabbed a fallen stake and rushed at Jefferson, but the XO batted him aside with one arm.

Jefferson pulled Tim toward his slavering jaws.

The pointed end of a wooden stake burst through Jefferson's chest with a spatter of blood. The vampire screamed, twisting and convulsing as he dropped Tim. He clutched at the blood-slicked stake and tried to pull it out, but it wouldn't come. With a prolonged hiss that ended in a pained gurgle, Jefferson fell to the deck, dead.

Standing behind the body was Jerry White. Both arms of his uniform were wet with fresh blood, his nose was swollen and bloody, and he had one hell of a black eye.

"Gentlemen," Captain Weber said, catching his breath and looking around the room. Of the eleven men who had started the expedition, only six were left. "The control room is ours."

Jerry's eyes rolled back in his head. His legs gave out under him. Tim jumped forward and caught him before he struck the deck.

CHAPTER FORTY-ONE

When Jerry White awoke and opened his eyes, he could see out of only one. The other was covered by a large bandage, as was his nose, and both gave him a sharp pain when he touched them. He sat up slowly and carefully, wincing as his sore body complained, and realized he was in a dark, tightly confined space. His heart raced as his mind conjured images of torpedo tubes and coffins, but after a moment his confusion passed and he realized he was in a rack in the berthing area. He was so tired and so sore that it took great effort for him to slide the curtain aside and let in the berthing area's red light. He was on the bottom rack of a triple-decker bunk—not his own, although the sailors who had shared it were likely dead now and wouldn't mind. The wounds on his arms had been bandaged, although the work looked rushed and sloppy. His injured knee had been set with a splint consisting of two wooden stakes and a whole lot of gauze. With Matson dead, he supposed the others had done the best job they could of patching him up.

The last thing he remembered was limping into the control room and staking Lieutenant Commander Jefferson before he could bite Tim. After that, the world had gone black. The fact that he was in a rack and not dead told him the vampires hadn't won.

The curtain in the doorway was pushed aside, and Tim walked into the berthing area. Jerry turned, wincing as every nerve ending complained.

"You're awake," Tim said, a big grin on his face. "The captain said it would be okay to come check on you. You look like something ate you and shat you back out."

Jerry tried to laugh, but everything hurt too much. "You're the one who almost got eaten, as I recall."

Tim sat down on the rack across from him. "Thanks for that. You saved my life. Again."

"I'll put it on your tab," he said. "Is everything …?"

"Back to normal? Hardly, but the boat is operational. As far as we can tell, Jefferson was the last of them. Captain Weber put a skeleton crew, including me, to work piloting the boat. The rest of the survivors have been doing a search. They haven't found any more bloodsuckers, but they did find bodies. A lot of bodies."

"Damn," Jerry said.

Most of the bodies, Tim explained, had been piled in the captain's stateroom, which looked like something out of the Jonestown massacre, but the search party had only to follow their noses to find more in the auxiliary engine room, the garbage disposal room, and the wardroom. They checked the torpedo tubes as well, but all they found was the missing part of Lieutenant Duncan's corpse.

"I take it we have you to thank for Duncan losing his head?" Tim asked.

"I never did take kindly to bullies," Jerry said. He nodded at his knee. "Who do I have to thank for this?"

"One of the ensigns had some emergency training from back home, and it turns out Oran Guidry knows a thing or two about patching people up after a bad fight. You're probably going to need a cast on that knee, but the splint will have to do until we reach land."

"How long will that be?" Jerry asked.

"To be honest, I don't know. Getting out of Soviet waters is our first priority right now. We may be shorthanded, but everyone's pulling their weight. We had to train some men to work the essential stations in the control room. I've got Aukerman, a PO from engineering, covering sonar while I'm down here. I made him promise if he hears so much as a peep to come get me. They're learning on the job, but it's slow going. I think you'll be the only one getting any sleep for a while."

"How many of us are left?" Jerry asked.

"Not a lot. Twenty-three. When we searched the boat, we didn't find any more survivors. Only the crewmen who were in the reactor room survived."

"Christ," Jerry said. "There were a hundred and forty men on this sub when we launched."

"We're practically a ghost ship now," Tim said. "I guess we're just like our namesake, like you said—the colony where everyone disappeared."

"Can I ask you a personal question?" Jerry said.

"Shoot," Tim said.

"When you were in the control room with the vampires, were you scared?"

Tim nodded. "Scared enough my poopie suit almost lived up to its name. What about you?"

"I wasn't," Jerry said. "It's the strangest thing. I knew what I had to do, and I figured either I would do it or I would die. I was … calm. When I saw Jefferson, I just came up behind him and …"

"Staked him."

Jerry nodded. "I was close enough to Jefferson that he could have knocked my block off, but I wasn't scared. I don't know why."

"The same reason you weren't scared to run into that burning engine room on *Philadelphia*," Tim said. "You're braver than you give yourself credit for."

"Or stupider," Jerry said.

Tim grinned. "Or maybe it's because Jefferson wasn't the first XO you had trouble with."

"*Philadelphia*'s XO wasn't a vampire—just your garden-variety asshole," Jerry said.

"What happened on that boat, Jerry?" Tim asked. "You never told me."

Jerry sighed. He settled back against the pillow, groaning with discomfort. "It's a long story. Maybe some other time."

"If I've learned one thing on this underway," Tim said, "it's that you never know how much time you've got left. Best not to put things off."

"Yeah, I suppose you're right about that," Jerry said. "Back on *Philadelphia*, I was friends with a radioman named MacLeod. This guy had always wanted to be in the submarine service, ever since he was a kid. It *meant* something to him, and he worked his ass off to get there. But to join the navy, he had to hide who he was. Do you know what I mean by that?"

"I've heard a few stories," Tim said.

"Personally, I didn't care about that stuff. MacLeod was a good sailor and a friend," he said. "I don't know how, but our XO, Lieutenant Commander Frank Leonard, found out. Only, he didn't report MacLeod. He held the knowledge over him instead. He rode MacLeod hard, even harder than Duncan rode me. He was on the guy's back about *everything*, chewing him out, treating him like shit. But that wasn't the worst of it. Leonard had a taste for drugs when he was off duty—coke and pills mostly—and whenever we were in port, he would turn MacLeod into his errand boy, making pickups from his dealer. It didn't just put MacLeod's career at risk if he got caught; it could have landed him in jail. But it was either that or Leonard would spill the beans about him being gay, so MacLeod thought he didn't have a choice. He bit the bullet and did as he was told.

"I was furious when I found out about it. I wanted to report Leonard, but MacLeod begged me not to. He said if I did, the navy would find out the truth about him and kick him out. That same fear of being found out was why he never went to the COB to complain about Leonard. But I did it anyway. I knew I couldn't prove anything about the drugs without MacLeod's help, so I did what little I could. I filed a formal complaint about the way the XO was treating him. There was an investigation. Leonard had been up for a promotion at the time, but after the investigation he was passed over. It was his third time getting passed over, and you know how it goes in the navy: three strikes, you're out. That was the end of his career. Of *both* their careers, it turned out, because MacLeod was right. The truth about him came out in the investigation and he was discharged, just like he always feared would happen. He never spoke to me again. I thought I was doing the right thing, but I wonder sometimes."

"It was a tough call to make," Tim said, "but you definitely did the right thing. If that was who Frank Leonard was, he didn't deserve to be in the navy."

"Yeah, but MacLeod *did*. That's what stinks."

He took a deep breath through his mouth. He hadn't expected to tell this story to anyone, on *Roanoke* or anywhere else, ever again. He just wanted to put it behind him, but he was surprised how good it felt to get it off his chest.

"Anyway, I learned my lesson: keep my head down and don't get involved. That was the plan for my time on *Roanoke*. Guess that went right down the shitter, huh?"

"I'd say risking your neck to kill vampires and save your crewmates is getting pretty damn involved," Tim stood. "Get some rest. I'll come back to bother you some more later."

"No rush," Jerry said. "I feel like I could sleep for a week."

Tim turned around to leave the berthing area, but a sailor appeared in the doorway, breathing hard, as if he had run all the way from the control room.

"Spicer, the captain wants you back in the sonar shack now!" the sailor said. "We've got a bear on our tail!"

CHAPTER FORTY-TWO

Tim's first thought was that the Victor that had tailed them before was back. During the time the crew lost control of *Roanoke*, it had strayed fifteen miles north along the coast of the Kamchatka Peninsula, which could have given the Victor plenty of time to find them again. The captain had changed their bearing as soon as he had control once more, setting course for the closest American territory—the Aleutian Islands to the east, 1,200 miles off the tip of the Alaskan peninsula. But for the moment, they were still in Soviet waters. If they wanted to get out in one piece, they were going to have to shake the Victor off their tail.

Captain Weber had already ordered *Roanoke* rigged for ultraquiet by the time Tim arrived in the control room. The screw was slowed, and their speed was reduced to two knots. The control room was still rigged for red, casting everything in a crimson tint. The bodies, both human and non, had been cleared out to make room for the captain's skeleton crew: a quartermaster, one man in Fire Control, a diving officer, a planesman, and a helmsman. That was it. There was no officer of the deck or chief of the watch. The surviving crew of *Roanoke* was stretched thin, which left the watchstanding sailors to take their orders directly from Captain Weber himself.

"Spicer, I want your eyes and ears on the Victor," the captain told him.

"Aye-aye, sir," Tim said, bolting for the sonar shack.

He took a seat in front of his console and slipped the headphones on. The vampires had broken the lights in here too, but there was still plenty of illumination coming off the display screens, which apparently hadn't bothered their eyes as much as the overheads. It was Aukerman who had first spotted the Victor. Seated at the next console over, the engineer turned emergency sonar tech pointed out the anomalies in the cascading waterfall display, although Tim had already spotted them as soon as he sat down.

There was surface traffic as well. Two ships floated 500 feet above them, to their north and east. Tim concentrated on the noises they made, identifying one of them as a destroyer, probably Kashin class, a guided-missile ship built in the 1960s. He pegged the other ship as even older: a Sverdlov-class cruiser, a gunboat from the 1950s. That was a stroke of luck. The Soviets could just as easily have had planes patrolling the skies and dropping sonobuoys that could pinpoint Roanoke's location in seconds. They could have had ships dropping acoustic gear that actively pinged every cubic inch of ocean around them. Instead, the Soviets had sent two antiques to patrol these waters. Their outmoded technology was probably the only thing that had saved Roanoke from being spotted already—spotted and torpedoed. The ships were ancient by technological standards, but that didn't make their weaponry any less lethal.

Still, as long as Roanoke stayed below the thermocline, he was confident the surface ships wouldn't see them. The submarine on their tail was another matter. The Victor didn't look as if she had spotted them yet. She wasn't running on quiet, just patrolling as normal, but that could change in a matter of seconds.

Captain Weber came to the door of the sonar shack, silhouetted in the red light from the control room. He wore a somber, tense expression. "We've drifted right into Victor fucking Central, Spicer, and the timing could not be worse. Has she detected us yet?"

"There's no indication she has, sir," Tim said.

"Excellent. Keep an eye on her. If that submarine increases her speed so much as half a knot, I want to know about it."

***

With only twenty-three men left aboard, the submarine was eerily quiet. Twenty-three *living* men, Jerry reminded himself. There were a whole lot more corpses being stored in the wardroom and the empty staterooms until they could be dealt with properly.

The berthing area wasn't far from the mess, which normally would be so filled with boisterous conversation and sailors horsing around that Jerry wouldn't expect to get a moment's peace. Instead, it was deadly silent, which, he discovered, was worse. He strained his ears to hear anything, even the sound of Guidry in the galley, making cold sandwiches for the remaining crew, but there was nothing. Even the culinary specialist had probably been put to use somewhere. He got the feeling the whole middle level was empty except for him.

And then he heard them—footsteps in the corridor outside. They stopped right outside the berthing area.

"Back already, Spicer?" Jerry called. "I didn't think the Soviets would give up that fast."

In the murky red light, he saw something small appear at the side of the curtain. From a distance, it took him a moment to recognize fingers grasping the doorframe. A shape pushed through the curtain without bothering to move it aside. The red light fell across the man's face, illuminating his features. Jerry stiffened.

Warren Stubic, the torpedoman who had frozen to death in Lieutenant Abrams' freezer, walked into the berthing area.

***

Tim studied his sonar screen. *Roanoke* was a small target in a vast ocean, and a moving target at that. As long as they remained at ultraquiet, barely making a sound as they drifted out of the Victor's sonar range, the Soviets didn't have a prayer of finding them with their outdated equipment.

Still, the worst thing a sonar tech could do was get cocky, because that led to sloppiness, which led to mistakes. Tim forced himself to focus. His mind was still moving in a thousand different directions, trying to process everything that had happened—the horrible deaths, the sudden revelation that vampires were real—but he pushed himself to concentrate on the Soviet submarine instead. He couldn't let anything distract him or they could wind up dead on the bottom of the ocean. He sure as hell hadn't survived a horde of hungry vampires just to become fish food.

So he watched the screen and listened to the sounds the Victor made—and it didn't sound right. She was traveling at nine or ten knots, not trying to be stealthy, her engine banging and clanging. But something was missing, something important that he couldn't put his finger on. He had memorized all the common sound signatures that Soviet boats made—it came with being an experienced sonar tech. But this sounded so unusual, so off, that he reached for the console and hit a few buttons to record it. It was standard operating procedure. When sonar techs heard something they didn't recognize, they recorded the sound and compared it to other audio recordings later, to identify it.

But as he listened, it came to him what was missing from the Victor's sound, and he sat bolt upright in his seat.

As far as he knew, the US Navy was the only submarine service with quiet boats. Soviet subs ran loud. No other militarized nation with a navy even had nuclear-powered subs. They still had diesels, loud as trucks underwater. American subs ran quieter than the rest of them because their screws were specially designed and shaped to reduce cavitation—the formation of air bubbles—and therefore remain quiet enough not to be detected by sonar.

The Victor's screw wasn't causing cavitation. Tim could hear her engines, but her propeller was as silent as their own.

And that just wasn't possible.

***

Too late, Jerry realized that they had been wrong. Jefferson wasn't the last of the monsters. All this time, in the quarantined isolation of the torpedo room, in the same dark space where the vampires had hidden themselves before launching their attack, PO3 Warren Stubic had lain frozen in his body bag. But the cold hadn't killed him, because cold didn't kill vampires. It had only left him dormant, hibernating while he slowly thawed. Now he was back, the one who had brought this curse onto *Roanoke* in the first place, patient zero of the vampire outbreak. And Jerry was alone with him in the berthing area. Alone and incapacitated.

But something was wrong with Stubic's eyes. No inhuman glow came from within them, and they didn't appear to be focused on anything, not even on Jerry. Being frozen solid had damaged his eyes somehow. Stubic was blind.

Jerry's rack was at the back of the berthing area, built into the farthest bulkhead from the doorway, but he couldn't stay there. Confined to such a tight space, he was a sitting duck. He tried to slide out of his rack as quietly as he could, but the injured knee was too sore and too stiff for him to move silently. He squirmed his way to the edge of the rack, then dropped to the floor. He stifled a cry as his broken nose, fractured eye socket, and broken knee all felt the impact. But it didn't matter—Stubic heard him anyway. The vampire's head snapped in his direction, and the lips pulled back in a rictus grin to reveal long viperine fangs.

The berthing area was wide enough for two rows of freestanding bunks between the rows built into the bulkheads. If he could keep the bunks between himself and Stubic, he might be able to make it out. Jerry grabbed the corner of the nearest bunk in the middle and pulled, dragging himself along the floor.

Stubic groped his way into the berthing area. "Don't bother trying to hide from me. I can hear you."

Jerry pulled himself farther along the floor. Stubic moved through the bunks and sniffed the air, trying to catch Jerry's scent.

"Who are you? Spicer? Goodrich? No." Stubic inhaled voluptuously, like a kid smelling candy. Then he grinned, his fangs glistening in the red light. "White."

Shit. Jerry glanced at the curtained doorway of the berthing area—too far away for him to make a break for in this condition. He thought about shouting for help, but that would just give Stubic his exact location, and he knew how fast these creatures could move.

"Aren't you tired of always following orders, White? 'Aye, sir. No, sir. Please, can I have some more, sir.'"

Stubic was inching closer. Jerry pulled himself forward, gritting his teeth against the pain in his injured arms. He slid from behind one bunk to behind another, but the doorway still seemed miles away. Stubic cocked his head, listening to the sound of Jerry's coveralls sliding against the deck, and gave a wry smile.

"Instead of doing what you're told, wouldn't you rather take what you want instead? Answer only to yourself and your desires? Wouldn't you rather be at the top of the food chain, instead of the bottom?"

Jerry's arms hurt so much, he could barely move them, but he had to keep going. He grabbed the foot of the bunk and pulled, sliding himself around it. Stubic paused, tilting his head to listen. The smile remained on his face, sharp and malevolent.

"I can make that happen for you, White. I can give you the gift of the green-eyed queen. I can make you like me, and then you'll never have to follow orders again."

Green-eyed queen? What was he talking about? Keeping his eyes on his pursuer, Jerry continued pulling himself toward the doorway. Suddenly, Stubic moved, fast as a cat, from where he had been standing amid the bunks. Jerry turned, and there he was, standing right before him, blocking his way. Jerry's heart sank. Stubic had known where he was all along, and had only been toying with him.

In a single arcing movement, Stubic picked Jerry up off the deck by his coveralls and slammed him into the side of a triple-decker bunk so hard that the curtain rod came loose and fell to the deck with a loud metallic *clang*. Jerry's face and broken knee shrieked in agony.

He gritted his teeth against the pain. "We killed the others. We'll kill you too. One blind vampire can't take over an entire submarine."

Still holding him by the coveralls, Stubic grinned, his lips pulling back from his fangs.

"Who said there would only be one of us?"

***

"Captain, sir, there's no cavitation coming from the other sub," Tim reported, moving one earphone of his headset aside so he could hear. "I don't understand it. The engine sounds Soviet, but the screw isn't making any noise at all."

"That doesn't make sense, Spicer," Captain Weber said from the door of the sonar shack. "A bear's screw is loud as a lawnmower. They're reliable that way."

"I know, sir. Is it possible she's one of ours? We're close enough to Alaska that they might have come looking for us."

The captain shook his head. "The navy wouldn't risk sending another boat into Soviet waters just to find us."

"Then I really don't understand what this is, sir," Tim said.

The captain straightened, his eyes widening in realization. "This is it, Spicer. This is what they sent us to find! The prototype submarine. She's real, and we've found her."

Tim looked at the screen again, at the shapes the sonar vibrations were creating within the cascading colors. The next generation of Soviet submarine? Was it possible? He felt as if he were looking into the future. Ten years from now, twenty, thirty, would some other sonar tech be sitting where Tim was and looking at the same readings on their screen, listening to the same sounds? And if they were, would they have learned about this very moment during their training—the moment a US Navy submarine picked up the first of a brand-new class of Soviet submarine on sonar?

"Are you recording her?" the captain asked.

"Aye, sir," Tim said. "She still hasn't detected us. If she had, she wouldn't be running this loud."

"Keep an eye on her," Captain Weber said. "And keep recording. I want to bring back as much information as we can."

A loud metallic *clang* in Tim's earphone startled him, reflected in the sonar display by a sudden bright flare. Aukerman winced in pain and threw his headphones off.

"What the hell was that?" Aukerman asked.

"Whatever it was, it came from inside *Roanoke*," Tim replied.

"Shit," Aukerman said. He slipped his headphones back on.

On the screen, the readings for the Soviet submarine shifted.

"Captain, sir, I think she heard us," Tim announced. "She's turning our way."

"Has she engaged active sonar, Spicer?" Captain Weber asked.

"Not yet, sir."

Then he heard something else on his headphones—something that made him go cold. The unmistakable sound of torpedo tube outer doors sliding open.

***

"This is how we survive," Stubic said, pinning Jerry against the bunk. The vampire's blind, unfocused eyes seemed to look through him, into his soul. "We feed and multiply and spread the gift of the green-eyed queen. And what better place for us to thrive than in the darkness of the ocean?"

"My friends will stop you," Jerry said through gritted teeth. "Even if you kill me, they will take you down. It's over. It ends here."

Stubic laughed—a hideous sound that raised goose bumps on Jerry's flesh.

"You're missing the point, White. For my kind, there *is* no end."

Stubic's groping hands found Jerry's head and pushed it to the side, exposing the neck. He bared his fangs and leaned in.

***

Captain Weber stood behind Tim's chair and looked at the sonar screen. "If this bear detects us, we're as good as dead. *We* broke into *her* house. If she shoots us, it's a freebie. And we'd be fools to fire on her first with those ships on top of us."

He was right. If *Roanoke* torpedoed the Soviet sub, the two ships on the surface would hear the explosion and drop their acoustic gear. *Roanoke* would be located, torpedoed, and its presence labeled an act of war. With both superpowers' fingers on the button, Tim could imagine things escalating quickly.

He said, "Sir, my best guess is that she's about ten miles out and closing. Her torpedo doors are open, but she's still on passive sonar. She may not know for sure yet that we're here."

"We're going to have to *sneak* out of here." Weber ducked back into the control room and said, "Maintain current speed and depth. Slow and low, gentlemen—that's how we'll get out of this."

On the sonar screen, the Soviet sub adjusted its bearing, diving to *Roanoke*'s depth until it was aligned behind them. Tim's chest tightened. His throat went dry. Had they detected *Roanoke*, or was this just an unrelated change in their bearing? It was possible the bear was trying to lose itself in *Roanoke*'s baffles—the cone of water directly behind the sub, which the hull-mounted sonar couldn't hear through. It was an unintentional blind spot caused by the need to insulate the sonar array from the noise of the submarine's own engines, and one the Soviets had learned to exploit. It was also possible she was lining up to fire a torpedo at them. If only there were some way to know for sure whether they had been detected—some other way than being fired on.

The only way to get the bear out of *Roanoke*'s blind spot was to clear the baffles, but that would mean taking a sudden hard turn to look back into it. Not only would that take them off course, but changing their bearing that drastically would definitely alert the Soviets to their presence. And as the captain had said, considering how close *Roanoke* was to the Rybachiy sub base, the Soviets would have no qualms about firing on them.

The Soviet sub blinked in and out of sonar as she passed through the baffles. Tim's whole body tensed. He glanced over at Aukerman, who looked as nervous as he felt, and was probably wishing he were back in the reactor room.

According to the sonar readings, *Roanoke* was passing right under the Sverdlov. The cruiser was thirty years old, and Tim hoped she was hard of hearing. If her listening equipment was as out of date as the rest of her, they would pass by undetected. If not, acoustic gear would rain down all around them.

He held his breath, and then they were past the Sverdlov. Tim sighed with relief. But the sub was still behind them, still searching for them. Tim strained his ears for any sound of torpedoes being readied, but so far the bear had taken no further aggressive action.

"Stay the course," Captain Weber told the crew at the helm. "Slow and steady."

Tim didn't understand how he could sound so calm. With each passing second, he was more convinced the Soviets would spot them and that would be the end of it. Either they would be destroyed like the South Korean 747, or they would be forced to surface so they could be boarded, the crew taken prisoner and probably tortured for information while Soviet engineers took *Roanoke* apart.

The sub winked in and out of sonar. Tim wiped the sweat from his forehead. Next to him, Aukerman did the same. In his headphones, the Soviet sub sounded so loud, Tim felt as if he were sitting in its engine room.

He thought back to those long winters of his childhood, how he had stared into the seemingly unending darkness and prayed for daylight. It had come eventually, as it always did, but there were times when he felt its return as a personal triumph, as if the sun had deigned to come back only because he had prayed hard enough. It was a childish way to think, believing the strength of his wish had somehow affected the world around him. But now, after everything else that had happened, with their lives hanging in the balance once more, he found himself feeling that same yearning with the same intensity, as though he might get them out of this alive if he just prayed hard enough.

***

Stubic leaned closer, his sharp teeth inches from Jerry's neck. Jerry winced. He couldn't let this happen. He didn't want to die, didn't want to become one of these creatures. But he was pinned against the locker and too weak to fight.

His hand grasped for anything he could use as a weapon, anything to make Stubic let go of him, but what could he possibly bring to bear against the vampire's unnatural strength? His hand brushed the gauze of the splint on his knee—and then one of the wooden stakes splinting his leg.

He slid the stake up and out of the gauze, doing his best to ignore the screaming pain in his knee. With all the strength he could muster, he drove the sharp end into Stubic's chest.

The blind, glassy eyes widened in surprise. Stubic hissed and drew back, releasing him. Jerry fell to the deck. The pain in his broken knee was worse than anything he had ever known.

Stubic dropped to his knees, hands grasping the stake protruding from his chest. Then, to Jerry's horror, he laughed and began to pull the stake out.

"You're too weak to drive it in all the way, White. Why fight me? Think how strong you'll be when you're one of us. Not just the new strength in your transformed body, but strength in numbers. Our kind is connected in ways you can't imagine. Our bodies. Our minds. I can hear the green-eyed queen in my head, urging me to grow our numbers, to fill the darkness of the ocean with our kind. When you rise, you'll hear her too."

"If I wanted to hear what a vampire was thinking," Jerry said, "I wouldn't be sitting here praying for you to shut the fuck up already."

He threw himself on top of Stubic, taking him down to the deck, the weight of his body pushing the stake deeper into the vampire's chest. Stubic screamed as it pierced his heart. Blood sluiced from his mouth. He convulsed, his limbs smacking against the deck, but this time there was no escape from the stake. Jerry leaned on it with all his strength until Stubic quit thrashing.

He looked down at the dying vampire. "If you really do share your thoughts with each other, tell your green-eyed queen you failed, and that she can kiss my still-living human ass."

Stubic's blood-slick lips stretched into a smile. He spoke his last words then—words that chilled Jerry to the core. And with a last wheezing, triumphant laugh, the vampire died.

***

"Captain, she's slowing and turning around!" Tim shouted.

Captain Weber came into the sonar shack and looked past Tim to the screen. "We're not out of the woods yet, Spicer. Let's make sure she keeps going."

They kept watching the screen for another fifteen minutes. Tim heard the torpedo doors close again, after which the bear continued sailing away and didn't turn back. He couldn't believe it. It was as though his prayers had been answered. The Soviet sub hadn't detected them, and neither had the surface ships. No torpedo had been fired. No one had been captured and interrogated. *Roanoke* had the proof it had been sent to find: that the prototype submarine existed. And the Soviets were none the wiser that a US nuclear sub had violated their sovereign territory.

The captain clapped Tim on the shoulder and announced, "We're clear."

Tim let himself breathe again. Seated at the next console, Aukerman let out a spontaneous cheer and high-fived him.

CHAPTER FORTY-THREE

They had to keep sailing slow and low, even through international waters, to avoid detection by the Soviet boats that patrolled nearby. It took 26 hours for *Roanoke* to reach a suitable place to surface in US waters—a spot 30 miles off Attu, the westernmost of the Aleutian Islands, and the westernmost point of land in the United States. By then, the battle lanterns mounted on the bulkheads had started to lose power. They were never intended to be the boat's sole source of light for days on end. The crew used some of the Supply Department's extra six-volt batteries to bring light back to the essential parts of the submarine—the control room on the top level; the galley, mess, and head on the middle level; and the torpedo room on the bottom level—and stockpiled all the remaining batteries they would need to keep the lights burning on the long trip home.

Before they surfaced, Captain Weber ordered *Roanoke* up to periscope depth. The instrument rose out of the floor, and he peered through the eyepiece, searching the surrounding waters. When he determined it was safe, he gave the order.

"Rig for surface."

When Tim heard those three beautiful words from where he sat in the sonar shack, he had to fight back the tears. After being trapped in the dark, confined space of the sub with those creatures, the idea of breathing fresh air again, of seeing the sky again, was overwhelming. For a moment, he feared he might lose the fight and start weeping right there in front of his sonar screen. He supposed no one would fault him if he did.

The surviving crew had been dealing with their stress as best they could. Some spent what little rack time they had curled in a fetal ball behind the privacy curtain and crying softly to themselves. Others channeled their emotions into food, eating second and third helpings of the cold sandwiches, canned goods, and cereal Oran Guidry prepared for them.

The bodies of the dead had been stored with as much care as possible in available rooms on the middle and bottom levels. There were a lot of bodies, more than Tim wanted to think about, and their numbers included the eight crewmen who had become vampires. As much as Tim hated it, there was just no room to store the vampire bodies separately.

When they had a moment to spare, crewmen gathered outside those makeshift morgues, ignoring the stench that emanated from them. Some bent their heads in prayer. Others yelled curses at the vampires and banged their fists angrily on the bulkheads. It was another of the strange ways the crew dealt with what happened. But it wasn't enough. Everyone's nerves were on edge. Arguments broke out over nothing, and Tim had personally broken up two spats in the mess that were about to turn physical. The men needed to get back on land. They needed this underway to be over. So did he.

Jerry was still confined to his rack in the berthing area. Whenever Tim could, he left Aukerman in charge of the sonar shack and went down to visit his friend. Jerry was in even worse shape than before. The fight with Stubic had aggravated his broken knee and briefly reopened the wounds in his arms. He slept a lot, which was helping him heal, but Tim figured he wouldn't mind being woken up to hear the good news that they were back in US territory.

"Spicer," the captain said, coming into the sonar shack after the submarine had breached, "join me on the bridge."

"Aye, sir!" Tim said, springing out of his seat.

The two of them put on their parkas and climbed the ladder to the bridge. Tim could barely contain his excitement. His breath came quick and hard. His need to see the world outside the submarine was stronger than he had realized. Tim opened the hatch that led out to the sail, and the two of them stepped up. The freezing wind hit him like a cold slap in the face, but he didn't care. It was fresh air, and he was outside. That was all that mattered.

The North Pacific was quiet, a blessing on a body of water known for its squalls. Tim looked around at the frigid stillness that surrounded them. In the distance, the dark snowcapped mountains of Attu Island rose against a sky clear and lit up with stars. The thin crescent moon hung so low it looked almost fake, like a stage prop in a high school play. Tim had hoped to see the sun, but when winter hit the Aleutians the sun didn't cross the horizon for weeks at a time.

"I want to bury them here," Captain Weber said, his breath steaming the air in front of him.

Tim nodded. "It's a peaceful place for it, sir."

The captain took a deep breath of cold air. "After what they've been through, these men deserve a peaceful place to rest. And a beautiful one. I can't think of a more peaceful, more beautiful place than this."

Tim looked out at the quiet, still waters and agreed.

There were 78 corpses aboard *Roanoke*. With 23 survivors, that meant the vampires had flushed 39 men out of the torpedo tubes. Many of them had been stuffed into those tubes alive, then drowned once Matson flooded them. Tim couldn't imagine the extent of their terror at the end. Their deaths would have been mercifully quick, but that didn't mean they hadn't died in fear. None of them deserved that. If only there was a way to go back into Soviet waters, collect all those bodies, and give them a proper burial at sea like the others …

Captain Weber had a pained, mournful look on his face. "The men will be buried with full honors. All of them."

For the second time that day, Tim fought back tears.

***

The captain set the entire crew to work loading the dead into body bags. When they ran out of bags, they wound the corpses in sheets from the racks. Tim couldn't cover them fast enough. The expressions on the faces of the dead were not peaceful ones. These men had died in terror, confusion, and agony. He would never get their faces out of his head, he knew. He would see them every time he closed his eyes.

Their faces were one thing; their wounds were another. While some had only two small puncture marks on their necks where the vampires had fed, others had simply been murdered in the quickest manner possible, their throats torn out entirely. He could see into their necks, see the shape of their tongues and the muscles that connected them to their throats. Several times, he had to pause his work for fear of vomiting. He never actually threw up, but some of the others did.

Once they finished winding the victims into their shrouds, it was time to wrap the vampires' bodies. The other crewmen didn't want to touch them—not out of fear, but out of anger. The sailors called them monsters, bloodsuckers, and worse, saying they didn't deserve a burial at sea with the others. Tim felt differently. They were as much victims as the people they had killed. Petty Officers Warren Stubic and Steve Bodine, Lieutenant Commander Lee Jefferson, Lieutenant Gordon Abrams, Seaman Apprentice LeMon Guidry, Senior Chief Sherman Matson, Lieutenant Junior Grade Charles Duncan, Ensign Mark Penwarden—these men hadn't been monsters, not even Duncan. They had been *good* men, most of them, navy men, until they died at the hands of vampires and became vampires themselves. These men had been their crewmates once, turned into monsters against their will, and in death, the men they had once been still deserved respect.

Unfortunately, other than the captain, Tim and Oran were the only ones who felt that way. Oran, in particular, wanted to make sure his brother's body was treated with respect. Together, the two of them wrapped the vampires' bodies in sheets while the other crewmen turned their backs in silent protest, until finally the captain ordered them to help.

After the dead were prepared for burial, the crewmen returned to mop and scrub the wardroom, the garbage disposal room, the officers' staterooms, the auxiliary engine room, and any other spaces where the bodies had been stored, until no sign of them remained. Not that it would matter. Tim knew that nothing short of an exorcism would get the crew to return to those rooms. Captain Weber had been avoiding his own state-room since the pile of bodies there had been taken away—even after every surface was scrubbed with bleach. He didn't even use the captain's egress or the fore ladder anymore. No one did.

When the time came, the men carried the dead to two of the hatches that led to the top hull, one in "the box" behind the reactor room and the other behind the control room. A rope system was devised to haul the bodies up the ladders, one by one. It was a lot of heavy bodies, but the crew didn't stop until all 78 corpses were accounted for, lying shoulder to shoulder along the top hull, aft of the sail.

When the time came for the ceremony, the surviving crew gathered on the top hull, standing at parade rest. It was bitterly cold, without a breath of wind. The sea remained calm as if it too was honoring the dead it was about to receive. Tim only wished Jerry could see it too. He knew how badly Jerry wanted to be there, but the captain had ordered him to stay in his rack and rest.

After the horror the men had faced, anything that smacked of tradition would help things feel normal once again. Flying flags above the dead was a long-standing tradition, so by the light of the Milky Way, they flew the navy banner, the US flag, the Hawaiian flag, and *Roanoke's* own banner. No one spoke. *Roanoke* sat on the northernmost edge of the North Pacific Ocean, covered with the bodies of the dead, as quiet and motionless as an ice floe.

Seven sailors, wearing full dress whites under their parkas, lined up with short-barreled Mossberg 500 pump-action shotguns taken from the second weapons locker. The only one who refused to wear a parka over his uniform was Captain Weber. He didn't even allow himself to shiver. This was his boat, his crew, and he clearly blamed himself for the deaths. He refused to let himself be comfortable in the freezing Arctic air.

At the captain's command, Tim and the other men saluted the fallen. Captain Weber read the service out of the *Navy Military Funerals* handbook.

"O God, whose days are without end, and whose mercies can be numbered, make us, we beseech Thee, deeply sensible of the shortness and uncertainty of human life; and let Thy Holy Spirit lead us in holiness and righteousness all our days: that, when we have served Thee in our generation, we may be gathered unto our fathers, having the testimony of a good conscience; in the communion of the Christian Church; in the confidence of a certain faith; in the comfort of a reasonable, religious, and holy hope; in favor with Thee our God, and in perfect charity with the world; All which we ask through Jesus Christ, our Lord. Amen.

"O God, we pray Thee that the memory of our comrades who have fallen in battle; may be ever sacred in our hearts; that the sacrifice which they have offered for our country's cause may be acceptable in Thy sight; and that an entrance into Thine eternal peace may, by Thy pardoning grace, be open unto them through Jesus Christ our Lord. Amen."

When he was finished, tradition dictated that it was time to commit the bodies to the deep, but first Captain Weber wanted to do one last thing. He put down the handbook and picked up a cigar box that had been sitting at his feet. He opened it, pulled out the fallen sailors' dog tags one by one, and read each name aloud. He included the names of the sailors who had become vampires, drawing a stifled sob from Oran Guidry when he heard LeMon's name. But no one made a peep in protest, not even the men who had turned their backs earlier. It took a long time to read out 78 names, but the captain didn't pause, not even to blow warm breath into his freezing hands.

Finally, when he was finished, Captain Weber moved on to read the committal. "Unto Almighty God we commend the souls of our brothers departed, and we commit their bodies to the deep in sure and certain hope of the resurrection unto eternal life, through our Lord, Jesus Christ, Amen."

The seven sailors in dress whites lifted their shotguns to their shoulders, ready for the salute.

The captain put the handbook down again, laying it on top of the cigar box at his feet.

On the hull, one of the bodies sat up. The body bag convulsed as the corpse inside began to squirm, struggling to get out.

"What the fuck?" Tim said aloud.

And then all the bodies sat up, all except the eight who had been staked or burned. Seventy bodies in all, seventy vampires trying to tear their way out of their body bags and tightly wound sheets. The men bearing shotguns acted on instinct and fired at the nearest vampires, but all it did was blow holes in their wrappings, making it easier for them to tear their way out.

The body in the bag closest to Tim pushed, stretched, clawed at the plastic.

"Fall back!" Captain Weber shouted. "Everyone back in the boat! Now!"

The crewmen sprinted for the two open hatches. But in the freezing Arctic air the salt spray from the ocean had turned to frost on the submarine's iron hull, and men slipped and fell, which only caused further panic. Tim lost sight of the captain. Nearby, a vampire tore free of its wrappings. It was a young redhead Tim recognized as Goodrich, the auxiliary tech. He hissed, baring his long fangs, and grabbed the leg of the shotgun-bearing sailor running by. The sailor turned his shotgun around and used it as a club, smashing Goodrich in the head with the buttstock.

Tim didn't see what happened next, because suddenly the hulking engineer Ortega was rushing at him. Tim had rolled Ortega's body in bedsheets only hours ago, and now here he was, on his feet. Tim could see Ortega's tongue moving through the gaping hole in his throat. One of the men blasted Ortega in the face, the shotgun pellets tearing through his skin. Ortega lost his balance on the slippery hull, fell, and slid into the water.

Tim bolted for the nearest hatch, the one leading down to the maneuvering room. All around him, body bags ripped open, but he didn't take his eyes off the hatch up ahead. By the time he reached it, the other hatch had already been closed and locked and the other sailors had already fled down into the submarine. He started down the ladder, then saw he wasn't the last sailor into the boat after all—there was one more still on the hull, an enlisted man running for the hatch.

Tim held it open for him, but he didn't know how much longer he could. One of the no-longer-dead bodies was tangled in its body bag and pulling itself toward him across the icy hull, hissing and grasping for him.

"Come on!" Tim shouted. "Move your ass!"

The sailor was almost there, four feet away at most, when a shape came rushing out of nowhere, fast as lightning, and tackled him so forcefully they both slid across the frosted hull and into the water below.

Damn. Tim had to act now. It was too late for the sailor. If the vampire didn't kill him, the freezing water would. More shapes raced like a flash toward Tim and the hatch. One of them—Keene this time—reached through the opening and tried to grab him. Tim slammed the hatch on Keene's wrist, crushing bone. The vampire yanked his hand back, and Tim pulled the hatch shut. He locked it, sealing the resurrected creatures outside.

Above him fists pounded on the hatch. So many of them.

CHAPTER FORTY-FOUR

Tim hurried down the ladder from the hatch, cold and out of breath. The dead had become vampires, every last one of them. If the captain had waited even one more day to bury them at sea …

Stubic had told Jerry something about him not being the only vampire still trying to take control of *Roanoke*. At the time, he had assumed that Stubic meant he was going to turn Jerry into a vampire. Now Tim understood what Stubic had really meant: 70 more vampires had been waiting in the wings.

He had to get to the control room. He threw off his parka and ran out of the maneuvering room, through the reactor room, and into the middle-level corridor outside. He climbed the main ladder to the top level.

The control room was in chaos as men scrambled to their stations. The captain had the conn and didn't even seem to notice as Tim sprinted into the sonar shack.

"Rig for dive!" Captain Weber shouted. "Make our depth six-zero-zero feet. When we reach that depth, make our speed twenty knots."

As the order was repeated and executed, the dive alarm sounded. Tim braced himself in his seat as the floor began to tilt.

"Gentlemen, we wanted to commit our dead to the sea," Captain Weber said. "It's time we did so."

Roanoke dived into the subzero depths while the diving officer ticked off the feet.

"Spicer, switch to active sonar," the captain ordered.

"Aye-aye, sir, switching to active sonar," Tim replied, working the dials and knobs in front of him. The cascade on his sonar screen blazed into sharper focus.

"I want to know when every last one of those bastards is off my goddamn boat, Spicer."

Tim concentrated on the sonar screen. As the active sonar pinged off them, it looked as though some of the vampires were falling away from the submarine and drifting off into the depths. When *Roanoke* finally reached 600 feet, they accelerated to 20 knots, and the rest of the vampires were peeled off the hull like leaves off the hood of a speeding car.

"The hull is clear, sir," Tim reported. "They're all gone."

"Any chance vampires can swim?" Captain Weber asked. It sounded like the setup for a joke.

"At this depth, they're frozen, sir, just like Stubic was," Jerry said. "The cold won't kill them, but it's enough to keep them dormant."

The captain nodded. "Then let's hope some well-meaning idiot doesn't find them and thaw them out."

On Tim's screen, the active sonar pinged off dozens of small shapes as they drifted away from the submarine. It was finally over.

***

Tim went down to the berthing area to visit Jerry a few hours later. Oran was there, leaning into Jerry's rack and helping him tighten the gauze around his knee.

"Had to do this once for Monje's knee after he got in a bad fight at school," Oran said. He went quiet for a moment, then sighed. "Anyway, don't you go fightin' no more rougarou. That leg need to heal." Jerry winced at the pressure on his knee.

"That hurt?" Oran asked. "I can go get some aspirin from sick bay ..."

"Nah, don't worry about it," Jerry said. "It may hurt like a son of a bitch, but I earned this pain. I'm okay with feeling it for a while."

"Crazy bastid," Oran grumbled. "Maybe you can talk sense into him, Spicer."

"I wouldn't even try," Tim said, laughing. "I just wanted to let you know the captain has set a course back to Pearl Harbor."

"Finally," Jerry said. "After this, I just want to sit on the beach and soak up the sun for a month!"

"You just make sure and heed what them medical officers tell you," Oran said. "Don't go running off to no beach like a *couillon* if they tell you to stay in bed."

"Let them try to stop me," Jerry said.

Oran shook his head. "Finding trouble—that's your habit."

"That's an understatement," Tim said. "There's more news, by the way. Captain Weber has made me acting chief of the boat."

"Congratulations, COB," Jerry said. "I'm sure Farrington would be proud."

"I hope so," Tim said. "It's the first time a petty officer first class has been made chief of a boat, I think. I'd better not screw it up."

"You won't," Jerry said. He leaned back in his rack. "Look at us. The USS *Roanoke*, making history left and right."

"Do you think they'll believe us?" Oran asked. "About what happened, I mean."

"They'll have to," Jerry said.

Tim wasn't so sure, although he kept his mouth shut. The navy would need someone to blame, but there was no longer any evidence of the vampires on board. It was more likely they would come up with an official story themselves: mutiny, a Soviet attack, or just a deadly virus that had swept through most of the crew—which, come to think of it, wasn't that far from the truth.

"I was thinking about all them rougarou we dumped in the ocean," Oran said. "What if they wash up on shore somewhere before the sun comes out? What if that's all it takes for them to thaw out?"

"I can't even think about that right now," Tim said. "Far as I'm concerned, I don't want to hear the word *vampire* or *rougarou* ever again."

"Nah," Oran said. "I bet the sharks and crabs and killer whales got 'em anyway. Gobblin' 'em right up in the water like little frozen snacks."

He laughed, but it was a nervous, doubtful laugh, as though he weren't entirely convinced.

Jerry smiled thinly but couldn't bring himself to laugh with him. As he lay there in his rack, Stubic's final words came back to him—words that still made him shiver.

"What makes you think this is the only submarine we're on?"

EPILOGUE

Waikiki, January 10, 1984

Petty Officer Second Class Kenneth McNamee, helmsman of the submarine USS *Swordfish*, SSN-579, stood on a Waikiki side street and pulled a business card out of his pocket. He checked the address on the card twice, making sure he had the right place. It didn't look like much—just a door at the far end of an empty alley. He would have thought it was a trick, but someone had made a welcoming aisle of lit candles up to the porch—just the kind of touch a Hawaiian brothel would add to class itself up. This had to be the right place.

He approached the door cautiously after making sure no one saw him enter the alley from the street. He wasn't worried just about the pickpockets and muggers who were sometimes in the employ of brothels. If the navy caught him here, he would be in some serious shit. And if they learned of McNamee's particular proclivities, the shit would be deep enough to drown in.

His unusual tastes had already gotten him in trouble once, back when he was a janitor at a public school in Paris, Illinois. He had lost that job, although it was no great loss. He couldn't think of anything more soul-deadening than pushing a mop through school halls day after day. It was probably why he had gotten bored and allowed his mind to wander, pick out an object for his affections, think about her day after day until finally …

The DA hadn't prosecuted him right away. He was an old-fashioned guy, the DA, with that old "boys will be boys" attitude. He had given McNamee a choice: go to jail or leave town. He didn't have to say it twice. Even if jail hadn't been the other option, McNamee would have left. Paris, Illinois, may have been named after the City of Lights, but there the similarity ended. It was a two-street shit-burg in the middle of nowhere, and he was happy to leave it there. Joining the navy had been a no-brainer too. His own pop had been a navy man, so why not follow in the old man's footsteps? As it turned out, those footsteps had led him to Hawaii and Naval Station Pearl Harbor.

An old Filipina woman opened the brothel door, and McNamee found himself in a small waiting room. On the walls were pictures of naked women and embracing lovers. Sculpted figurines stood on shelves and in corners, all of them erotically themed except for one: a grimacing face that was depicted as being made of feathers, or maybe flames. The old woman walked over to an elegantly crafted wooden table and sat behind it.

"Pardon me," he said. "Is this …?"

He didn't need to finish the question. "You're looking for a girl for tonight?"

"That's right, yes," McNamee said. "That's exactly right."

"Then you've come to the right place," the old woman said. "Tell me, what kind of girl are you looking for?"

He swallowed nervously and glanced around the room. They were alone, but he still felt unsafe saying the words aloud. He didn't think his tastes were all that strange or wrong, but it seemed the rest of the world felt differently. That meant he had to be careful. He answered her in a whisper.

"I—I like them young," he said. "Real young. Is that going to be a problem?"

"Not at all," the old woman said, much to his relief. "She can be whatever you want her to be."

She picked up a telephone from the table and spoke into it in a language McNamee had never heard before. The words made him shiver, though he couldn't say why.

She put the phone down. "She's ready for you."

The old woman pointed to a door behind her desk. He walked through it and found himself in a room lit entirely with soft candlelight. His date for the night sat on a sofa, wearing a delicately patterned silk kimono. She looked about 13 or 14, on the cusp of becoming a woman, which was just how he liked them. God bless Waikiki. You really could get whatever you wanted here, as long as you knew where to look.

The girl smiled at him, enticing and unafraid. Her jade-green eyes twinkled. She rose, turned around, and walked into a hallway that led deeper into the building. There were no lights in the hallway. He couldn't see where it led, and after a while he couldn't see her anymore. The shadows seemed to swirl and close around her. Afraid he might lose her, he hurried after her.

In the hallway, there was nothing but darkness ... and the sudden glow of eyes.

And then the teeth.

END

ACKNOWLEDGMENTS

This book began with a conversation. Several years ago, I had the pleasure of interviewing the late John Piña Craven, a former chief scientist for the US Navy's Special Projects Office, whose many accomplishments include helping recover a missing hydrogen bomb and locating a sunken nuclear submarine. He is also rumored to have played a pivotal role in Project Azorian, a clandestine operation to raise a Soviet submarine that sank 1,500 miles north of the Hawaiian Islands—thus changing his job description from scientist to spy. John told me a great deal about what can go right on a submarine … and what can go wrong.

I found myself a bit lost as I began work on this novel. Other than a tourist sub named *Atlantis*, and the *Finding Nemo* ride at Disneyland, I had never actually set foot on a submarine. Fortunately, I knew a few people who had. Gerald Shealey, who served on SSN-709, helped me a lot. He's also a good friend, even if he is a Golden State fan. Adam Bozarth, who served on Ohio-class boomers, helped as well. So did Karrin Peterson, who knows the navy and is a fine editor to boot. I also learned a thing or two from Harvey Hughes, who worked on 688s from the outside, as a navy deep-sea diver. Alex Baker built me a detailed scale model of a 688. Having that model on my desk helped me keep everything in perspective.

I want to thank editor Michael Carr and the dedicated team at Blackstone Publishing for turning this manuscript into a novel. I also thank my wife, Brooke, for putting up with this project, which took a lot longer than most of my other books.

Most of all, I want to thank the men and women—yes, as of 2016, women serve on US subs—who serve our nation in the "Silent Service." These are not only America's best and brightest; they're our bravest too. Thank you for living 18-hour days 100 fathoms below to keep us all safe.

Steven L. Kent

Nicholas Kaufmann wishes to thank Steven L. Kent, Richard Curtis, Michael Carr, and the amazing crew at Blackstone Publishing. Also, deepest thanks to Alexa Antopol for her continuing love and support.